Meredox of Archonia

TREPIDATION

A novel

By

Jarod Meyer

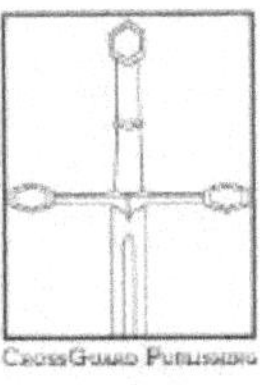

CrossGuard Publishing

CROSS-GUARD PUBLISHING
Iowa

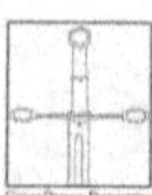

© 2021 CrossGuard Publishing

All rights reserved. This book or any portion thereof may not
be reproduced or used in any manner whatsoever without
the express written permission of the publisher, except for
the use of brief quotations in a book review or literary
publication.

PUBLISHER'S NOTE
This is a work of fiction. All names, places, characters, and
incidences are either the product of the author's
imagination, or are used fictitiously, and any resemblance
to actual people, alive or dead, events or locations, is
completely coincidental.

A product of CROSSGUARD PUBLISHING
Cover art: Andrey Vasilchenko
Cover design: Jarod Meyer
Editor: Christopher Guhl

Map Design: Jarod Meyer

TRADE PAPERBACK ISBN: 978-1-7341420-5-1

AMAZON KINDLE EDITION:

1st Edition. 2021

A note from the author

This story touches on the subject of an extremely important indivudal in history. Many religions hold this individual in the highest esteem, my own included.

I would like to remind everyone that this is a work of fiction, which means that it is not real and was never intended to be real.

I hope you enjoy the story.

Prologue

William flopped down on the meditation mat, his brow still heavy with perspiration. He watched Katrina's shapely backside disappear through the dark corridor. His mind reeling at the prospect of their intimate encounter.

Feeling his body against hers had done wonders to lift his spirits. He regretted that she couldn't stay with him longer but he had a lot of homework to do before the morning.

Between the sex and William's training with Meredox, his body was thrashed and he would need plenty of meditation before his journey to Dichonia. Before that, he needed to become familiar with his destination.

Very few people had spoken to William about this dark place. He imagined it as some sort of hell where fire and brimstone scoured the land, torturing the souls of the damned. Apparently there was only one documented journey to this underworld.

Rolling over to the other side of his meditation mat, William found the dusty tome that Achilles had provided him earlier that day. The thick, leather-bound book seemed to be in excellent condition despite its age. He wondered if that was because few had read it. Or if, like most things in Archonia, it had unique properties.

The purple binding smelled faintly of sandalwood as it creased open, revealing the elegant script of Meredox's own hand. The slant was heavy but William's mind eventually picked up on the shapes and patterns.

The first page indicated an interesting title, making William want to delve into the story. He hoped that it wasn't written in the style of a text book or he would not get far before meditation took him.

William's fingers ran under the script "Hunt for the Fallen." Then he turned the crisp page which plied apart with ease due to the thick stock.

Part One
Condemnation

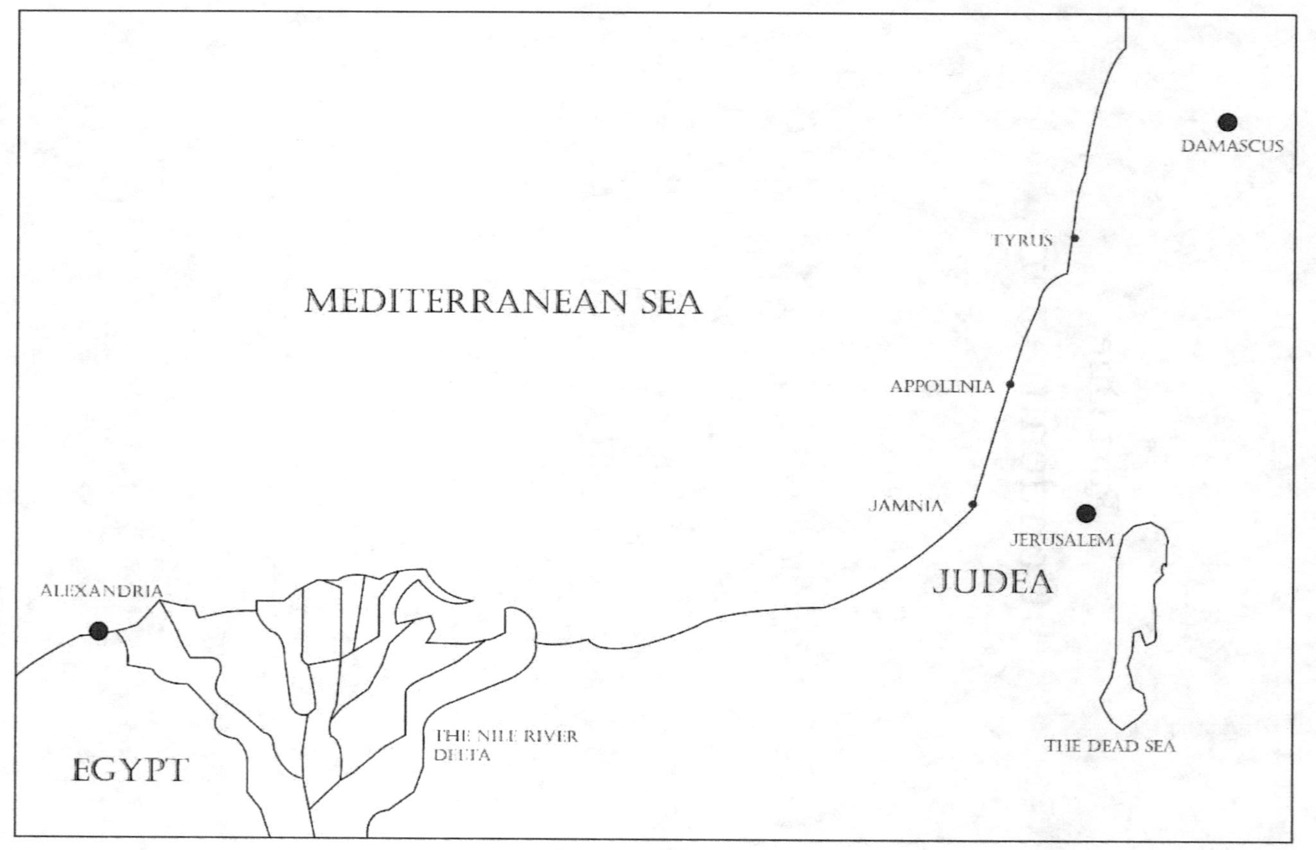
DAMASCUS
TYRUS
APPOLLNIA
JAMNIA
JERUSALEM
JUDEA
THE DEAD SEA
MEDITERRANEAN SEA
ALEXANDRIA
THE NILE RIVER DELTA
EGYPT

CHAPTER ONE
A Lesson in Trickery

Adomos' heart pounded as he lurched from rooftop to rooftop in the fading light of dusk. His worn leather foot wraps did little to shunt the pain of the loose pebbles and debris digging into his feet as he fled.

Starvation had set in more than a day ago and Adomos' body screamed at him to cease this taxing flight. His mind shouted back that he would surely be killed if he stopped for rest.

The con that Adomos' identical twin brother Diogenes had planned had gone horribly awry and soldiers were close at their heels. Without food or shelter, exposure would take them if the imperials did not.

Luckily, Adomos and Diogenes were born acrobats and these clumsy soldiers could do little to catch them as they sprang about the fine Roman-Egyptian stonework of Alexandria.

Lungs burning, Adomos spotted Diogenes crossing his path ahead. A simple feint would confuse the soldiers on the streets below and hopefully put a larger gap between them. Diogenes winked as he passed by and somersaulted from one roof to a lower one across the street. Adomos flopped to the stone, belly first to hide as the soldiers caught sight of his brother's daring maneuver.

Below, the imperials skidded to a halt. Having been chasing Adomos they quickly changed course nearly breaking their ankles as they turned hard. Large gasping breaths escaped his mouth as he lay prone, praying to the old gods that they had taken the bait.

After several moments, Adomos heard nothing as the armored soldiers disappeared into the growing darkness. Catching his breath, the surge of energy he had gotten from the fear began to subside and his belly begged him for food. He would need to find something before he met back up with Diogenes.

Adomos waited until the streets below him were clear, then swiftly rolled over grasping the ledge of the roof. Dangling for a moment, he felt a rush of wind before his sore feet hit the ground. He dusted off his crimson tunic and threw his shoulders back to appear confident and noble.

He and his Brother's Greek heritage made it easy to blend in with the Romans whose status here was higher than even the most noted Egyptians.

Moving casually down the bricked road, Adomos found a small establishment lit up in the dwindling hours of the evening. Bustling frivolity could be heard from within, echoing around the all but empty streets. He strode in casually with a smile. The tavern was teeming with locals all feasting on dinner and drowning their sorrows with wine.

Adomos shoved through the crowd, spotting a fat purse attached to a Roman's belt. The man's all-white garb with boasted golden trim. He deftly intercepted the stranger and offered him a traditional roman apology after bumping into him. His off-hand twisted inside the purse with ease and he pulled several Denarii out when he spun away.

Hastily stuffing them in his pocket, Adomos pulled them back out almost immediately as he sat down at an empty table space. The gold clanked against the wooden surface and the servant's head spun acknowledging the money.

"Good evening, sir. Would you like something to eat and drink?" the servant asked. His dark skin shimmered in the candlelight, fraught with perspiration from the toil of serving so many.

"Yes, whatever you have on hand is fine," Adomos replied, running his fingers through his hair.

The servant walked away nodding and Adomos caught a glimpse of the very man he just robbed sitting down at the table across from him. His stomach sank and he stiffened in a panic.

"Pardon, sir but I couldn't help but notice another well-dressed Roman patronizing this humble tavern. I'm afraid I haven't seen you around town," the man said.

Adomos exhaled, slowly trying to gather his wits. Lying never came as easily to him as it had to Diogenes. He preferred the honesty of a well-played illusion to the thin veil of a lie. His mind scrambled to construct his cover story. Something he usually had much more time in planning. The only thing that was blasting through his mind was the meeting spot he had memorized earlier that day.

I'm meeting Diogenes at the docks, past the White Mare. Mare, Docks

"Good evening to you, brother, my name is Mare eh Docks, I've only just arrived in town and I'm afraid I'm just passing through on my way deeper into the territory," Adomos replied.

"An explorer? Good man. I'd love to hear of your journeys, and your purpose here. Let me buy your dinner!"

Adomos felt the heat rising in his face as the stranger's hands moved towards his thick purse which he had only moments ago made lighter. Tossing some coins on the table, the man shoved the stolen pieces back towards him.

A great relief washed over him as the Roman didn't take any notice of his missing coins.

"How kind of you, sir. I don't even know your name," Adomos replied, scooping his stolen bounty back up and pocketing it.

The servant returned and dropped off a wooden goblet filled with dark red wine, and a plate of bacon with hard tack biscuits. Having casually taken a swig, Adomos nearly spit it out when the officer announced his station.

"Manius is my name. Legate to the empire's legions."

"Sir, you honor me with your company. I am but a humble historian. I have been commissioned to chronicle the far reaches of the empire in all its glory," Adomos replied, running his hands through his thick locks again.

"Ah an academic. I dreamed of being one in my youth but the roar of the legion called my name," Manius said, helping himself to a chunk of grease covered bacon.

"Do you know what that ruckus was about earlier? I was nearly caught in the middle of a skirmish. Your legionnaires were chasing some criminals I believe."

"I've no idea. I'm sure I'll hear about it in the morning. I have the evening to myself. A much needed rest from the rigors of the military," Manius said.

Relief greeted Adomos a second time and he eagerly chewed on his meal. Luck had finally favored him it seemed. For another hour or so he regaled the legate with made up adventures that he had partaken in during his years as a historian. When the man wasn't looking he stuffed a chunk of bacon between two pieces of biscuit and stowed them in his pocket along with the blunt knife he'd been provided with. By the time he stepped foot back out into the streets darkness had completely fallen, his belly was full, and he had coin in his pocket.

Not a bad turn of events.

Moving at a brisk pace, Adomos hoped that Diogenes hadn't thought him captured or killed. The lie had taken him longer than expected to establish. He trotted down the dim torch-lit causeway until he finally spotted the White Mare tavern. Then, pushing past it he heard the crashing seawater cause the docks to moan in protest.

Mare eh Docks

The boat they had secured passage on was a leisure vessel which stank of blood and sweat from slaves who broke their backs helping rich nobles cruise the sea. Adomos pulled himself up over the edge with some effort, scraping his elbow against the dry wooden planks of the skiff's railing.

Adomos slunk low and snuck down into the bowels of the ship where he heard a soft moan amongst the crates.

"Brother, is that you?" Adomos whispered.

"Thank the old gods, you made it. Come here I need your help," Diogenes said, his voice weak and panicked.

Adomos' eyes adjusted to the darkness and he spotted his brother leaning, barely conscious against a crate. A small candle flickered revealing an arrow shaft protruding from Diogenes' right thigh.

"By Aries, they stuck you. I thought you were faster than that," Adomos said, dropping to his knees and applying pressure to the bloodied area.

"Those damned auxiliary archers are getting better every year," Diogenes said, wincing in pain.

"It has to come out, there is nothing for it."

"I'm well aware of that, brother, do you have anything to bite down on?"

Adomos fished in his pocket for one of the silver Denarii he had lifted and offered it up. Diogenes took it and looked up at him incredulously.

"Where did you get this?"

"Took it off a legionary, a legate no less," Adomos replied, ripping a length of his sleeve off and tying it tightly above the arrow wound.

"You!? Picked a legate's pocket? Now I have heard everything."

Adomos watched his brother bite down on the coin. Then he gripped the crate above him and nodded, his eyes like black olives staring back. The arrow had lodged into the edge of his leg and hadn't dug deeply into the flesh. Still, the least damage would be done pushing it through.

Bracing himself against his brother to hold him down and get leverage, Adomos pushed until the arrow poked through the flesh a few inches from where it entered. Diogenes growled and writhed biting his teeth. With a clunk he hit the deck, his eyes drooping closed.

By the time he came around, Adomos had pulled the arrow the rest of the way through and was heating the knife he had stolen on the candle. Diogenes pushed himself up into a seated position gripping his wound.

"Of course you pushed it through," Diogenes said, moaning.

"Had I pulled it out you would be dead from loss of blood by now," Adomos replied, then without warning he applied the hot knife to the entry wound.

Diogenes cried loudly and after a few moments passed out again. Fear gripped Adomos seeing his brother's eyes roll into the back of his head. The shock was simply too great for him especially in his weakened state. A few more applications of the hot knife and the blood had sealed over the wounds. Healing would be a long process and he would be scarred but that was better than being dead.

Adomos helped his brother sit up a third time and then produced the meat and bread he snagged. Diogenes' eyes grew large and he didn't so much as say a word before sinking his teeth into the food. It disappeared faster than the pot in his show.

"Gods that tasted heavenly. Bless you, brother. Bless you.

Adomos sat down next to his brother and held him close. Diogenes shook for a while until his body warmth relaxed him.

"I'll always be here for you, brother. I promise."

CHAPTER TWO
The Road to Egypt

One month earlier...

Diogenes emerged from the barrel on stage to a mix of unsure applause and screams of confusion. This uneducated, uncultured rabble didn't understand or appreciate the illusion they just witnessed.

Regardless, Diogenes took a bow with a large, practiced smile on his face. It was one of his only roles in his twin brother's show of trickery and illusion. It had been wildly successful in the heart of Rome but on the road in these sparsely populated territories the spectacle was lost on these simpletons.

Even as his twin sat huddled in an identical barrel across the stage, Diogenes collected a paltry handful of coins from those audience members who weren't cursing at them for performing sorcery.

As the crowd left, Diogenes proceeded to pick up the various props that his brother used in his performance. When everyone was out of sight, he whistled, and Adomos popped his head out of the barrel, stretching.

"How did we do?" Adomos asked.

"Terrible. We might be able to feed ourselves for a day or two at best. You are not appreciated out here. You should be on the stages of Rome!" Diogenes said.

"Well, brother, your antics made sure that we would never perform in Rome again. That's why we are out here, if you remember," Adomos said, rolling the barrel off the stage.

"I was doubling our profits by lifting coin from the rich sycophants in that city. The only reason I got caught was because you got to be too well known. People thought I was the great sorcerer Salvias."

"Let's not have this fight again. Just give me the take. I don't want you gambling it away like you usually do," Adomos said.

Diogenes felt a surge of anger rise in his throat but he forced it back down. As much as he hated to admit it, Adomos was right. He had a problem with losing their money on games. He fished the handful of coins out of his pocket, leaving one for himself, and handed them over.

"What is this? A wooden coin? Fools can't even pay us with proper metal?" Adomos said tossing the coin into the dirt.

Diogenes dived after it, "Hey now, that's my lucky coin. Must've given it to you by mistake."

"That old thing. Why do you still hang onto it? We used those to practice our technique growing up. We have real coins to practice with now."

"Call me nostalgic I suppose," Diogenes said rolling the wooden coin over his knuckles then making it disappear with his palm open and facing the ground.

It re-appeared a moment later when he pulled it from his sleeve. The frayed edges had given him splinters plenty of times. Only added incentive to get the trick right. A rough likeness of his favorite hero had been carved into one side while the seal of Greece inscribed on the other.

"The damned thing reminds me of our time in the gutters."

"I liked Rome. I thought it was better than mother Greece," Diogenes said, finally pocketing his coin.

"Rome killed mother and father or did you forget?" Adomos replied spitting on the cracked wooden planks of their stage.

Diogenes didn't bother to reply. Adomos always made that comment when they talked about growing up on the streets of Rome. Instead, he finished picking up the show and packing their Plaustrum.

In the next hour Diogenes found himself back on the road. The sturdy Plaustrum rumbled down the Roman highway. He'd stolen it from a farm on their flight from the city and it had been a great stage for his brother's show. The oxen, Theseus, was getting on in seasons but remained a faithful companion. Not stubborn like the young beasts of burden who hadn't yet accepted their lot in life.

Diogenes could hardly believe that nearly four harvests had passed since they had been banished from Rome. He and his brother had survived on the small earnings from shows and his own skill at pick-pocketing. A near constant hungry belly had been normal for them most of their lives but being on the run had taken its toll on Adomos.

The hours rolled away and Diogenes decided to pull off the road for the night near a small oasis west of Jerusalem. The torch light from the vast city shone even from this distance. He had tried to convince his brother to make their next home there but Adomos had insisted the political tension in the area was mounting.

Judea had quickly become known for their new God. Between that and the new Roman gods, the old gods of mother Greece were a thing of the past. Zeus help them.

Diogenes curled up with Theseus for warmth as they settled in for the evening. The gentle snorts from the large beast had become a thing of comfort.

"Jerusalem is so close, brother. Why do you insist that we go to Alexandria?" Diogenes asked.

"I've told you more times than I care to count. Alexandria is the center of intellectual culture in the world right now," Adomos replied, flattening his hair with his fingers as he so often did.

"Yes, yes, you and your scholarly ambitions. Well then. Goodnight, brother."

The chilly desert air nipped at Diogenes fingers as he roused from his slumber. His eyes fluttered open and he jolted upright as he spotted a pair of strange eyes looking at him. Adomos was already on alert and he wore a serious look on his face.

Looking back over his shoulder, Diogenes spotted two more men, clad in dark clothing with daggers strapped to their hips. The short, curved blades and the manner of dress betrayed these men's heritage.

Desert men.

Diogenes tensed up again as one of their camels bleated loudly. The man sitting right in front of them was staring intently his curly black beard interrupted by an old scar which crossed his lips.

"Good morning, my name is Adomos. Peace be upon you," Adomos said. Diogenes looked at him feeling his lips tighten. His Syrian was not the greatest but he could keep up.

Did he just give his real name?

Diogenes remained silent, letting his brother handle the talking. He would only get them in to trouble by opening his mouth.

"And peace be upon you, as well. You know our words. Are you of the empire?" The scarred man asked.

"We are from the distant land of Hispania. We travel to the great city of Alexandria by way of Thrace and Rome before it. We are simple scholars," Adomos said, confidently.

Diogenes guessed that Adomos was trying to avoid eastern providences of the empire which had long histories of conflict with Syria but Hispania may have been a little far. It worried him that neither of them new the words in that land either.

"For learned men you travel foolishly. No caravan to guard your belongings," Scarface said.

"We have very little. You may take what you like but please leave us our lives," Adomos said.

Diogenes watched Scarface look him over and then he looked to his other two men. There was a short spindly man that seemed to have missed many meals. His dark cloth was faded by the sun but he proudly wore a bright red scarf around his neck.

"I saw your show two nights ago. In Tyrus. You are no scholars. And certainly not of a far off land like Hispania," the skinny man said.

Oh gods, no.

Diogenes' stomach twisted into knots as he watched Scarface signal his two companions to seize them with a wave of his fingers. Rolling to the side, he tried to avoid the grip of the skinny man. He somersaulted forward and came to his feet just in time to catch Scarface's elbow in his chin.

The ground met Diogenes roughly and he inhaled dust. A crushing weight fell upon him and he felt the men wrenching his arms behind his back. Frayed rope rubbed horribly over his wrists as he was bound.

Diogenes felt the bitter taste of blood in his mouth as they rolled him over. He spotted Adomos kneeling perfectly calm with hands tied. It looked like he was muttering something with his eyes closed.

"We do not enjoy hurting people. But I hate liars," Scarface said.

"Forgive us, we are wary with giving out our true origins," Adomos replied.

"Who are you really? Where do you come from? And how is it that you are skilled with pickpocketing?"

Diogenes winced as his brother shot him an angry glance. These could be some of the folks that he lifted coin off of in Tyrus but he couldn't remember.

"My name truly is Adomos, and this is my brother Diogenes. We are Greek, but grew up on the streets of Rome. The only way to survive there as orphans is to take what you need," Adomos said.

"My name is Bardeen," Scarface said. "My friends here are Noon Nabo and Zain Zaia."

"What is it that you want with us Bardeen?" Adomos asked.

"Zain was impressed with the acrobatics in your show. You are very skilled. I'm afraid Noon Nabo was equally impressed with your Brother's sleight of hand. You took many of his marks," Bardeen said.

Diogenes looked at the third man who wore a loose-fitted tunic, his face was wrapped with black cloth. The only thing visible were his dark eyes.

"We have very little left from our time in Tyrus. But as I said before you are welcome to it," Adomos said.

"Keep the gold. We have need of your skills." Bardeen replied.

Diogenes shrugged his shoulders when his brother looked at him. He considered himself lucky that these marauders hadn't simply slit his throat while he slept. He quickly realized his hands were shaking.

"How can we help you?" Adomos asked, calmly.

"My friends and I, travel to the great city of Alexandria. There we plan to plunder the city of its riches and sell the wares back here in Judea."

Diogenes snorted and all eyes fell upon him. In his best Assyrian he spoke up.

"We too travel to Alexandria."

"What if we do not wish to help you?" Adomos asked.

Bardeen frowned at him and produced his slender, curved dagger.

"Then we will kill you and take your belongings.

Diogenes's brother may never forgive him for being so eager but he'd already been imagining some fantastic heists in what was thought to be the second largest city in the known world.

"We're in," Diogenes said, a coy smile spreading across his face.

CHAPTER THREE
An Alien World

Socrates sat on a tall hill, the white grass surrounding him swayed gently in the breeze. The light from an unmoving sun shone down, warming his body. This seemed his only solace next to the thirst and hunger he felt.

Having been up here on this hill for days on end, Socrates hoped to answer some of the nagging questions about the strange heaven he had come to know. Almighty Zeus called it Archonia. He had come face to face with legendary souls such as Zeus on a regular basis since his ascension.

Not only from Greek history but people of all races, religions and creeds appeared in this world. Each shocked that their beliefs hadn't been accurate in the slightest. Socrates himself hadn't held stock in any religion. He was pleasantly surprised in a life after the mortal world.

Socrates' stomach rumbled again. It felt as though he was hungry, but it wasn't the emptiness he had felt during his time on Earth. Likewise, his thirst didn't seem to be deadly because he had gone far too long without hydration.

Looking to the sky, the alien sun hung low but remained steadfast at high noon. This made it difficult to keep track of time. Though it was already surmised that this world was timeless. Socrates still longed for the construct.

Socrates glanced at his notebook where he had been making marks frequently to track the passage of time. It was his guess that he had gone nearly ten days without food or water. He scribbled down his final conclusions.

After estimated ten days of fasting my body feels hungry but has not deteriorated. The strange spells of unconsciousness seem to revitalize my senses. I can conclude that our souls can indeed exist without physical sustenance. The only nourishment comes from these periods of meditation.

Rising slowly, Socrates silently blessed this world for returning to him his youthful vitality. Many things about him had changed after his ascension. Physically he was at peak form. Intellectually he had never been able to rationalize better.

After nearly two hundred years of enjoying this paradise, Socrates and several other notable men of intellect began to explore the sciences of this plane of existence. Together they were establishing the parameters of the world and testing the limits of their new bodies.

Making his way back to the growing city state they had dubbed the center of the universe or "Helios,"

Socrates stopped for a drink of water from a fountain which trickled softly near the northern most buildings. He scooped a handful of water into his mouth and the refreshing liquid hit his parched lips evoking an audible moan.

"Welcome back, Socrates," Aristotle said, standing tall a few feet away.

"Thank you, my friend. I am ready to address the guild," Socrates said, scooping more water into his mouth.

Socrates' thick black beard caught some of the water which hung heavy as he walked alongside his colleague. He gently brushed out the droplets as they made their way along the stone road. A mason was laying bricks which had been intricately carved into a large mosaic that would spread across the city. The level of detail staggered him as he gave the artist a wide berth.

Soon, Socrates found himself in the Guild's outdoor amphitheater. His other colleagues were already waiting for him. He hailed Archimedes and Plato as he took the main dais.

"The last of us has returned. I'm afraid we have all given our reports already on this study, Socrates. You appear to be the most thorough of all of us," Aristotle said.

"To be honest, brothers, the quiet solitude was enlightening. I found myself nearly lost in it. Alas I fear madness would've taken me had I remained alone on that hill much longer."

"Your findings, sir," Plato said.

"Yes, of course. My study has determined that the soul does not need physical sustenance to continue its existence in this life. It is, however, a sensory pleasure that I hope to never forget," Socrates said, patting his belly.

A mix of chuckles and grumbles echoed around the theatre as Socrates stood there with a smile.

CHAPTER FOUR
The Son of a God

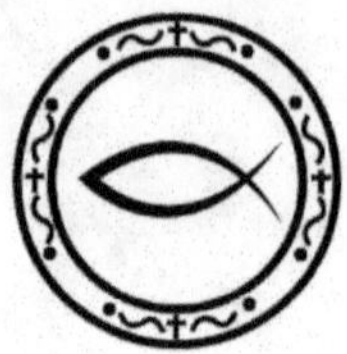

Yeshua's hands burned as he struggled to pull in the net. They must have hit a large pocket of fish because it was taking the whole crew to pull in the catch. His arms felt like they were going to snap under the pressure.

With a jerk, the catch nearly took Yeshua overboard, but he hooked his leg on a rope just in time. The extra leverage saved him from getting swept out over the edge. His fellow fisherman yelled and the commotion rose as they hoisted the full net up on deck.

Cheers of approval and joy went up across the boat as the net unfurled and hundreds of fish went sliding and flopping across the deck. Yeshua wheezed through his front teeth and blew on his hands to alleviate the pain of the fresh burns upon them. He wasn't a seasoned fisherman like the others. But he had to earn his keep.

As the others rejoiced, Yeshua went back to sanding down a fine chair that he had been crafting for the captain. His carpentry skills were the main reason he had been hired on. He had already made excellent repairs to the rest of the ship so there was little for him to do besides this.

A couple of minutes later, he finished the last part of the armrest, making it smooth to match the other side. He blew away the wood dust and sat down on his creation. It didn't as much as creak. He shifted in it and even the bobbing boat didn't make it move. Smiling to himself he rose.

Perhaps a coat of fish oil to seal it?

Just then, a spray of saltwater jumped over the railing of the ship and soaked him. He was already completely drenched so it mattered little. His hands stung anew however. The saltwater burning into his damaged skin.

Yeshua hissed but tried to find serenity in the waves on the horizon. He thought back on his life, trying to decide if he had made a real difference or just made a mess of the world.

Father. Have I fulfilled your purpose?

The sea continued to churn beyond the vessel but no answer came. One hadn't come in a very long time. Since he had decided to stray from the path that had been set before him.

Through his father's will, Yeshua had performed wonders. He was known throughout the world now as the son of God. Making the blind see, and the lame walk, he had begun a movement to change the world, making it one of peace, love and serenity.

Now Yeshua stood on the deck of a small ship filled with the stench of fish and the sound of vulgar fishermen. Doubt filled his mind. Through all his trials and wondrous feats his followers had lost their way.

With a heavy sigh, Yeshua grabbed the new chair and headed below deck. There he put it in place of the captain's worn seat which he would scrap for another project.

Suddenly, the sea froze, the long weatherworn planks of the boat stopped creaking and all the world fell still. Yeshua turned slowly, already aware that is father was with him.

"Hello, my son."

Yeshua turned and sighed. His father stood mere feet away, his long golden hair swayed from a breeze that wasn't there and his white eyes cut through Yeshua's flesh, peering into his soul.

"Father, you answered me today."

"I will always be watching you, Yeshua. How fairs the life of a fisherman?"

"It is good honest work, no death threats, or droves of desperate sick and wounded to attend to," Yeshua replied.

"Your disciples miss you, your brother is just not the same leader."

"My disciples have lost their way. They seek power with their newfound following. My brother leads them on a path which can only end badly."

"Joses is doing his best. He is spreading my words to the people as you once did."

"You must face the truth at some point, father. Men have wicked hearts. There will always be evil within us and..."

"I know. I thought to reset the world with my great flood but men have fallen back into their usual ways. I've sent them you, the perfect example of kindness and decency, and they twist your purpose."

"If you know this, then why have you come? Was I not right in choosing to leave the path?"

"You were right. Everything I have worked for will soon be destroyed. In three days' time they will arrest your brother and put him to death in Jerusalem. I thought you should know."

Yeshua's head flooded with emotion as the image of his father disappeared. He gripped at his chest where it felt like his heart would burst forth at any moment. He sank to his knees a solitary tear streaming from his eye.

For many moments he knelt there in silence. The rest of the crew must have still been busy gathering and sorting the catch. Nobody disturbed him for a long time.

Finally, he heard the men coming into the cabin and he rose to greet them. The captain praised his work and sat down in his new chair with a beaming smile. Then the crew broke out the wine and began their celebrations for the bountiful trip.

Yeshua's mind spun out of control as he thought of all the horrible ways they might kill his brother. Deep down he decided he couldn't simply wait for word of his brother's death.

When everyone began to settle down for the evening, Yeshua slipped away. The moon shone brightly over the sea and it helped him find east towards the shores of Judea. They were perhaps a mile or so offshore. It would be a long march over the wavy sea but he had done it before.

Yeshua's father had helped him to walk upon the waters and calm the seas. He looked down over the edge of the small ship where the whitecaps churned. He took in a big breath and jumped over the side.

The water consumed Yeshua and he frantically flailed his arms about until he broke the surface. Gasping for breath, he felt the chilly sea waters smacking up and filling his ears. The sting of salt filled his nostrils and he coughed trying to catch his bearings.

Yeshua splashed about and saw that the fishing boat had already passed him and was floating away. He screamed but the crashing waves rolling over him drowned out the sound of his voice.

Desperately, Yeshua fought to swim back towards the boat. His thick woolen clothing began to weight him down as it soaked up the sea. It made him slow like running through mud.

He cried again. "Father, help me!"

The boat floated further away with each passing second. The image of his father did not appear and suddenly a great curling wave fell over him, crushing him in darkness.

Jarod Meyer

CHAPTER FIVE
Alexandria

Diogenes looked back towards the road behind them. The miles of rough land seemed to be swallowing them but Theseus plodded on, pulling the Plaustrum now encumbered by three more bodies. Adomos had chosen to walk, lightening the beast's load. Their progress had been halved by these thieves.

As he looked back, Diogenes caught a glimpse of Bardeen, the thieves' self-proclaimed leader. He could smell the sour body odor from the front of the cart and the heat of midday only made it worse. Anger and doubt trickled through his mind as he fantasized ways of dealing with these Assyrians.

Diogenes then looked to his brother who must've seen the wheels turning behind his eyes. Adomos, being the more level-headed of the two, slowly shook his head. His natural stubbornness rose inside of him, however, and he couldn't help but defy.

"What is your plan once we reach the city, master thief?" Diogenes asked.

Bardeen's head turned quickly as if he was surprised by the question. "There are many temples and manses that we might plunder. We will have to scout them out and come up with a plan. As long as this wagon is full by the time we leave then all will be happy."

"You don't have a general idea of how we will go about that?" Diogenes chided.

"My men are skilled at cutting throats. If you and yours help us get past locked doors and high walls then we will do the rest," Bardeen replied.

Diogenes saw Adomos cringe. His brother wasn't the kind of person who wanted to hurt people. He himself had never killed another person but he often thought that if it came down to it, he could. Still the prospect of helping these murderers to kill indiscriminately seemed wrong.

"Well that sounds sloppy. The key to any good trick is misdirection," Diogenes said.

Adomos' head snapped toward him and he clearly mouthed "no." Diogenes didn't pay him any mind. He wouldn't be bullied this whole trip by these cutthroats. A simple display of strength would even the playing field and also make their lives seem more valuable.

Diogenes waited until they were on a particularly rocky patch of ground. The Plaustrum rumbled and jerked as the bumps shook it. All at once he tugged on Achilles' reins to halt their progress. Then he dug into his pocket for what little coin he had withheld from Adomos.

Turning and jumping onto the platform of the cart, Diogenes tossed the coins through the air over the heads of the thieves. The paltry few coins rang brilliantly as they hit the wooden planks and rocky ground.

All eyes including Diogenes' brother's eagerly followed the telltale sound. He, however, somersaulted coming to a seat right behind Bardeen who quickly realized his dagger had been commandeered.

Diogenes held his breath so he didn't have to suffer the horrible smell of the thief. Gripping the man's dagger in his hand he held it to Bardeen's throat until everyone realized what was going on.

"And that, my friend, is the power of misdirection," Diogenes said.

Diogenes waited for everything to sink into the minds of the others. Bardeen's two goons reacted by pulling their daggers and waiting for a command. The leader held up his hands stopping them from doing anything foolish.

"I see that you are more dangerous than you let on, acrobat. If you harm me my men will take their vengeance swiftly," Bardeen said.

"I don't doubt that but are you willing to risk your neck?"

Bardeen didn't reply.

"I have no intention of hurting you, Bardeen. But I won't have your daggers threaten me for the duration of this trip. Know now that we are on even ground. Let us begin to build trust with one another," Diogenes said. Then, he released the man and flipped his dagger so that the handle was facing him and offered it back.

Diogenes smiled as Bardeen looked back at him with wary eyes. Slowly the man began breathing again and took the dagger.

"Very well, Diogenes. You have skill and cunning as well. Tell us what you think the plan should be."

"First of all, help me pick up my coin," Diogenes replied.

For the remainder of the day the mood lightened. Diogenes had earned the thieves' respect and in so doing formed somewhat of a comradery. By evening Theseus had pulled them all the way to the great river delta of the Nile.

The Rocky lifeless terrain gave way to lush greenery and signs of civilization. Diogenes and the rest of the group stopped at the first sign of fresh water and filled their skins to the brim, drinking as much as they could in the meantime. Though they had stuck mostly to the coast of the sea, water was still a precious commodity.

Diogenes accepted some dried mutton and crusty flatbread from their new companions. It filled his belly, satisfying him for the time being. Their own food stores were non-existent and he had conceded that he might not eat again until Alexandria so this was a welcome treat.

Moving on, Diogenes walked beside Theseus leading him across small bridges and along paths built amongst the river delta. They made it to the main channel and bartered their way across on a small skiff.

The sun was nearly below the horizon as Diogenes stepped foot on the other side of the river and that is when he saw it. The great lighthouse of Alexandria. The famous port city glowed under its radiant light. Even miles away he could appreciate its majesty.

"I didn't know men could build things so tall," Noon Nabo said, staring in awe.

Diogenes walked over and tugged his brother into a half hug as they both looked at it. They had been travelling for years and had talked about seeing the great lighthouse.

"We've run out of daylight. Should we press on to the city or make camp here?" Bardeen asked.

"I say we push on," Zain said, excitement glowing in his eyes.

Diogenes agreed and silently hoped to spend his coin on good food and drink. He pulled Achilles forward finding the highway. The road was much better kept on this side of the delta and they made great time.

Torches began to light their way when they got about a mile outside the city. The large Roman buildings loomed overhead. Whitestone and columns holding up sturdy ceilings. Diogenes appreciated the subtly Greek stylings.

"Reminds me of home," Adomos said, walking up and stroking Theseus' head. The beast puffed in approval and muddled on.

"I'm sorry for what happened in Rome," Diogenes said. The apology was a long time coming. He had been holding it in for years. He saw Adomos look at him with a stunted smile. His brother didn't reply. Perhaps it was sheer exhaustion.

Soon, Diogenes heard music and the familiar rumble of city life. Salesmen shouting into the night. Slave traders trying to get their last minute sales in before leaving port. Entertainers swallowing fire, juggling balls, and all manner of things. He could picture it all without even seeing it.

"Do you think we could get a show in before the city begins to sleep?" Adomos asked, his face defying his sheer excitement.

"Yes, brother, I think we could," Luxor said, thumbing his wooden coin.

Bardeen and the other thieves didn't argue with them. They looked weary from the road but seemed agreeable to watching a good show.

Diogenes led Achilles into a fairly busy thoroughfare. He covered his face with a hood and kept his head down so as not to reveal that he and his brother were twins. In the meantime, Adomos began calling for viewers. His brother shouted out above the crowd that a magical show was about to begin. He boasted of his mysterious powers of sorcery, offering small sleight of hand tricks which evoked wonder from many.

Moving carefully, Diogenes began to set up the stage. He placed Adomos' set of rings on a small stand, then situated their two oaken barrels for the final trick. Finally, he put up the curtain. After the show was set, he proceeded into the crowd which was gathering around and placed small tokens in their pockets. Noting which ones were which so Adomos could call them out. He listened intently for any valuable information that his brother might be able to divine from thin air about the viewers.

When Adomos wasn't looking, Diogenes did lift some coin from a well-dressed Roman woman. He fingered the gold letting it settle in his pocket, then made his way to the stage where he got in the barrel to wait for the final trick.

Diogenes was used to the cramped space in the barrel and snuggled into his favorite position, knees tucked to chest. There he produced his coin and counted it out. Along with what he had withheld from their profits and what he had just attained, he had around five Denarii which would afford him a decent set of new sandals and a full belly.

He heard the planks of the stage creaking and stowed the money. Adomos leaned over into the barrel.

"Details please," he whispered.

"The fat Egyptian with the blue sash has my wooden coin, make sure to get it back. I put the carved elephant in the dark-skinned child's pocket. The Well-dressed Roman woman in red is from Neapolis and talked about her uncle Graccus taking her to a show like this as a child," Diogenes whispered.

Diogenes felt Adomos ruffle his hair in approval and then put the lid on the barrel.

The crowd got silent as Diogenes heard his brother begin the show. By now he had memorized it and could picture Adomos going through the motions. The opening speech still made him laugh.

"Good evening patrons. Those fortunate enough to be with us tonight are about to witness greatness! I, the mysterious sorcerer Salvias, have travelled across the river

Styx and back learning to harness the power of magic! Join me this evening for the show of a lifetime!" Adomos said.

Diogenes heard the clanking of the seemingly solid metal rings which Adomos strung together impossibly. And knew that the show had begun

Next, Diogenes heard the telltale sound of the clay pot being set on his barrel. Adomos would hold a small cloth in front by two hands.

"Watch closely as I make this clay pot disappear!" Adomos said.

At that point Diogenes reached out of the slot carved into the back of his barrel and grabbed the pot, pulling it inside with him. The crowd outside gasped then applauded.

From there the show went into Adomos guessing what was in the crowd's pockets. The little boy was amazed that the elephant carving had magically appeared. Graciously, Adomos let the boy keep it.

Damn I'll have to carve another.

When it came to his wooden coin being found in one of the man's pocket that he had placed it in, Diogenes was relieved to hear his brother cry out.

"Sir, please give me that coin with all haste! It is cursed and must be kept safely within my protective care."

Finally, Diogenes heard his brother preparing for the final trick.

"And now, using my mystical powers I will transport myself from one barrel to another across the stage before your very eyes!"

Keeping a keen eye out a small hole in the side of the barrel, Diogenes waited until the lid on the other barrel settled in place and then burst from his hiding place with the familiar practiced smile.

Unlike the dullards from the countryside these city dwellers erupted in applause and looked simply astounded. He felt the normal tinge of guilt that his brother couldn't enjoy the crowd's response to his show but it was fleeting as he bowed and held out their collection pot.

The take was inspiring. He counted at least thirteen Denarii among some other foreign currencies which could still be valuable. His smile became genuine and his cheeks tensed up so much they began to hurt.

Diogenes pulled the curtain up and the crowds began to disperse. He helped Adomos out of the barrel and made sure to put his hood back down so nobody saw him outright. If word got out their big act could be ruined.

"Quite a show!" Bardeen said, approaching the Plaustrum from behind the curtained side.

"Quite the profits," Zain added, his mouth muffled by his face wrap.

Diogenes looked to his brother with a wary eye. "Of course we will share our earnings, we have to make sure we all have full bellies for our joint venture," Adomos said.

His brother's high level vocabulary was wasted on these ruffians who looked like they hadn't received any semblance of a proper education.

Diogenes dumped the pot out in his hand and separated the coins into two groups. Then, he tossed a handful to Bardeen who pulled up his shirt and caught the whole lot, scooping it up with a crooked smile.

The group was suddenly interrupted by the clearing of someone's throat. "Ahem," the prominent female voice rang out.

Diogenes bowed away so his face was hidden while his brother turned to greet their patron. The Roman woman, he had stolen from before the show.

"Good evening to you, sir. I enjoyed your show," She said, her attendants flocked around her, a palanquin waiting behind to carry her away.

"You honor me with your patronage, my lady," Adomos replied, bowing low.

"I haven't seen such a show since I was a girl. I am mystified as to how you guessed where I was from. Have you been following me?" she asked with a coy smile.

"If only I were lucky enough to remain close to such a lovely example of the feminine form. I'm afraid I am simply gifted in the art of close observation."

Sly tongued demon.

"But in the show you claimed to be a great sorcerer who could read minds!" she said, flashing a flirtatious smile.

"My lady, If I truly were a sorcerer I'm sure the legion would have strung me up long ago for practicing dark magic," Adomos said.

"Indeed, well your tricks were amazing nonetheless. Like nothing I've ever seen. I'm surprised you don't perform on the stages in Rome," she said.

"We have been to the city once or twice but I so desired to see the beautiful sights of Alexandria," he said taking her hand and brushing his lips lightly against her knuckles.

Diogenes shook his head as it hung low under his hood.

"Well, sir you must grace my husband's home with your entertainment."

"And who might your fine husband be?"

"You may have heard of him. He is the prefect of all Egypt. Aulus Avilius Flaccus," she said, turning and getting up on her Palanquin aided by her attendants.

"It would be an honor. When would you like us to call on the Prefect?" Adomos called after her.

"He is throwing a party tomorrow. I'm sure he will need entertainers. One of my attendants will send word with directions to our home," she replied as they lifted her into the air.

"My lady, we have not discussed payment?"

"Your compensation will be ample and you will accept it," she replied absently looking forward towards the crowds ahead.

Diogenes watched her and her entourage leave and everyone was silent. Glances were exchanged until everyone was out of earshot. Almost immediately after, Noon Nabo leaned into Bardeen snickering.

"What a fortunate turn of events! We can swindle the prefect of Egypt tomorrow night and be on the road home the next day!" Bardeen exclaimed.

"I just secured a show and my reputation in this city and you mean to ruin it?" Adomos said, eyes narrowing.

Very rarely had Diogenes ever seen his brother get upset or even mad. But when he did there was nobody that could match his fury. He jumped into the conversation in order to steer it in another direction.

"I'd have to agree with my brother that it would be foolish of us not to milk this udder for all its worth. We could sustain ourselves for months on a reputation made at the hands of the prefect," Diogenes reasoned.

"Your reputation. But what about us? What if you let it slip that we are Assyrian thieves and we get arrested? Besides we do not like it here. We desire to return to our homeland," Bardeen replied.

"Bardeen, you must understand how difficult it will be to rob a prefect. He will have legionaries posted at every doorway. You and your men wouldn't get far," Diogenes shot back.

Diogenes watched the thieves discuss amongst themselves for a long while as he and Adomos packed up the show. All the while Adomos shot them disgusted looks. He, however was ecstatic because Bardeen's idea of turning them in would be the perfect way to swindle these thieves out of their lives.

All it would take would be some convincing and they could be the most popular performers in the providence within a week.

CHAPTER SIX

Death is the only Guarantee

Socrates leaned over his desk perusing the guild's notes. His eyes grew tired but through force of will he could keep them open for days on end. He was re-reading, for the third time, the other's account of their experiment on food and water. Their inductions seemed to closely match his own.

The only one Socrates threw out completely was Euclid's who tried translating his data into a numerical equation. The man had only lasted a day without food and water so his findings were laughable at best.

Socrates rubbed his forehead as he walked over to the window of his office which had been knocked out of the yellow stone with a hammer. The crude structure was a temporary home until the architects could complete the construction on his new Parthenon.

There, Socrates hoped to educate all the souls who never had a chance to do so in their mortal life. It would be his masterpiece. A university for learning about not only things from the previous life, but of this one as well. The guild was hard at work forming his curriculum.

He heard the delicate footsteps of his longtime friend approaching through the cool corridors before he heard him speak.

"They are ready to begin the next experiment," Aristotle said.

Socrates turned slowly placing the notes back on his shabby wooden desk. Then, with hands behind his back, he walked alongside his friend towards the theatre once more.

"The man has been convicted of his crime?" Socrates asked.

"Long ago, it seems that they have been holding him for nearly ten cycles," Aristotle said.

Socrates felt his brow crinkle. He tongued the inside of his cheek trying to rationalize their experiment but it wasn't going to be innocent in the least. Even for academic purposes killing a man was horrible in his mind.

"What could he have possibly done to affront the people? So far as we know there is little reason or cause for suffering in this life."

"He rapes. We do not know if it is a problem in his head or if he simply enjoys the act of being malicious but several souls have come forward as victims. Furthermore he does not deny his actions. Instead they seem to give him a sense of power and purpose," Aristotle replied.

"Atrocious. Well perhaps he can aid us in determining whether we are indeed immortal in this world."

"The wars surrounding the creation of Archonia state..."

"History can be changed. Lies can be elaborated throughout centuries. We need to document the knowledge in a controlled environment. I do not like it any more than you do," Socrates interrupted.

Socrates walked in silence next to his companion for the remainder of their trip. The guild amphitheater was not far from their offices. The others were already waiting on him as he approached the scene.

In the center of the stage on the lowest level of the sunken-in circular rows of seats there knelt a young man. Long golden locks of curly hair puffed from his head hanging in front of his eyes. His hands were bound behind his back as where his legs in the kneeling position. The thick ropes had been fashioned from the strong fibrous grasses that inexplicably grew in the southern plains.

Standing over the man was none other than Zeus and Achilles. Both renowned warriors and leaders in their time. One thought to be a god and the other thought to be the son of a goddess.

Achilles wore his hair long, braided behind him in a militaristic style. He wore his breastplate and greaves as if he was still on the battlefield where he fell at Troy. Zeus stood a full head taller at an unnatural height which he claimed to be gaining with each passing cycle in this afterlife. His unusual white hair made him seem like a wizened old god. When in reality he had been a man like all the rest of them.

"Good day, gentlemen. Thank you for bringing the prisoner. We ask that you make the proceedings swift, without added cruelty and suffering," Socrates said, calmly.

Without another word Achilles sword sang as it left its sheath. Socrates was surprised at the callous display and wasn't fully prepared for the experiment to begin.

"Hold, sir. Please allow me to inspect the prisoner first. He is still a man and I will hear it from his own mouth that he is guilty of his crimes," Socrates yelled.

Achilles stowed his sword, his face not indicating any emotion. Socrates approached the prisoner and pulled his chin up so that he could look in his eyes.

The young man's face was covered in a peculiar grin. Not a fleck of worry was on his mind. One side of his pale lips was curled up in a smile as Socrates inspected him. His pupils appeared perfectly normal indicating he was not under the influence of any foreign substances.

"What is your name, young man?"

"Pontius."

"And do you rape, Sir?"

"I do."

Socrates was flabbergasted by this emission but he didn't show it. He held the boy's face firmly in his grasp studying his aqua colored Iris's and a vision flashed into his mind.

Socrates saw the naked form of a woman crying out in agony as he pushed himself inside of her again and again. Shaking his head, he stumbled back wincing. Aristotle moved in but he held a hand up to keep him at bay.

"I'm fine."

This strange power had come to Socrates within his first hundred years in Archonia. He didn't remember exactly when it began but he had not told a single soul for fear that they thought him mad.

Somehow Socrates could relive the memories of another in perfect detail. Sometimes by sight and other times by touching them. This man's eyes had told the story.

"Pontius of Archonia you are convicted of rape and are hereby sentenced to death. Your passing will aid us in defining the rules of this world. I hope that you can find some semblance of humanity in this fact that it might relieve you of your sins. Do you have any last words?"

"Damned hypocrites! I bet you've all raped! I know you've murdered!" Pontius shouted, looking back at Achilles. He continued to shout profanities all the way up until Achilles relieved him of his head.

Socrates cringed as the blade clanked against the ground, soaked in blood. The man's head flopped to the stone as blood rhythmically pumped from the stump of his neck. It flowed out in a wide puddle and the scene was silent.

The rest of the guild was busy taking notes of the event. Diligently, they recorded their findings for the final report, but it was abundantly clear that death was indeed possible in this life.

Fear returns to the hearts of men.

CHAPTER SEVEN
Lost in the Desert

Yeshua sputtered as his body rejected more seawater. The salty liquid flowed from his throat emptying his stomach in the coarse sand. Behind him, a wave rolled in and collapsed over top of his back as he faced away from the sea. His legs buckled and he was swept further up on shore.

Staggering to his feet, Yeshua walked a handful of steps onto dry land before falling face first on the firm ground with a sigh of relief. Several minutes passed as he simply tried to catch his breath. He knew his father had saved him. It was the only possible way he was alive.

Turning over, he coughed more, spitting and hacking whatever saltwater was left in his system. Then he pushed himself up onto two legs and looked around. The flat, barren land offered nearly no vegetation. He guessed from their fishing route that he had washed up somewhere on the Plain of Sharon.

Joses and his disciples were in Jerusalem which would be to the south, Yeshua hoped. Looking to the sky, he found the sun and began to walk south. Almost immediately he tripped on his sandal which had snapped and come loose in the sea.

Yeshua knelt down, trying to rewrap the leather but it was all but destroyed. He pulled the wet remains from his leg and tossed it away. The pebbles underfoot cut into his skin without mercy.

After ten steps, Yeshua was hopping on one leg, his other foot shooting with pain. He ripped free the shreds of his sash and tied it around his barefoot with some difficulty. Then plodded on.

I will save you brother. Father guide me.

Yeshua marched south and prayed that he wasn't far from Apollonia. The seaside town was north of where they had set out of and he knew there would be some friendly faces there that would help him.

Despite his disguise as a lowly fisherman, if he drew the symbol of a fish in the dirt, his followers would know who he was. From there he could make his way to Jerusalem and his disciples.

As he continued, Yeshua discovered that he had bruised his ribs badly on a rock when he was being tossed around near the shore. As his breathing increased from his hike, his side began to bother him more and more.

In addition, the seawater left him parched. He would need to find freshwater somewhere fast. His lips were already dried and crinkled from thirst.

Father grant me strength.

After hours of walking, Yeshua's body began to shout at him. Though he had been well-fed and watered on the boat the pampered lifestyle didn't prepare him for such a thirst. His feet and legs hurt. His ribs throbbed with every step, and he could barely swallow.

Yeshua shuffled forward, hoping that south was where he needed to go. The sun beat down against his already darkened skin, pulling every drop of liquid from his body. Soon the world spun and he began seeing things in the rocky desert.

For nearly ten minutes Yeshua walked towards what looked like a small pond sitting in the middle of the ground before him. The mirage tricked him and no matter how much he walked it would not get closer.

Suddenly his body collapsed. His mind barely registering the sand that met him, burning against his face. He rolled on his back, sucking in air, his chest paining him with each breath.

"Greetings traveler. Can I offer you water? You seem in dire need," a deep, gravelly voice said.

Yeshua held up his hands which seemed to be the only thing he could do. The sun became blocked by a large blur in his vision and soon he felt something being pushed to his face. The familiar scent of wet leather greeted him as stale water trickled into his mouth. Unconsciously, he grabbed the water skin sucking down as much as he could.

"Slowly, friend. You mustn't guzzle."

Yeshua fell back with relief, licking his lips. After a minute the lifesaving water seemed to slowly revitalize him. He winced in the sunlight and looked at his savior. The stout man had a wide girth, his curly black beard hugged closely to his chiseled face. Immediately he recognized this man from his time in Galilee.

"Ananias!"

"Hehehe, indeed, my friend," Ananias said, helping him sit.

"How is it that you have come by me in the middle of the desert?"

"Your father sent me. He begged that I bring you something to drink. And who am I to refuse the almighty?"

Thank you father.

"Ananias, when last I saw you, you were to be executed. How did you escape?"

"A tale for another time, my friend. Let us be on our way to Apollonia," he replied.

Yeshua didn't argue. The burly man helped him up on to a short, furry camel where he nearly passed out again. Even with a belly full of water, sun fatigue had set in. His limbs were exhausted.

As Ananias took the camel's leader rope, Yeshua did a double take as he spotted the man's eyes. They seemed a peculiar white, but at second glance they appeared normally. Without giving it a second thought, he flopped forward onto the saddle and slept.

A jolt nearly tossed Yeshua from the saddle as he was startled awake. The camel bleated, galloping towards a well ahead. It began slurping water and Yeshua jumped down doing the same, right beside the beast.

After drinking his fill, Yeshua looked forward to the small lights of Apollonia. Ananias was nowhere in sight. He waited, thinking that the man's camel had run ahead to drink, but he never appeared from the darkness behind.

Strange.

Yeshua hadn't dreamt of him, after all his camel was right beside him.

This was father.

Eventually, Yeshua turned back and slurped some more of the wonderfully cool water. Then, got to his feet walking into town. He led the camel who seemed satisfied as well. Not worried in the least that his master was gone.

Yeshua could hear someone shaking a tambourine and another playing some sort of stringed instrument. The sound filled the air lifting his spirits a bit as he came into the torchlight.

The light fell over him illuminating his disheveled appearance and suddenly the music stopped. Several young women who had been dancing all ceased, everyone turning towards him.

Yeshua held up a hand in greeting and pushed forth his camel as a sort of offering. A man in colorful robes stood up and bellowed.

"Welcome traveler. You look like you need a good meal. What is your name?" he asked, with a half scowl on his face.

"My name is Yeshua, son of Joses of the town of Nazareth, then he drew a fish in the dirt with his toe.

The group of people erupted in cheers and the song picked back up. The girls moved in around him and pulled him toward the man in the bright robes who was likely their father.

"Thee Yeshua? We had received word that you were in Jerusalem with your followers. Surely you are not an imposter are you?" the man asked, his eyes narrowed.

"It is I. I assure you. My brother Joses did indeed travel to Jerusalem with my disciples. I'm afraid we bear a certain resemblance from our father.

"Then allow me to welcome you to my home. My name is Matthias," he said, embracing him. Quickly the man recoiled.

"I apologize for my appearance. I come from the sea and through the desert. It was a trial which tested my faith," Yeshua said.

Matthias nodded in understanding and waved his concerns away with a broad smile. He pushed Yeshua down into a seated position next to him and before he had settled in comfortably, a beautiful woman set a platter before him filled with dates, bread, and a small cup of sour wine.

Trying to remain polite, Yeshua ate slowly even though he felt as if he could eat the platter along with the food. After he had emptied the tray, another girl brought him a second glass of wine which he made quick work of as well.

The fermented fruit soon had Yeshua's head spinning. The singing and dancing ensued, and he began to relax.

"What drove you to seek a spiritual journey in the desert this day?" Matthias asked.

"To be honest, sir, I was hired to be a fisherman on a vessel which launched from Jamina harbor. I Left my disciples to live a solitary life of peace. Their Journey is becoming something that I do not abide," Yeshua responded.

Honesty was not a choice for Yeshua, he had been taught by his father since birth to be the epitome of goodness. In so doing, his father hoped that he would teach others this way of life.

"You abandoned the beliefs that you spoke so fiercely of all your life?"

"I did not abandon them. I still hold every belief dear to my heart, but my disciples are twisting my words. They have been gathering new companions who wish to use our message of peace to gain power and lands," Yeshua replied, sadly.

"This is true. Word from Jerusalem is that you and your followers go against the Rabbai there. The Jews are getting ready to retaliate. Tensions have never been higher.

"So I've heard. That is my destination. It is my hope to find my brother and flee these lands."

Matthias must've been able to see the sadness that Yeshua was clearly feeling. The elder patted him on the shoulder.

"You may rest here tonight. I have no need of your camel. Please take it tomorrow along with my blessing. For tonight, relax and enjoy the festivities. My daughter is married on this day."

"You are a good man, Matthias, I pray that good things will always come to you and yours," Yeshua said, then he sat back against a plush pillow laid out behind him and enjoyed the festivities.

The Heist

Diogenes passed under a massive stone archway leading Theseus up the personal drive of Aulus Avilius Flaccus. The anticipation bubbled up within him, threatening to overflow.

He walked slowly, so that the sun had plenty of time to recede behind the horizon. This work would need to be done at night. If the worst should happen a flight in any sort of daylight would likely prevent a successful escape.

Though Diogenes believed that the plan would go off without issue, his brother was not so confident. Adomos had used all their money from last night's show to bribe a dock guard then barter passage out of the port city on a cruise vessel should anything go wrong.

The boat is past the White Mare Inn, on the docks.

Scoffing at the waste of money, Diogenes plodded on. The prefect's courtyard wreaked of incense which barely covered the odor of feces accumulating in the drive. The result of all the guest's arrivals by chariot. Diogenes worked hard to dodge the piles as he made his way closer to the front entrance.

Diogenes' hood was pulled low and he looked to his companions who worked to keep a low profile as well. Only Adomos stood tall, his features clear for all to see. Once at the gate, he heard his brother greet the host at the door who ordered them to continue to the left and circle around to the rear of the house.

Following the path, Diogenes whispered to Adomos.

"Do not fret, brother. Everything will go according to plan."

Ignoring the comment Diogene's brother marched ahead, still upset by the presence of the thieves and their intentions to ruin his show.

Diogenes looked over his shoulder to where Bardeen was motioning for him to come over. He felt his mouth twitch in annoyance but he lagged back to where they walked.

"That balcony, we will lower the loot out over there, Noon will make sure the Plaustrum is ready and parked under it after you begin your show," Bardeen said.

"How do we know you will not simply leave with our Plaustrum and ox?" Diogenes asked.

"You have proven your honor to me, Roman, I will do the same tonight. Just make sure that the moment your show is done you get back as soon as you can, we must put leagues between us and this place," Bardeen said.

Diogenes nodded but in his head he had already formulated a scheme to betray these thieves. Adomos hadn't approved of either plan. He simply wanted to perform and be remembered for his tricks.

Eventually, Diogenes pulled on Theseus' reins and slowed him to a stop near the stables in the back. There, a service entrance played host to a number of servants and vendors who were helping with the party. There, he unloaded his barrel with all of Adomos' props.

Diogenes looked back at Noon Nabo who remained with the cart, while his two fellow thieves grabbed some crates from another wagon and began hauling them up the stairs into the villa. Adomos was speaking with the man clearly in charge of the servant staff because in addition to his formal attire, he wore a frantic look. Likely brought about by the sheer chaos of the night's festivities.

Rolling his barrel along the finely ground stone pebbles which made up the drive, Diogenes met up with Adomos as he had just finished gathering the details of their job.

"Right, well we don't go on for an hour so we can relax for now," Adomos said.

"Can we take our props up and wait? Bardeen has already gone in."

"Zeus save me! Those damn thieves are going to get us killed. I told you this was a horrible idea. We should leave now," Adomos replied, his eyes darting around.

"I have things under control, brother. You just focus on having a good show. We'll toast our success by the end of the night with the wine of a prefect."

Diogenes watched his brother stomp off, while he sat on his barrel near the short staircase leading inside.

Noon was fidgeting near the cart, clearly anxious to get it moving. He shook his head, waving the thief off when the man looked to him for direction.

Eventually, the courtyard fell quiet. All the servants were now inside, diligently working save for a stable boy who was tending to the animals. Even Adomos had entered to get a feel for the performance space. Diogenes waited patiently as Noon casually walked over and throttled the boy with a length of rope.

Diogenes hoped that the cutthroat hadn't choked the life completely from the boy but there was little he could do to prevent the thief's actions at this point. His plan was for them to do all the work of plundering the villa, then he would raise the alarm. Finally, while everything was in chaos, he would drive away with Theseus and the loot.

Rising quickly, Diogenes carried his barrel up the short staircase. Keeping his eyes to the ground, he was stopped by some legionnaires inside the first door.

"For the show," he indicated raising the barrel. The soldier looked inside the barrel where he saw the harmless props and after a short inspection he motioned Diogenes inside.

Passing down a short corridor, Diogenes spotted Adomos waiting cross-armed on the other barrel. He ducked down another corridor before his brother spotted him. If that was where he was supposed to be then he wanted to go where he wasn't supposed to be.

Eventually Diogenes came to an intersection of hallways several cubits away from the entrance. He set down the barrel and looked both ways almost immediately spotting a leg protruding from behind a tall potted fern. The leg sported a Roman greave and it was clear that Bardeen and Zain were being reckless.

Diogenes hustled over to the hidden body and found it lying in a pool of thick blood. He shuddered at the sight of the lifeless corpse. Suddenly, he spotted Bardeen, hauling a large decorative vase towards the balcony window down the hall.

Snapping his fingers, Diogenes scared the man nearly to death. The thief looked at him incredulously and he pointed at the leg sticking out in the hall. The thief shrugged, tying the handle of the vase to a rope. Then, he watched as Bardeen lowered over the balcony edge.

Diogenes sighed, then scooted the already stiffening leg behind the plant so that it couldn't be easily seen. After that, he rolled his barrel back down the hall to where his brother waited to begin the show.

Coming to a halt, Diogenes slapped his brother on the back. "Everything is going according to plan."

"Until it doesn't," Adomos replied.

"What do you want me to do? I'm trying to make the best of an unfortunate situation," Diogenes shot back.

"We could've turned these thieves in when we first got here. They hadn't committed any crimes yet. Now they've killed two men. The prefect will believe us. Especially after your spectacular show."

"Two men!? By Hades we will be strung up as murderers now!" Adomos hissed.

Diogenes held up his hands as if to calm him and winced, looking around to see if anyone had heard the outburst. When he was satisfied that they hadn't he continued.

"We are not murderers. We are being held hostage and once we show the Romans that we are indeed honest performers they will believe us."

"Yes, but then you intend to rob them blind anyway," Adomos shot back.

Diogenes felt his face tighten into a scowl. His brother simply didn't appreciate the value of money. Since as far back as he could remember he had taken care of the both of them with his pick-pocketing skills. They barely earned enough to live with the show's paltry earnings.

Soon, Diogenes spotted the master of ceremonies waddling up to them, his short plump figure seemed comical with his face painted like a fool.

"You're up, sorcerer. The crowd is extremely coarse tonight. Good luck," the man said, wiping sweat from his paint covered brow.

"I haven't had time to case the crowd or set up tricks," Diogenes said.

"I already did," Adomos replied.

Diogenes felt stung. It was always his job to place the objects and set up the tricks. He didn't say as much, instead he simply waited in the hall until his brother had set up the curtain then he placed his barrel and got inside.

Through his hole he was able to appreciate the life of the high and mighty. Beautiful white marble walls and columns were painted with red and gold trim. Exotic plants that he had never seen before dotted the area, growing in intricately sculpted pottery. The smell of wine and food drifted in the air which hung heavy with the smoke of incense.

The show proceeded and Diogenes' stomach twisted into knots, anxious for it to be done so he could carry out his plan and have the thieves arrested. When it came time for Adomos to guess the objects in the crowd's pockets, Diogenes peeked out his hole to see if he could catch a glimpse of the people his brother had chosen.

"And now my friends, I will divine the impossible by sensing what is in your pockets! But wait! What's this? My mystical powers are sensing something else," Adomos said aloud.

Diogenes had never heard him deviate far from his lines before and he felt himself tense, his breath frozen in his chest.

"Thieves! Murders and thieves in the villa!" Adomos shouted.

The crowd gasped and Diogenes did with them. His brother seemed to have had a plan of his own. There was silence for a moment following.

"Please, your eminence, I do not jest. There are thieves at the back entrance," Adomos insisted.

"Commander, inspect this claim. I'm not sure how a showman could hold such knowledge but I won't take any chances.

Diogenes felt his hands shaking as he waited. The crowd remained silent for the most part, then they heard some yelling coming from down the halls. Even in the barrel he could imagine what was going on.

There was a clattering of armor and then a soldier's voice. "Sir, the sorcerer does not lie, my men have apprehended two thieves. A third has fled into the night."

"Bring them before me that I might cast judgement!" cried a deep voice that could only be Aulus Avilius Flaccus.

Balling his hands into fists, Diogenes felt helpless sitting inside his barrel. He knew that this is what Adomos was counting on. If he came out most of their tricks would be ruined. Though it wasn't his show, the tricks were important to him.

Diogenes heard cursing and the cries of who he assumed was Bardeen and his goons. They were shoved into the view of the hole in his barrel and he spotted Bardeen and Noon. Zain was absent from the group.

"You have been caught in the criminal act of theft. From a prefect no less. You are hereby sentenced to death for your crimes, to be carried out tomorrow morning at my convenience," Flaccus said.

"We were tricked! A spell has been cast on us by this sorcerer!" Bardeen bellowed.

"Surely you don't believe that this man possess some divine power?" Flaccus asked.

"Don't take my word for it. Ask the real sorcerer in the barrel." Bardeen replied.

Before Diogenes could react, there was a legionnaire ripping the top of the barrel off and pulling him out roughly. He caught sight of Adomos who wore a panicked look on his face.

"What is this!?" Flaccus demanded.

"Your eminence. This is my brother, my twin brother. He is part of our act. I'm afraid many of my illusions depend on him," Adomos pleaded.

"Sir! This one has blood on his trousers," A legionnaire said, pointing at Diogenes feet.

Diogenes' throat went dry and he felt his body begin to shake again. "That is dried clay dust from the desert," Diogenes lied. Somehow he had gotten blood on his pants when he moved the dead legionnaire.

Damn.

"Lies! You are in league with these murderers?" Flaccus demanded.

Diogenes felt his tongue go numb as he looked upon the Prefect. The tall full-bodied man was standing, draped in a crimson toga, his bushy grey eyebrows accented the hatred in his eyes.

"No. your eminence, why would I reveal their whereabouts to you if we were in league with them. This blood must be from something else, perhaps the bottom of this barrel had some wine still in it..." Adomos tried to say.

"That is no wine cask that I have ever seen. But I can't be sure why you could have possibly revealed them if they were in league with you. Take them all, Praetorian. I will take no chances in having thieves running around my city. They will all be put to death in the morning," Flaccus finished, plopping down in his cushioned seat.

Diogenes mind was still processing the prefect's statement when the legionnaire holding him was sent sprawling to the floor. Then, he heard the shout that he and his brother would use as delinquents growing up on the city streets and his body reacted with practiced movements.

"Scatter!" Adomos cried.

CHAPTER NINE

The Energy that Binds Us

Socrates shuddered, still working to get the image of the rapist's lifeless head from his mind. Dutifully, he finished his notes.

The deceased left behind a body just like in the mortal life. This body was merely a husk, or imprint left behind as evidence of his existence. It was able to be burned just like any other flammable matter.

Scrawling out the last of his findings, Socrates leaned back and sighed. He quickly wondered if his efforts were futile. Already there was word across the land that souls were beginning to manifest many supernatural abilities. There could very well be no limits to a soul's potential in this world.

In fact, Socrates had a meeting with two such individuals today.

"Socrates, we are late," Euclid said, bursting into his room.

"Apologies, time slips away from me and because the blasted sun doesn't move I cannot discern the time. We need to have a sun that moves with the hours. Or some other method of time keeping besides these useless hourglasses," he said flicking the crystal time piece which sat expended on his desk.

Passing swiftly outside, Socrates realized that somehow he was able to make it to his chariot in much less time than he used to. His initial hypotheses was that he was getting faster somehow. Perhaps it was his legs but he guessed that it was more likely related to his mind.

Euclid caught up a few moments later and Socrates lashed his horses into action as the mathematician jumped on board. The short man wore far too many layers of fabric which draped over his thin form. A finely kept beard adorned his chin which he stroked with regularity.

"Fine horses. Wherever did you find them?" Euclid asked.

"A soul named Geirr summoned them from thin air. He is one of the men we will be meeting with today. He claims to have been blessed with magical abilities which allow him to create all manner of beasts," Socrates replied.

"Astounding."

Socrates didn't elaborate further, he was much more interested in some of the other stories which were surfacing about latent abilities springing up within the populous.

The ride through town was short and these beasts too seemed unnaturally fast for horses. A trip which normally would've taken hours took half the time.

Soon they came to a small plot of land outside the city where some of the other guild members had already congregated. A blast rang out across the plains spooking the horses and even he shook with fear as a large ball of fire curled into the air.

"That is the other person we are reviewing today. One that wields the destructive potential of fire," Socrates added.

"So it seems," Euclid replied cowering in the chariot.

Despite the sound the horses carried on at the heed of his whip until they rolled up to a small farmhouse surrounded by lush crops.

Socrates stepped off the chariot and approached a sizzling divot in the ground which had been scorched by fire. Smoke still rose from the hole and standing before it was a dark-skinned woman with wild eyes.

"Mahari, this is Socrates, he is the elected leader of our guild," Aristotle said, acknowledging his approach.

"Do you like my fire?" Mahari asked him, her irises appearing a strange yellow.

"It is, unique. We wish to know how you summon it. If the ability can be explained."

As he said this, Socrates heard the neighing of another horse which galloped through the fields carrying a lone rider. The Nordic man wore thick furs and leathers and seemed to have come straight out of a Greek nightmare of the barbarous people to the north.

"Greetings Geirr. Thank you for coming," Socrates said.

"Hmm." The man grunted and as he did, the horse beneath him disappeared in a flash of grey light. Socrates hastily scrawled this on his notepad which he pulled from his robes.

"What other sort of things can you create Geirr?" Plato asked, approaching him.

"Mmm...Whatever I can think of. Sometimes it doesn't turn out how I want it," Geirr said, then he waved his hand through the air. Grey light seemed to pour from his fingers. Droplets of water spattered the ground but instead of absorbing into the soil they bounced away as if they were hardened beads.

"And you, my dear, have the power of fire?" Socrates asked.

"Yes, I can turn anything I want to fire and ash," she replied, then with a snap of her fingers another loud boom echoed across the field and a plume of fire rose into the sky.

"The power to create and the power to destroy," Aristotle said, rubbing perspiration from his brow.

"These acts of magic are incredible!" Euclid exclaimed.

"Magic is merely science that is not yet understood," Socrates replied.

"This is beyond any science that we could possibly imagine," Plato insisted.

A flash of light interrupted the conversation and a tall golden-haired man appeared. His head was longer than that of a human and he seemed to have an extra finger on each hand, but with each encounter he looked more and more human.

Gasps let out amongst the crowd. Not all his guildsmen had seen the Archon before. Socrates remained calm.

"Socrates is correct. These abilities do not stem from some mystical force that cannot be explained. May I share some knowledge with you? Or do you prefer to reason things out?" Gabriel asked.

"My friends, and colleagues. Allow me to introduce to you the great Archon. He prefers the name Gabriel. His true name, he says, defies our capacity for understanding.

Murmurs trickled throughout the souls present in the field. Some looked scared while others looked intrigued.

"Surely you will not offer this information without some form of reciprocation. Isn't that your people's custom?" Socrates asked.

Socrates watched the Archon's lovely face curl into a smile. Every time this strange being had chosen to appear to them there was always a reason. While his wisdom was helpful, in the end it seemed to profit the Archon in some way.

"I would only ask that you begin instituting regulations for this world that I have created for you," Gabriel said.

Ah there is the catch.

"But this world is free from hunger, free from strife. There is no need for people to be governed," Socrates replied.

"It is free from pain and suffering as it now stands, but a forest, left unchecked, will grow too wild to control."

Riddles and analogies.

Socrates couldn't disagree. The world did need some semblance of order. Without established guidelines people could run rampant. The rapist they had put to death was evidence of that. He hung his head and sighed, motioning to the group.

"We will hear what the Archon has to say," Plato announced.

"Thank you, my friends. I assure you this will be enlightening," Gabriel said, then he walked over to stand between the woman and the man who had displayed their powers.

"The physical world that you came from had two forms of energy. Potential energy and kinetic energy. That is to say. Energy in motion and energy at rest. This dimension that you have named Archonia is one of energy that is constantly in motion. The bodies which your minds have manifested were created from this enormous pool of energy.

"Even now each one of you has the potential to draw upon this power and shape it. Geirr uses this energy to create things by shaping it into matter, while Mahari unleashes the energy into kinetic blasts.

"Socrates, even you have begun to utilize the energy to connect with those around you, reading the fluctuations in their actions and movements and even delving into their stored memories," Gabriel finished.

The group's heads turned on Socrates, who felt heat rising into his cheeks. The whole of the lecture had been lost as the Archon made mention of his growing abilities. He silently hoped that it wouldn't affect his status or reputation in the guild.

"We could all learn these abilities?" Euclid asked.

"In time, yes. Unfortunately, I cannot teach you."

"Cannot? Or will not?" Socrates asked, calmly.

The Archon smiled once again and disappeared into a burst of light, his white eyes leaving a throbbing blur in his vision for several moments.

"Such an enigmatic creature," Aristotle said, breaking the silence.

CHAPTER TEN
Cunning Disguise

Adomos shook his head as a beam of sunlight fell through the cracks of the ship's deck hitting his eyes. He winced and ducked out of the light where it took a moment for his eyes to adjust.

While they did, Adomos could feel the moisture below him and the slow sway of the ship as it floated at sea. Looking down, he spied his brother still snoring lightly. The leg wound looked puffy but seemed to have stopped bleeding.

The heist has been a complete failure as Adomos anticipated. The wondrous city of Alexandria was now lost to them. He and his brother were on the run once more.

Curses.

Lightly, Adomos shook Diogenes awake. His brother groaned and gripped his leg as he came around.

"By Hades, brother can't you let a poor wounded wretch sleep a little longer?" Diogenes said trying to put his head back down.

Adomos shook him a little more firmly "We need to honor our side of the contract we're due up on deck. Besides we need to disguise ourselves."

Diogenes sat up a little straighter but kept his eyes shut. "Fine, what is there to disguise ourselves with?"

"You'll have to shave your head. I'll shave my beard. Well look properly different," Adomos replied picking up the knife still stained with his brother's dried blood.

"I always have to shave my head, why don't you do it this time?" Diogenes replied, grumbling.

"I thought we agreed you look better bald?"

"We're twins!" Diogenes said.

Adomos thought for a moment and then smirked to himself.

"How about I let you sleep as long as it takes me to shave my beard off and shave your head? Do we have a deal?"

Diogenes flopped back over and began to snore loudly and Adomos took that as his answer. Gingerly, he put the blade of the knife up to his chin and began to scrape it across. The blunt instrument did its job but hurt the entire time as he dragged it over his flesh. The uneven edge bit into it at times, causing speckles of crimson to form.

Then, Adomos turned to his brother and began sheering strips of his hair off. Taking far more care with the process than he did with his own face, he soon finished without even waking his wounded companion.

Finally, Adomos shook his brother awake again. The familiar groan ensued then Diogenes sat up and felt his head.

"It's cold. What are we doing for names?" Diogenes asked.

"I came up with a fairly good one last night for that legate," Adomos said, running his fingers through his hair.

"You did? Tell me?"

"Maredocks."

"What? Like a horse and the port? How would you spell that so that it doesn't look fake?"

"hmm... good question. M-E-R-E-D-O-X I suppose."

"You always come up with the most unusual names. I think I'll stick with something simple. We're coming from Egypt. What about Luxor?" Diogenes asked.

"You think people will believe you've been named after an enormous city in Egypt?"

"It's certainly more believable than that made up name, Meredox," Diogenes chided.

"A pair of Greeks who were raised in Rome, acting like Egyptians. Who knows, maybe it will work," Meredox said, laughing.

Meredox helped his brother up off the floor and out into the underdeck. There, he found around thirty men straining and sweating as they swept large oars through the waters around.

This was a leisure vessel of a noble aristocrat. The captain had hired them and a handful of others to make the trip fast and pleasant without the need to wait for a favorable wind.

"There you are, scum! Sit down and get to work. I should whip you for stowing yourselves in the underdeck," a squat man barked, lashing at them with a leather strip.

Meredox shoved his brother out of the way and took the brunt of the assault.

"Calm yourself. We will pay the difference," Meredox exclaimed offering up the gold he still had in his pocket.

The stout man looked Meredox up and down with a sneer. His puffy cheeks hung low like the jowls of a canine and he even drooled like one.

"Sit down and row!" the man snapped, snatching the gold from his hand.

Meredox nodded and sat in an empty spot. Only one man pulled on this oar and he seemed relieved to have help. Luxor sat in the row across along with two others and he seemed barely able to make his strokes. A trickle of blood ran down his bald head where he had nicked him during the shave. Nobody made mention of their appearance though.

Hours passed as Meredox rowed. The old wooden oars splintered and rubbed into his hands causing them to slowly blister. His stomach grumbled loudly but sounded normal as the other's around him gurgled the same.

"May we break for food and drink?" Luxor asked loudly.

The rest of the men rumbled their approval and begrudgingly the oar master conceded.

"One minuta and then you're back at it," he growled.

Luxor nearly fell off his bench and Meredox caught him. Helping him over to the grain bin, he scooped a bowl of mush from the barrel and began feeding Luxor by hand. The bland meal was flecked with flakes of white fish and seasoned only by a mild amount of seawater.

Meredox cringed as he chewed on a mouthful but tried to be grateful for the sustenance. Luxor eagerly stuffed his face after a few more moments of help and then leaned against the bulkhead wincing in pain.

"I don't know if I can keep this up. My leg is burning. I feel dizzy."

"Here drink water. This torture will be done soon and we will be back in Judea," Meredox said offering his brother a water skin.

Luxor gulped the liquid down so quickly that all of it couldn't fit in his mouth and fell out the corners of his lips. Someone else grabbed the bladder before he was finished and began sucking on it too. The other crew members seemed to resent them. It was likely because of the Roman clothing and the hours they had missed in the morning row.

After the Minuta, Meredox was back at his seat. This time the others had taken up all the spots and left him and Luxor their own oar way in the back. It was cramped and chilly. Water soaked their feet which seeped in through a loose plank.

Luxor could hardly crank the oar at this point and Meredox found himself straining to maintain control of it. More than once he dipped the oar into the water and it jerked from his hand ripping the flesh on his palm further.

Squeezing his eyes shut and trying to ignore the pain, he continued rowing. Sweat dripped down his brow but he dare not wipe it away or the oar would be torn from his already feeble grasp again.

After another hour, Luxor was slumped back against the rear of the ship. Passed out from fatigue. Meredox felt numb to the pain, his body signaling shock. The world around began to spin and he felt close to passing out when the oar master shouted.

"Oars in!"

Chest heaving, Meredox lugged the large piece of wood into the ship and let it flop on the deck. Then he fell back next to Luxor who jolted awake.

"I think we're here, brother." Meredox said, gasping for breath.

"Gods, your hands, Ad...."

Meredox shook his head and put a hand to his mouth. Luxor slowly took it away, nodding.

"Meredox, your hands. They need attending to. Let's get on shore," Luxor said.

The roles were now reversed and Luxor worked to get Meredox to his feet. All the other servants or hired oarsmen exited to the top deck after the nobility had been cleared. When it came time for him to exit, the oar master stepped in his way.

"Where do you think you're going, slaves!?"

"We are not slaves. I have a deal with the captain. Our service for passage to these lands," Luxor said.

"I've heard of no such deal and I'm the master down here!" the man shouted, his jowls shaking as he did.

Meredox, growled and whispered "Coin."

Meredox watched Luxor instinctively reached for his wooden coin and hide it between his fingers on the back side of his hand. Holding his palm aloft for the oar master to see.

"It is not wise to cross us, we are sorcerers. I could make this ship appear," Luxor said producing the coin with a flick of his wrist. "Or disappear," he added, clapping his hands and letting the coin fall up his sleeve.

The art of illusion was all about distraction and normally Luxor provided the distractions. Their old trick worked and the oar master looked at him stupefied by the simple trick. The man's eyes on his brother, Meredox cocked back and threw his body behind a punch. The oar master's head jolted with a thud and he flopped to the deck in a heap.

Luxor didn't think twice and jumped into action stripping the oar master's clothes off. Brute stirred as his pants were being stolen and Meredox stomped the man's fat greasy face for good measure.

Looking up in horror at his brother's rash violence, Luxor donned the slacks with a grimace. They fit oddly but Meredox could already see the plan forming in his brother's eyes. He stooped down and grabbed the leather strap and looped it around his own neck then handed the end to his brother.

"Guess I'm your servant now," Meredox said.

"Always have been," Luxor replied, winking.

The sunlight hit Meredox like a wave. They had arrived late in the day but it still felt warm. The light seemed to lift the weariness of his plight for a moment as he stumbled up on deck. The gentle smell of seawater filled his nostrils and the sound of the gulls met his ears.

The leather strap choked him a bit as Luxor moved forward at a quick pace. Nobody seemed to notice the new oar master and his slave servant exiting the boat. If they did, they didn't care.

Meredox just wanted to put as many cubits between them and the ship as possible. Just off the docks, the streets of the coastal settlement were bustling with people. Luxor wound them through the buildings made from mudstone and straw into the market where he expertly lifted a tunic, sash, and mantle for him.

Hastily, Meredox ducked into an alley and put the colorful new clothes on. They exited the alleyway as equals, leaving the leather strap and the nightmare of Alexandria behind them.

CHAPTER ELEVEN
The Road to Religion

Meredox paused, his heart thumping against his chest. The organ beat as if it were trying to escape the very flesh which bound it. He watched his brother approaching the markets.

Jamnia had a bustling market rich with bounty from all over Judea. Unfortunately, the merchants punished thieves with little regard for status. If Luxor was caught lifting even a single date, he would lose his hand, or worse.

Meredox watched his fool of a brother go for the most conspicuous prize he could find. Right in the middle of the thoroughfare sat a large melon stand. The plump fruit made his stomach rumble even from thirty cubits away.

How in the name of Aeries are you going to snatch one of those? Idiot.

Sucking in a long breath, Meredox moved forward quickly. Shuffling through the crowd, he resigned that he would need to give his brother a good distraction. No amount of charismatic talking could get him out of trouble if he was caught.

"I need melons sir! How much?" Meredox exclaimed. Luxor caught his eye, rubbing his bald head where stubble had already began to regrow.

"I will be with you in one moment, sir, I was assisting this gentleman," the merchant said.

"Bah, I have much coin. I am more worth your time. But look! Your produce is rotten. I desire the very best of melons," Meredox chided.

The Merchant's eyes narrowed and his mustaches furled into a frown. Puffing out his chest as his face grew a darker shade of red, he turned away from Luxor who expertly snatched a plump melon from the stack and slid it under his tunic.

"I have the best melons in Judea. How dare you say otherwise, Sir! They are two prutahs a piece and I can guarantee you will be back for more!" the merchant said triumphantly so the crowd around could hear.

Meredox leaned in to the vendor and whispered. "For two Denarii I can ensure that you sell all your melons within the hour. Do we have a deal?" he asked extending a hand.

The merchant looked at him with a wary eye but couldn't pass up the opportunity to sell all his fruit before the sun took it. He shook Meredox's hand and almost immediately the show proceeded.

"If you can guarantee the quality of your fruit then why not a sample?" Meredox asked loudly.

Meredox watched the merchant stroke his mustaches which were bushy and flecked with gray. Finally the man shrugged his shoulders and picked up one of his melons. Reaching behind, the man produced a long knife and expertly sliced the fruit into several pieces. Then, he handed one to Meredox.

Trying to contain a smile, Meredox sunk his teeth into the rich fruit and a sweet explosion of flavor erupted in his mouth.

"This man speaks the truth! The best melons in all Judea! Come try your sample and fill your wagons to the brim with this bounty!" Meredox exclaimed.

Chewing on the rest of his piece, Meredox watched the people flood to the stand. The samples were gone before he was halfway done. By the time he tossed the skin of the melon on the ground, the man had sold over half his fruit.

Soon after, Meredox found his brother hunched down in a seated position like a vagabond chomping away at his stolen melon. He tossed one of his two Denarii at his brother's feet who gave him an incredulous look.

Then, Meredox cracked his own melon on a stone splitting it open and digging in.

"Where did you get that?" Luxor asked, his mouth still full of fruit.

"The melon? A gift from the merchant for helping him sell all his wares before midday. The gold was my earnings for the deal I struck to sell all of them within the hour," Meredox added, with a grin.

"I don't know how you do it, brother. You deserve to perform in the great cities," Luxor replied, wiping his mouth.

Meredox sat in silence as they finished eating their hard earned breakfast. His blistered hands still hurt from the oars but Luxor's leg was looking better with each passing hour.

"I guess crime doesn't pay as well as honest work. All I got was a melon and you came away with gold *and* a melon," Luxor said, sadly.

"I've been trying to tell you for years, brother. If we keep our hands clean then we can earn an honest living," Meredox replied, combing his hair down with his free hand.

"Then let's do it. We can go to Jerusalem and build your show back up. I promise I will never steal again. We can start anew," Luxor said, rising with bits of melon still in his scraggly beard.

"You know I don't like the idea of Jerusalem. There are too many fanatics from too many different religions all vying for power. Muslims, Jews, and now these followers of the Christ child. Not to mention the Roman occupation. One false move in that town and you're a dead man."

"But we won't be making any false moves. Let me help you, brother. I will work an honest job and we can have your rings remade. I can find some new barrels. We can make your show bigger and better than ever!" Luxor pleaded.

Meredox held up his hands and nodded in understanding. The guilt was clear in Luxor's eyes. Silence created a void between them for many moments until he responded.

"Fine, let's go see the great city of Jerusalem. We've seen the other two greatest cities in the world," Meredox sighed.

Meredox watched his brother's face brighten and he wrapped him in a hug. Then, he led the way out of the alley back out into the markets. The crowds were at full peak and he watched his brother closely to see if he could resist picking pockets.

To his delight, Meredox's brother held his hand, instead making his way to a nearby stable where he bartered passage to the city in a merchant caravan. The travelling group was small but the wealthy merchant liked servants. He and his brother would be attendants and see to whatever needs the merchant asked for.

By the next morning, Meredox was loading a cart full of salted fish, spices, and whatever else was needed. Their section of the caravan consisted of the merchant Caiaphas who had one son and one daughter. He and his brother. Plus one lone stranger named Yeshua who rode a camel and seemed to be otherwise destitute.

Caiaphas was a slender man which was unusual for a wealthy merchant, who always had plenty of food on hand. He kept his face clean shaven which made him seem far too young to have such lavish possessions.

Meredox watched as Caiaphas paid the Caravan guard his portion of the escort fee and then he made his way back to the cart.

"Greek! Help my daughter into the cart," Caiaphas barked.

"My brother and I are Egyptian, sir," Meredox replied, offering the young Judean woman a knee so she could get up onto the cart's seat.

"Nonsense. I have a keen eye for such things. Besides, despite your best efforts I can hear your accent. Now I don't know why you are trying to be deceptive but as long as you honor our contract I will have no need to make a fuss over your heritage," Caiaphas replied then leapt up into the other seat of the cart. Meredox bowed his head and began to walk as the oxen pushed forward.

Throughout the day, Meredox helped push the cart out of ruts and led the oxen around hazards. Meanwhile Luxor was busy catering to Caiaphas every whim. Bringing him the water skin, a cup of wine, or even food from his stores.

At midday Meredox watered the oxen when the rest of the caravan stopped to dine properly and let the beasts rest. The oxen lapped water vigorously from a large leather sack which he held in front of their snouts. The midday sun beat against his neck offering little respite even at rest.

"May I water my camel as well?" the man named Yeshua asked.

"Yes, of course." Meredox replied.

Meredox felt a calmness surrounding the man, and his face suggested a gentle kindness. He transferred the water bag to the camel and appraised the man's clothing.

"You have fallen upon rough times?" Meredox asked.

"Yes, I was washed ashore after jumping from a fishing vessel, then I had to brave the desert shore alone for nearly a day."

"You jumped?" Meredox asked, incredulously.

"I did. I needed to get ashore, my brother is in grave danger. I had only just received word," Yeshua replied.

"How did you receive word on a fishing vessel in the middle of the sea?"

"From my father."

Meredox let the man's camel drink its fill then he stepped away moving over to where his brother had finally been dismissed for a rest.

"Stay away from that one," Meredox said, pointing at Yeshua. "He is a madman."

"I'll keep that in mind. I have to say, this merchant keeps fine food. Perhaps I should work for him while we rebuild our show," Luxor replied.

"I don't think he is a very good fellow. We can find better people in the city. Besides we are much more educated than most of these Judeans. We can find jobs at a higher level in society."

Meredox sat and rested next to Luxor. After the luncheon the caravan was back on the move. For such a large group they seemed to be making good time. This route must've been a regularly traveled path.

Walking up at the front, helping his brother steer the oxen, Meredox was pleased that they didn't hear much more from Caiaphas for the rest of the day.

In fact, the rest of the week went by without any problems. Meredox soon found himself within sight of Jerusalem once more. The last time they had been so close, those blasted thieves had taken them hostage. The thought of them soured his mood.

"It will take us another day to reach the city. We will camp here for the night," Caiaphas called.

Luxor shouted to Yeshua who didn't halt his Camel's progress. "The merchant has called for camp!"

The bearded man turned and with somber eyes nodded. "I heard, but I must make it to the city before the morning," Yeshua said.

Meredox watched the man ride off alone ahead of the caravan.

Fool will get himself killed.

Meredox watched Luxor lumber back over and began setting up the merchant's tent among other things. Meanwhile, he once again saw to the care of the oxen. Soon they were hunkered down for the evening as the hairs on his arms raised from the chill in the air.

Morning came much the same as it had the past week and by midday Meredox heard Caiaphas greeting fellow vendors outside Jerusalem's gates. He and Luxor saw this as an opportunity to slip away unnoticed. They didn't want to let Caiaphas try to settle accounts with them on food and water for the journey. They had eaten and drunken more than their fair share.

"Wow, so this is Jerusalem!" Luxor, said, awed by its unusual stonework.

Meredox appraised the buildings, unable to find a common theme amongst them. There were Jewish, Islamic, and even some Roman influences amongst the masonry. Though the makings were inferior to that of a true Roman city, this towering urban center impressed him.

"This place smells worse than Rome," Meredox replied, not conceding to his brother's wonder.

"Please, brother. We are here to start fresh. I promise you will learn to love it," Luxor replied playfully hitting him in the arm.

Shaking his head, Meredox followed his giddy companion deeper into the city. A shiver ran up his back as they stopped at a fountain for water. Looking back his heart skipped a beat as he saw the familiar outline of a man draped all in black with his face covered.

Meredox stiffened and grabbed Luxor by the arm.

"Zain Zaia," Meredox hissed.

Luxor jumped to his feet and Meredox's eyes got wider as he realized the Assyrian thief was flanked by Roman Legionnaires. Everyone locked eyes and there was no trying to act casual or slip away.

"Run!" Luxor shouted.

CHAPTER TWELVE
Helpless

Yeshua dismounted from his camel, and tied it to a sturdy palm near a small pond. A full moon rose high over the Moab, east of Jerusalem. It shed a pale light on the garden of Gethsemane.

Patting his steed on the hump and rubbing his hand over the soft coat, Yeshua started through the lush greenery around. It was a beautiful night for the Passover and even as he walked silently towards his destination, he remembered fondly, the meals he had shared with his many disciples in this very place.

Tonight, Yeshua's brother Joses would be having dinner with them in his stead. He wondered if they had gathered some fine fair to partake in. He knew they would be gathered at the Cenacle and he hoped to find them there.

According to his father, Yeshua had until tomorrow to persuade them to flee with him to safe lands. He plodded along with a hobble. He had never been able to find a replacement for his mangled sandal.

Suddenly, Yeshua heard voices. He ducked behind a date Palm which was surrounded by a small shrub and listened.

"He prays in the garden I assure you."

Yeshua's heart jumped as he recognized the voice of his long-time friend Judas Iscariot. Peering through the branches he saw the man accompanied by several personal guards of the Sanhedrin.

I'm too late.

Checking that there were no more followers, Yeshua crept quietly and slowly back into the garden, following the group of men. His footfalls were each a gamble as he did his best not to be discovered. His mind raced with possibilities on how he would get to his brother.

Eventually, Yeshua saw the fires of a camp. His brother was among the only people there and even in dark he felt a pang of terror as his brother's features took form against the torchlight.

Sinking to a crouch, Yeshua waited.

"Hello, Rabbi," Judas said, kissing Joses on the cheek.

Yeshua squinted in confusion.

Why did he address him as such?

"Blessings, Judas, why have you come with the Sanhedrin's guards?"

"They demanded I bring them here. They seem to think that Yeshua, the son of God is camped among us," Judas replied, chuckling.

Oh calling him Rabbi was a cover.

Yeshua adjusted himself into a more relaxed position while he waited patiently for the Sanhedrin to leave.

"We know who you are, Yeshua, son of Joses. The Pharises will see you arrested this night for your trouble-making," said one of the men, armed with a pike and short sword.

Yeshua watched as Judas' eyes went wide and he took off into the tree line. Joses froze momentarily and that was all the time the men needed to surround him.

Father why?

Silently, Yeshua watched as the Sanhedrin guard bound Joses and led him into the night. The few others in the camp stood there dumbfounded and in shock.

After several minutes he heard his old disciples arguing and finally, Yeshua emerged from the brush. He recognized Andreas, Maththaios and, Te'oma among a small group of others who he did not know. When the group caught sight of him they all stopped.

"Who has come to our camp now?" Te'oma asked, squinting into the darkness beyond.

"It is I, brothers, Yeshua."

Gasps came from his old followers and they all rushed to greet him. They smelled pleasant, especially compared to him. He gripped at least two of them as tightly as he could while the others hugged him from all sides.

"Yeshua, the Sanhedrin took Joses only moments ago," Maththaios exclaimed.

"Yes, I saw. My father warned me that he was in danger. That is why I have returned. To stay this mad course which you have all been set upon and lead you to a peaceful life away from these lands."

Yeshua felt their bodies recoil his words stinging. He waited patiently for their reply which he knew would be harsh.

"So you still believe as you did before you left us? That our cause is lost and that we are misguided?" Andreas asked, a look of sadness on his face.

"You are all good men. The very best in my opinion. I simply cannot be a part of your plans in Jerusalem. I will not stop you. I only ask that you consider coming with me. I will be taking my brother though. Will you help me get him back?"

"If it is your intention to take him, then we will not aid you, brother. He is the mantle on which we rest all our hopes. The ideals that you created and stood for all those years depend upon your face. If the Jews kill Joses they will only light a fire under our cause. People will flock to us in support," To'ema said.

Yeshua hung his head. After all he had done for these men, they would turn his name and face into a martyr for a lost cause. He turned without another word and walked back into the wilds of the garden. Nobody followed him, nobody called after him.

How low have I fallen?

"Not as low as you might think, young one," his father said.

Wiping a tear from his face, Yeshua spotted the glowing outline of his father who had appeared to him in the form of the angel Gabriel that he had grown to enjoy.

"Father, tell me what I must do to save Joses."

"There is nothing that can be done for Joses. There might yet be something we can do for our message."

"The message has become fouled by the minds of greedy men, Father, I will hear no more of it," Yeshua, shot back more forcefully than he had intended.

"Yeshua, there is a way to take back what your disciples have twisted. You could do something that echoes throughout thousands of years."

"And what is that?"

"Tomorrow, Joses will be dragged before the Pharises, they will likely torture and kill him."

"Why are you telling me this?" Yeshua asked sinking to his knees convulsing sobs overtaking him.

"The one thing that all men fear is death. If you conquered death, they would all listen to you," Gabriel replied.

"Conquer death? Is this some power you have? To bring people back who are dead?" Yeshua asked.

"Not you, but your name. As twins you and your brother could perform the greatest illusion the world has ever seen. Joses dies and you appear, free of the grip of death days later. The world would remember that for as long as there are men alive to tell about it," Gabriel finished.

"I do not desire fame, or immortality. My only desire has ever been to teach men to be better. To do better."

"And many will, after you take back your name and show the world who you are. I have helped you perform many supernatural feats on your journeys. I hoped that seeing righteous acts come from a human being instead of myself would allow humans to more easily follow the example. I can see now that I was mistaken. I do not possess the power to bring someone back to life that has already passed into the next world," Gabriel said.

"But, father, you could stop him from being killed in the first place!" Yeshua shouted.

"Your brother's suffering will make people see the error of their ways. Then you will show them the light."

"No!" Yeshua yelled to the night. But his father was already gone.

A sleepless night did little for Yeshua's mood. As he rose from the sand next to his camel his stomach rumbled, protesting the serious lack of nutrition his journey had caused him.

Moving through the brush Yeshua found a date palm that had a few fruit still left on it. The handful of dates helped provide him with a little vigor to face the day. Returning to his little camp he gingerly pulled handfuls of water to his face. The liquid tasted of his camel and sand as he slurped it down.

Finally, Yeshua wrapped his sash around his face to hide his features the best he could and then he headed towards the city. The walk was arduous due to his tattered clothing and lack of rest but he found what he was looking for without difficulty.

Much must have happened in the night because a crowd was gathering before the great palace of the Roman governor Pontius Pilate.

Yeshua, keeping his head low, entered the crowd and got as close as he dared in order to listen.

"I can find no guilt in this man! Even Herod Antipas finds no crimes committed. Why good people, do you wish to see him arrested?" Pilate asked.

The on-lookers shouted and cursed throwing rotten food towards the dais which Pilate stood. There, Yeshua saw his brother bound and kneeling, his face calm and emotionless.

To his left, Yeshua heard a Jewish man speaking to this companion.

"Not five days ago this man was welcomed into the city as a king by his followers. Now, they ask for his death," the man said chuckling.

Yeshua's heart throbbed, tears threatened to surge from his eyes, but he gritted his teeth and balled his hands into fists holding them back.

"I will give you all a choice, good people. I have here a known seditionist and murderer named Barabbas. Will you see him released in place of Yeshua?" Pilate asked.

The crowd roared. They had been worked into a frenzy. Yeshua wondered what his group of disciples could have possibly done to rile the people against them so much.

Or was it someone else?

A man shoved past Yeshua roughly and he nearly lost his balance. There was no apology. Craning his neck he tried to see through the arms flailing in the air, their owners calling for his brother's death.

Yeshua felt the dates in his stomach threatening to come back up as the crowds called for the murderer's release. The man named Barabbas looked dumbfounded, but laughed as he walked back into the group of people.

The Roman governor shook his head in amazement. Yeshua didn't know if he could watch anymore but he was frozen in place whether out of fear or some desire to jump up on the dais and stop this.

Yeshua watched Pilate whisper something to his attendant and soon a small bowl was brought from inside his palace. He dipped his hands into the bowl then wrung his hands together.

"I wash my hands of this man's blood, let it be upon you." Pilate said, then receded into his home.

Yeshua watched helplessly as the people from the crowd rushed up onto the dais and grabbed Joses.

CHAPTER THIRTEEN
Wood and Blood

Meredox plowed into a woman carrying a basket atop her head, his feet skidded across the heavily trodden dirt street as he regained his balance and pushed his legs to their limit.

With no time to stop, Meredox lost track of his brother. His lungs burned as he sprinted through the streets looking for an escape. Somehow, the trouble they stirred in Alexandria followed them here.

Hurtling through a merchant stand Meredox dove through a second, head-first, rolling into a somersault. From there, he ducked down an alleyway.

The mudstone buildings converged and soon Meredox was in a narrow corridor. To his dismay, the Romans where close behind. He took a sharp left turn down another passage and his heart stopped as he realized there was no exit.

Knowing that he had little time, Meredox braced his arms and legs against the sides of the buildings trying to shimmy his way to the rooftops. Each movement hurt as he pushed against the stone trying to gain leverage.

Meredox spotted the Roman's turning the corner and in a last ditch effort he leapt trying to reach the edge of the rooftop. His finger's missed by less than a cubit and he slid back down to the dirt, his legs buckling from underneath of him.

Knuckles rapt against Meredox's nose and bright colors overtook his vision. He vaguely felt strong arms binding his wrists. His senses began to clear as they picked him up from the ground.

Moments later, Meredox still hadn't caught his balance and threatened to tip over several times as they dragged him back out into the busy streets. There, over the throbbing pain in his nose, he spotted Luxor. They had captured him too.

"Didn't get away this time you little rats!" a legionnaire said.

Twisting his head, Meredox spotted Zain amongst the group of ten or more legionnaires who subdued them.

"You sold us out?" Meredox spat.

"This citizen reported seeing two criminals who fled Alexandria several nights ago. They tried to rob the prefect's own home," a roman officer said, sternly.

"Did he tell you that he and his ilk forced my brother and me to be a part of their terrible plan? We are simple stage performers. We are not criminals," Luxor said.

"Then why did you run?" Only guilty men run."

Meredox didn't have an answer and neither did his brother. They slipped up. Too many years of running from authority made it such an innate reaction that they hadn't stopped to think things through.

"Meredox and Luxor, you are under arrest for the murder of a stable boy and a soldier of Rome. You are hereby sentenced to death at the stake," the officer said.

"Murder!? We didn't murder anyone, it was those Assyrian cutthroats. They waylaid us on..." But Meredox was cut short.

"I'll hear no more of this, take them away."

A fist connected hard with Meredox's abdomen. Air rushed from his mouth and his body curled over in pain. The blow would've dropped him to the ground but strong arms held him up.

Meredox felt a sharp pain in his back as something prodded at him to move forward. The searing pain jolted him into action. He heard Luxor curse while moving down the busy street.

Passersby jeered at Meredox as the soldiers escorted them ever closer to their punishment. Spitting and throwing things at them while they did.

We don't even know these people.

Meredox tried to rationalize the situation but his mind kept reverting back to their sentence. He had seen a staking before and it was barbaric. Warm liquid trickled down his leg at the prospect. It wasn't anything he could have stopped. He didn't even realize he was making water.

"Look at me, brother. I'm here. Everything is going to be fine," Luxor said.

The hollow words barely registered with Meredox who had all his life simply wanted to bring joy and happiness to a few people with his illusions.

Soon, the crowds thickened and it seemed like Meredox was being led into some sort of spectacle. Hundreds of people were gathered berating someone being scourged. The man knelt slumped on the ground, tied to a thick wooden post.

Another criminal?

Crimson strips crossed the criminal's back while Meredox could see chunks of his flesh flung carelessly about the yard. He felt the feeling in his hands and feet leave him as he realized they might be doing this to him in mere moments.

Thankfully, the soldiers pushed them toward a pile of large wooden stakes.

"Pick one, criminals. You get to carry your own sentence," the officer said.

"We don't get a trial? What kind of madness is this land subject too?" Luxor cried.

Meredox watched helplessly as the soldier back-handed his brother who fell to the ground in a heap. He was too terrified to even react to Luxor's pain. Instead, he simply stood there gawking at the large thick pieces of wood that had been nailed together.

The sharp pain prodded Meredox in the back again and he jumped forward falling onto one of the stakes. A soldier untied his hands and he hugged the nearest chunk of wood, worried that if he disobeyed they would take him back to the scourging post.

With tremendous effort he hefted the stake onto his shoulder and tried to move. The long end dragged on the ground making his progress slow and arduous. Looking over his shoulder, he spotted Luxor putting up more of a fight.

Unfortunately between their serious lack of nutrition and an accumulation of wounds, Even Luxor, who loved a good scrap, could do nothing as three fully armored soldiers beat him into submission.

The fear and confusion soon returned and a non-Roman soldier began whipping at Meredox's back with a strap of leather to get him moving. He winced, looking behind where Luxor now had his own stake draped over his shoulder. Alongside him, the feeble man that had just been scourged was also being forced to bear his own stake.

Meredox could see the open wounds seeping into the wood as it rested on the man's ragged body. Then, he noticed that they had wrapped thorn covered vines into a halo and forced it roughly upon his brow. With all the blood upon this man's body, he scarcely knew how his legs were holding him up.

The leather struck Meredox again and the man spoke something in Hebrew that he didn't understand. They were in a part of the world that was not familiar to them and it was treating them mercilessly.

Meredox marched on, each step taken with great difficulty under the weight of the stake. His brother soon caught up looking more determined than he felt.

"Do you have any ideas on how to escape, brother?" Luxor asked.

"No, there are soldiers everywhere, this man that is with us seems to have committed some sort of atrocity. Nearly the whole city has turned up to watch his demise," Meredox replied, his words shaky as they left his lips.

"Do you not recognize him? He travelled with us in the caravan. He is the one who called himself Yeshua," Luxor replied, grunting as he readjusted his burden.

Meredox looked back and studied the man. Through the veil of pain and blood his face did appear familiar.

"He seemed off, but not someone who could have committed terrible crimes," Meredox said.

"Move it!" a soldier shouted and Meredox's legs buckled under the blow from his spear. The hard packed dirt of the Jerusalem road met him roughly and the heavy stake crushed down on his leg.

Meredox cried aloud in pain. The soldier lifted the stake but made sure that he was back on track carrying it moments later. The area of his thigh which had taken the brunt of the fall screamed at him in rhythmic time to his heartbeat.

"Leave him alone you bastards! You've already condemned innocent men this day, there is no need to torture us!" Luxor shouted.

After what seemed like a full hour of sheer torture, they passed outside the walls of the city and Meredox found himself at the base of a large hill. The dread filled him and he knew before anyone told him that this would be his final resting place. Each step ushered him closer to his death.

Meredox, dropped the stake and ran. He made it a full three strides before many sets of hands from the crowd shoved him backward. He fell again this time the stake dug into his back as he sprawled against it.

A strong flexible switch clapped against Meredox's skin as one of the Hebrew soldiers struck at him, cursing in the foreign language. Covering his face and curling up, he waited until the assault subsided before reverting to his punishment.

The stake seemed twice as heavy this time when Meredox moved to pick it up. After a significant amount of struggling he hoisted it and was soon making his way up the hill. Suddenly, the pain and movement subsided for a moment. The scene around him seemed surreal.

Shaking his head, Meredox squinted into the crowd where he could have sworn he just saw the man named Yeshua. He looked back to confirm that the criminal was still behind him bloodied and beaten.

"Meredox!" Luxor shouted above the crowd.

Looking around, Meredox realized that the others had stopped and that they had reached the top of the hill. He watched as his brother dropped his stake and ran over to him. Strong arms wrapped around his, and Luxor buried his head into his.

"I'm sorry, brother. I'm so sorry for everything. I pray that I will see you on the other side of the river Styx," Luxor finished, and then he was ripped away.

Cold steel pressed into his chest as he was forced to watch four soldiers hold his brother down on the stake. With a hammer, they drove thick iron nails through Luxor's wrists and ankles. Meredox shuddered at the sound of his agonizing screams. They were quickly drowned out by the roaring approval of the on-looking crowd who seemed to be relishing every ounce of misery.

Meredox didn't put up a fight when it was his turn. His mind was still in shock, trying to comprehend what had gone so horribly wrong. Strong hands pressed his arms roughly against the sun warmed wood.

The pressure came first as loud jarring thuds erupted from the hammer and nail. Then a searing pain followed, pulling Meredox out of the numb state and hurling him back into reality.

Meredox's screams were all he could comprehend as the loud noise tried to take his mind off the sheer agony bombarding his body. He looked over and shuddered as he saw the iron rivets protruding from his wrists. It took two men to hold his legs still while they bore the nail into his ankles.

Every small shudder became torture as they hefted Meredox's stake upright. A slight drop jarred him and the holes in his body lengthened as his flesh gave way to the force of the stake coming to rest in the hole they dug for it.

Every muscle screamed for relief and finally as if an answer to his prayers, his mind began to shut down. The pain slowly faded as he drifted off into darkness.

CHAPTER FOURTEEN
Sweet Release

Luxor gritted his teeth and adjusted himself into the most comfortable position he could. The blood from his wrists and ankles clotted but any small movement could tear them back open.

The sharp burning sensation resurged with every breath but Luxor worked to push it to the back of his mind. For the moment, however, he found a small amount of respite.

Looking to his right he spotted the criminal Yeshua hanging upon a stake, passed out from pain and or loss of blood. His brother hung on the far side and he could see movement beginning to come back to Meredox's head.

"Brother!" Luxor shouted.

Luxor growled as Meredox didn't respond. Instead, the man named Yeshua stirred and responded.

"You should let your brother find rest if he can."

Looking above the man, his crime was displayed for all to see.

"So you are the king of the Jews? The son of a god?" Luxor spat.

"I was born of the one true god of Abraham," Yeshua replied.

"Then why not save yourself? Save all of us?" Luxor mocked.

"I have asked my father for help, but my suffering is for a purpose. My death will make the world see and my resurrection will make the world understand."

Luxor stared blankly at the scrawny man hanging helplessly on a stake. Even under this much duress, his madness showed.

"If you were so omnipotent why did you travel as a beggar in a caravan with us?" Why not reveal yourself then?"

"I have never before met you and your brother, my friend. You must have been mistaken," Yeshua replied.

"It was you, oh mighty king. We rode together in close proximity for days."

"That's not possible...Unless..." Yeshua said stopping.

"I have a twin brother, is it he that you saw?"

Luxor's mouth dropped open and a new wave of pain overtook him.

A twin brother? Like us?

"Be calm criminal, this is no devilry, my brother and I were born at the same time and we look exactly alike. It must have been him that you travelled with. Please tell me, what did he say to you?"

"I am no criminal! I was wrongfully accused. And I know it is no sorcery, look closer at the man who hangs on the other side of you, my brother and I share the same face as well, though we have disguised it as best we can. Your brother said that he was on his way here to save you. He talked about some mad plan that you and yours had to take over the city."

"Our plan was not to incite unrest. I was to spread the gospel of peace that my brother and I have worked to show the world."

"Your plan seems to have failed, Yeshua." Luxor said, groaning in agony as he accidentally shifted.

"Please, friend call me Joses. It is my true name. I was wearing the face of my brother to continue his good works."

Luxor didn't care much for this man's schemes or his plights. He only cared about his brother. He looked at his twin and sadness flooded him. The feeling remained there for several agonizing hours while they hung.

Every minute prolonged the agony and at times Luxor wished for it to simply end along with his life. Then at other times his mind raced trying to plot a means of escape. He even went so far as to try pulling his wrist free from the nails which bound him. But the pain was too great and the metal spikes seemed to be caught on the bone in his wrist.

Crying aloud in pain, Luxor finally saw Meredox look up to him.

"Brother, I'm scared, Meredox said.

"I am too, Brother." Luxor replied.

Only now did Luxor notice that there were people gathering around the hilltop. Those villains who had initially watched the torture and ridicule had gone. Before them now were a handful of women, one was weeping for Joses. Some part of him wished that he had found a woman to love but he had only ever had his brother.

Luxor thought back on his life then, it seemed to play out before his eyes. His difficult years on the streets of Rome, his travels abroad doing shows and stealing just to eat. Finally, this last chapter where, despite all their toils he and his brother were coming to a violent and bloody end.

The clatter of armor interrupted Luxor's thoughts and he saw the Roman guards approaching with spears.

"Sorry boys, it's hot and you lot are taking too long to die," a soldier said, then he jabbed Yeshua with the spear. The man writhed in agony for a moment but then it seemed a wave of relaxation overtook him as the rest of his blood spilled over the dirt.

Luxor tensed up, his heart pounding as a soldier approached him. The cold metal spearhead pierced into his stomach and he could feel his body jerk, trying to reject the foreign object. He thought he heard himself cry aloud but his lifeblood was running down his chest

His mind shut down, his muscles relaxed and the world grew dim.

Yeshua watched in horror as the soldiers lowered the body of his brother. The only person who had ever truly understood him. A man he had known since the very first moment he opened his eyes.

Still hooded by his sash, Yeshua followed the group of people who had taken custody of Joses and were now ushering him to his final resting place. Among them he recognized Joses' lover Mary. He had always teased his brother about choosing a woman with the same name as their own mother.

Keeping his distance, he watched them for the rest of the day caring for the body and anointing it with oils. It was evening time when they laid Joses to rest. From the shrubbery growing nearby, he wiped a tear from his cheek as they rolled a great circular stone over the door of his tomb.

Now what, father?

Yeshua received no reply. Apparently this wild plan would have to be contrived by himself alone. After darkness had completely fallen he approached the stone and tried to move it away. The enormous rock was far too heavy and after several moments of straining he gave up.

"I'll move that for you in time." His father said, once again appearing to him with the long golden flowing hair of Gabriel.

"I've been thinking, and I have a deal for you, father."

"A deal? Interesting."

"If I do this last thing for you, if I complete my purpose which you set me on from the moment I was born will you reunite me with my brother?"

"I will. I will also make this promise to you. Because I have tried and failed to make men understand a peaceful way of life I will no longer directly interact with mankind. Your message will be my final teachings and they can choose whether or not to follow them," Gabriel said.

"What must I do?" Yeshua said hanging his head.

"First you must undergo some pain as you brother did. I will give you the choice however. Would you like me to inflict these wounds or will you do it yourself?" Gabriel asked, and then he motioned to a rock nearby where a hammer and nails mysteriously appeared.

"I must bear the scars of his suffering in order for this ruse to be believed?" Yeshua asked.

"It will convince more people. Make for a better story," Gabriel replied.

"I don't think I could possibly harm myself..." And as Yeshua said this, white light pierced his wrists and ankles. Searing pain erupted throughout his entire body and he screamed at the night, dropping to the ground in a heap.

Smoke rose from the holes punctured into his flesh, and he felt tears streaming down his face. Soon, the pain subsided as a white light seeped into the openings and mended the flesh. Relief took him and he sprawled out wide armed on the ground.

"That was but a fraction of the pain Joses endured. I hope you appreciate his sacrifice," Gabriel said.

"Joses! Where is he? Does he live on?"

Gabriel didn't respond, instead he rolled the stone away from the tomb with a single finger and motioned with an open hand that Yeshua should enter.

Yeshua jumped up from the ground and rushed inside. There he smelled the overwhelming scent of blood mixed with clove oil. There, wrapped in linens, lay his brother. Gently he unwrapped the bindings on his face and stroked Joses' brow.

"You must discard the body," Gabriel said.

Spinning around, Yeshua felt his lips curl into a frown.

"I cannot throw my brother away like refuse."

"It is merely the flesh that his spirit has left behind. You must do this. I will not do everything for you. How then will you learn and appreciate?"

"This seems cruel, Father."

"Every man prays to a god to grant their wishes and lift their burdens. When they themselves have the power to do so. If you want your Brother's death to mean something then you need to put in a little of the work. Enduring pain is not enough."

Yeshua cringed at his father's statement. Gabriel was a harsh teacher who had put him and Joses through many trials. These obstacles made them stronger and wiser. He quickly wondered how many times he had done the hard work without knowing if it would be worth it in the end.

Deciding that it wasn't worth scouring his memories, he began unwrapping his brother's clothes and then hefted his body up. Drained of fluid it felt light. An unnatural stiffness had set into the flesh making it awkward to carry him.

Eventually, he found a small ditch and placed him gently upon the ground. Then he gathered some kindling and made a fire. He choked on the putrid smoke as Joses' body burned. It was the most horrible stench he ever encountered.

Yeshua gagged as he bore witnessed the skin melting from the bones and wept from his sorrow, Gabriel simply watched.

Three days passed and Yeshua anxiously awaited the moment his great performance would begin. Gabriel had insisted that it would take time for the news of his death to spread across the land. It was paramount that everyone believed him to be gone. This and only this would elevate his supposed resurrection to that of a true miracle and not some trick.

In the early morning, Gabriel gave him the nod and he exited the tomb after the stone was rolled away once more. He began to walk back towards the city when he caught sight of Mary and two other woman walking towards the tomb.

Stopping, Yeshua doubled back, following them at a distance. He heard the cry of surprise and grief as Mary dropped to her knees. The scene probably looked like a desecration of his brother's tomb.

Yeshua did not want her to suffer in grief for a moment longer but he stuck to the script that he and Gabriel had put together.

"Woman, why is it that you are weeping?"

"Sir, if you have carried him off please tell me where you have laid him and I will take him away."

"Mary..." Yeshua said.

His brother's lover turned around and she froze as she laid eyes upon him. It took several moments for her mind to catch up and process what she was seeing, then she lunged at his feet.

"Teacher!" she exclaimed.

"I have not yet ascended to the father. Go tell the others," Yeshua said.

End of Part One

Part Two
Trepidation

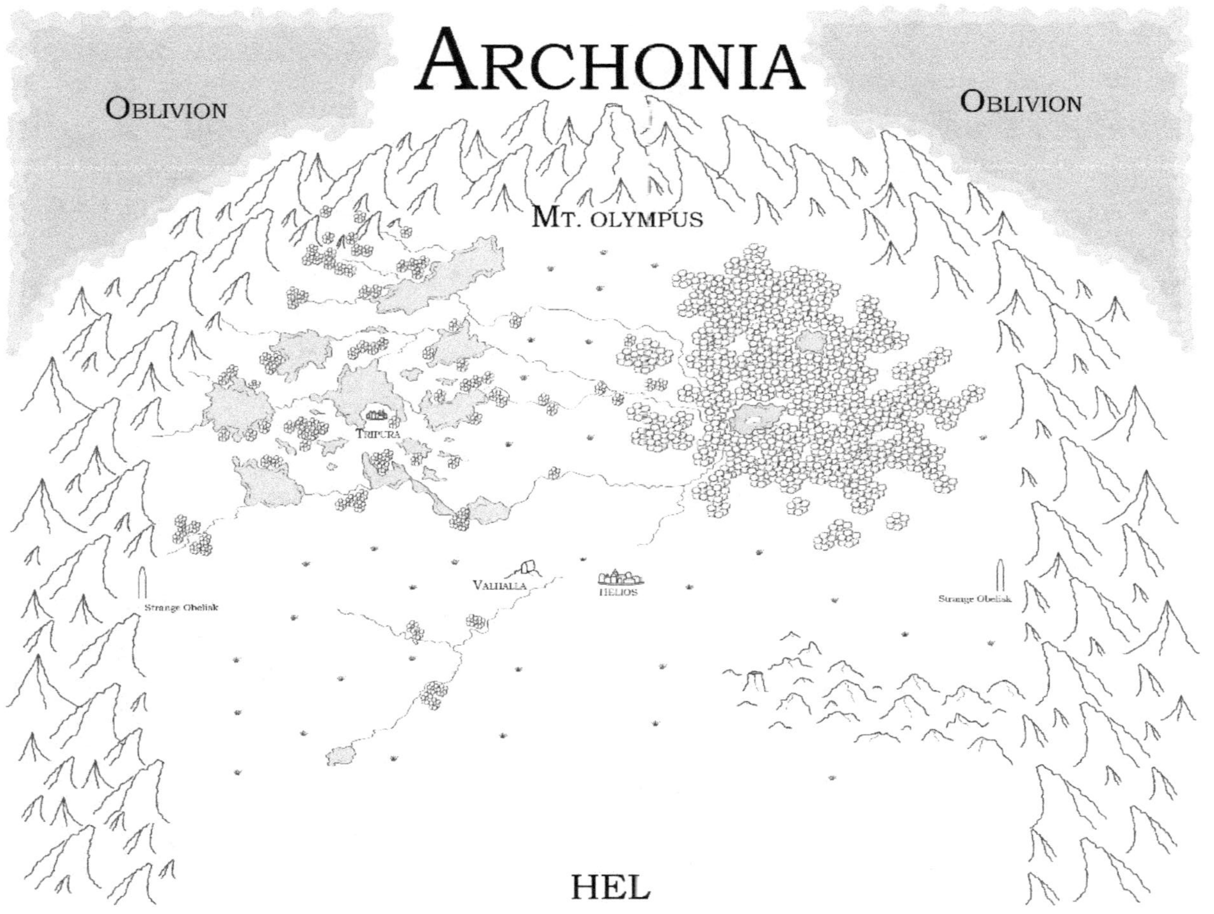
ARCHONIA
OBLIVION
OBLIVION
MT. OLYMPUS
TRIPURA
VALHALLA
HELIOS
Strange Obelisk
Strange Obelisk
HEL

CHAPTER SIXTEEN
A world of spirits

Meredox gasped as he jerked upright, his chest heaving in and out. His mind still flooded with the pain of his gruesome death. Looking down at his hands, he found that there were no holes in his flesh and no blood upon his clothes.

Was it all a dream?

Scrambling to his feet, he felt an immense numbness, he realized the world around him was drawn in shadows. The countryside appeared as if all the color had been drained.

Meredox inhaled and there was no smell. Where once the hilltop was filled with the stench of rotten flesh and blood he could sense nothing. As if the sensation had been stolen from him.

This must be a dream.

Walking a few awkward steps forward, Meredox tried to find an answer to this strange absence of feelings.

Turning around, he spotted the stake which he had been hanging upon only moments ago and suddenly he froze.

Oh gods. I'm dead.

Before his very eyes, Meredox's own body still hung from the large wooden planks. His form sagged, completely devoid of movement. Looking back to his hands, he studied their pale outline. Many belief systems had spoken of a life after death. Was this it? This numb, colorless existence? Would he be like this forever?

"Oh gods! Where am I!?" Luxor shouted.

Meredox looked over to where his brother's body also hung. Below was the glowing outline of Luxor, slowly taking form. He rushed over and laid a soft hand on his brother's upper arm.

"Luxor, we've passed. We are on the other side now," Meredox said.

Tears in his eyes, Luxor wrapped Meredox in a hug. The normally comforting action felt bleak.

"This is all my fault," Luxor said.

"Death was the only thing certain about life, brother. Wherever we are now, at least we are together."

Meredox felt his brother sniffling into his tunic which was still tattered and torn. The action seemed hollow somehow. Luxor's spirit left no tears and he could scarcely feel his brother's embrace.

"Always the optimist, Meredox. Where are we? What is this place?"

"I do not know. It feels as though we are behind a thin sheen of cloth, still looking upon the world we came from. Somehow I feel... Empty," Meredox said.

Suddenly, Meredox saw movement to his right. His neck swiveled and he set eyes upon several figures. A group of men and women were approaching. He jabbed Luxor in the side and subtly motioned towards them. Only then did he spot two other groups of people moving their way.

The space beyond the hill seemed dark, almost non-existent. Meredox quickly wondered where these figures had come from.

"Hello? Who are you?" Luxor asked, puffing out his chest and facing the nearest group.

There was no response and Meredox began to feel uneasy as the people converged around them. Men and women alike all wearing grim faces marching slowly.

"Luxor I don't think these spirits are friendly," Meredox hissed.

Quickly Meredox made a move, scrambling towards where they had been staked. He grabbed Luxor pulling him along but skidded to a halt as he spotted more spirits ahead of him. They were surrounded.

"What do you want from us?" Meredox bellowed.

Gripping Luxor's arm he stood back to back against his brother. The spirits moved in, their eyes locked upon him. New fear rose in his heart. Could they be hurt in this world? Could they perish a second time?

Without warning, the march ceased. At least twenty souls surrounded them, standing no more than two cubits away. Tension was thick in the air as each spirit sneered at them.

"Leave this place, vermin. You criminal scum are not welcome here with our lord," a man declared.

Their lord?

Meredox didn't respond but he thought perhaps they meant Yeshua or Joses, whatever his name was.

"We are not criminals, friends. We were falsely accused by the Romans. My brother and I were simple stage performers. See?" Luxor said, then he took out his wooden coin which he somehow still had in his pocket and tried to perform a simple sleight of hand trick.

"Lies! Take them!" a woman shouted.

Arms shot out, wrapping around Meredox's wrists before he could react and from behind someone began choking him. Thick calloused fingers squeezed against his neck. Unlike the rest of his senses, pain didn't seem to be blunted in this strange world. While restrained like this, there was little he could do to fight off the person throttling him.

No! Get off him!" Luxor said, but soon someone had him by the neck as well. Luxor gagged, the hands crushing down upon his throat with no relief in sight. His vision began to blur again but a burst of light erupted from behind the crowd of murderous spirits. Air rushed into his body and he coughed as he was released.

Meredox winced at the sight of the bright light and their attackers shrunk away from the heat which seemed to be pulsing off a figure. Unlike the rest of the world this person was filled with color. Long curly golden locks swayed gently with the waves of heat pouring off his body.

"These men speak truly," the figure said, his voice a beautiful tenor, ringing like a chorus of string instruments.

"An angel of the lord!" a man cried, dropping to his knees.

"My name is Gabriel. I have come to take you to the land that was promised."

The group of people rejoiced, while Meredox and his brother shrunk away from the golden figure, clad in a fine tunic with shimmering trim.

Behold, your teacher, Joses of Bethlehem, brother to Yeshua, and my son." Gabriel said.

Meredox looked over and spotted Joses standing tall beneath his cross. The crowd erupted again, with shouts of joy. As they did, the façade Joses was putting on faded instantly. He collapsed to the ground and began to wail loudly.

A flash of light burst outwards again, momentarily blinding Meredox. Slowly, the world spun back into view and the crowd and the golden figure had disappeared. Joses remained slumped on the ground, crying loudly, convulsing with each sob.

Meredox trotted over to him, crouching low and placing a gentle hand on his shoulder. Joses grabbed him, pulling up to grip tightly around his waist. After a few moments, he returned the man's embrace letting him release his anguish.

"There there, your suffering is at an end," Meredox said, patting him on the back.

Looking over his shoulder, Meredox saw his brother staring awkwardly at the scene. He didn't say anything or try to stop him he just waited until the man's tears had all ran out.

"After all the years I devoted to those people. They let me be scourged and hung like that." Joses said, sniffling.

"People are cruel, my friend," Meredox replied.

"I'm sorry, I was doing my best to hold it together there. I'm just done. I'm done with people. I mean no offense to you and your brother," Joses said, pulling away.

"You don't need to explain yourself, Judean. For as long as I can remember the only person I've ever been able to depend on is my brother."

"Well at least he was there for you. My brother fled from his problems. He left me alone so that the wolves might devour me."

"The man Yeshua we encountered seemed determined to find you and take you away. He even went ahead of the caravan travelling by night to seek you out. Perhaps he did not abandon you completely."

Another flash of light burst to his left. This one was far less vibrant. The golden figure had returned, striding over to them with sure, steady steps.

"Yeshua did not abandon you. He still fights for our cause. Your message will change the world," Gabriel said.

"Leave me be, Father. I want no more of this. I have served you faithfully throughout my life. This second life is mine to live. Please just take me to the promised land so that I might find peace," Joses finished, hanging his head in defeat.

"Would you like to come with?" Gabriel asked looking to Meredox.

Meredox and Luxor turned to one another not sure if the strange being was speaking to them, for he didn't turn his head from his supposed son.

"Yes I speak to you, Adomos."

Meredox winced at the sound of his given name but ignored the comment. Instead, he processed his situation.

"What is this promised land?" Luxor asked.

"Many people call it many different things. Heaven, Paradise, the promised land. Ultimately it is a place I have created for mankind's souls to live in peace after their mortal years have passed."

Meredox was speechless still. Luxor looked equally so. They would be foolish to turn down such an offer. Still for some reason it seemed too good to be true and he pressed the issue.

"You created this world? Are you a god? How do we know that you speak the truth?"

Gabriel offered a little smirk "Perhaps I acted like a god to the men of the mortal world. While I have abilities and knowledge that far surpass anything that you could comprehend there are still limits. In the next life we have been labeled as Archons."

"We? There are more than one of you?" Luxor asked.

"All these things will be explained to you in good time, Diogenes." Gabriel said.

Meredox exchanged a worried look with his brother but neither of them wanted to be left behind for the angry spirits that still lingered in this shadowy place. He watched his brother walk forward first.

"We will join you, Archon." Luxor said, confidently.

As he did, a heat embraced Meredox like a thick blanket and pulled him into a white light which blasted out over the edges of the hilltop. He lost sense of sight and sound as he was thrust upwards at a terrible speed.

CHAPTER SEVENTEEN
Paradise

Luxor felt like he was falling, the sensation had always brought him a mix of terror and joy. Never before had he fallen from such a great height. A strange world took form thousands of cubits below and it rushed toward him faster than he could take in the details.

Letting out a scream, Luxor shielded his eyes, fearing that he would die from the fall. Just before he reached the ground, everything slowed. His feet settled amidst long white grass. He tried to take a step but his wobbly legs buckled. Falling to his knees, he took a moment to orient himself.

"Brother!" he cried.

Luxor heard no reply. Swiveling his head he saw no one else around him for as far as he could see. Not even the strange Archon who had brought them here. The only sight was endless fields of long white grass.

"Hello?" he called.

Rising to his feet he found that his balance had returned. He trudged a few steps through the thick grass. Despite its spiked appearance the plant was soft to the touch. The gently waving stalks tickled at his bare skin.

Luxor looked to the sky finding a bright glowing sun hanging above him. By the look it appeared to be midday. Squinting, he put a palm over his eyes like a visor and scanned the horizon. The waving fields seemed hypnotic as the wind passed over them. He just barely spotted a break in the sea of grass and had to look twice to make sure.

Miles away, there appeared to be some sort of settlement. Or at least something other than grass. Taking a moment to think, Luxor ultimately decided that this would be his best option.

Barefoot and dressed in the scraps that remained of his clothes, Luxor made his way across the fields towards his destination. He walked for what seemed like nearly an hour before stopping to take a short rest.

Looking back to the sun, Luxor realized it hadn't seemed to move. Then, he scanned the horizon again. This time for any signs of food or water. He would need something soon if he was to keep up this pace. There was nothing. The only change in the endless rolling hill was ahead.

Luxor pressed on, his mouth growing parched with each passing minute. The temperature held a comfortable level, nothing like the sweltering heat of Judea. The cool breeze invigorated him but soon he felt the low rumble of his stomach calling for nourishment.

Marching on, Luxor began to give up hope of reaching his destination which seemed to still be so far away. Suddenly, he realized that someone was watching him.

Luxor's head spun, locking onto the silhouette of a man astride some sort of mount. He was shrouded by the sun as he remained motionless at the top of a hill. Squinting, Luxor waited. After many moments of simply staring at one another, he finally raised his hand hailing the strange figure.

As his eyes adjusted to the light, Luxor caught sight of the man who began to descend from the hill atop a large brown bear. He felt his eyes widen and his body tense up at this sight. Bears were not to be trifled with, any man knew that.

The stranger looked terrifying, clothed in furs with blue paint marking his face. The only hair he had was a long golden beard speckled with brown.

"Hello der, little man. You lost?" the man bellowed in a deep, rough voice.

"I am. I've only just arrived in this strange world and my usher seems to have abandoned me," Luxor said.

"Hmm... Ya I see dat. You're filthy. Grom here could smell ya over dat der hill."

"Can you help me?"

"Vats your name, little man?"

"I am Luxor. What can I call you?" he asked sticking with his most recent cover for sake of ease.

The bear rider regarded him with a strange look as he offered his name. It was as if he was trying to figure something out for a moment before he spoke again.

"I'm Runi. Dis here is Grom," he said, scratching his bear's neck. The animal snorted and shook its head, leaning into his affectionate gesture.

"A pleasure to meet you, Runi. Do you have water? My thirst grows by the minute."

"Grab one of dose der stalks. Grip it ard and give er a yank," Runi said, leaning against the front of his saddle as if he was bored.

Luxor looked down at the grass around him. He yanked one of the long grass stems out near the bottom. The roots came free fairly easily. They wcrc plump like an onion or potato but squishy.

They're filled with water.

"You can eat dat whole root, little man."

Luxor didn't think twice and put the whole bulb in his mouth. His teeth cut off the stalk and he tossed it aside. Water squirted from the side of the root as his teeth chomped down and his throat rejoiced. Even the mild taste of soil didn't stop him from enjoying the intense sweetness of the root as he chewed and swallowed it down.

Grabbing several more, he took a moment to eat while Runi studied him.

"Can you tell me about this world? Or where I am?" Luxor asked, grinding away at the refreshing roots.

"Dis is Clan Bjorn territory. Meh brothers and I have a settlement over yonder," Runi said, spitting over the side of his bear.

"I need to find my brother, is yours the only settlement in this world?"

"No, lots of people. Lots of territories. Who's yer brudder?"

"We both just came here. His name is Meredox."

"Aint ner heard of no mare docks. I'll ask around. We should move though. Get back before dark," Runi said, then he turned and kicked his bear into motion lightly with his heals.

Luxor scrambled to his feet wiping away bits of dirt that had settled on him, from his eating of the roots. He caught up to Runi in moments feeling refreshed and ready for the rest of the hike.

The trip started quiet. Luxor noted Runi's stoic behavior. He had seen some northerners during his time in Rome. They were mostly slaves brought down to fight in the games. Runi would've made a grand gladiator in the arena.

"Where you from, little man. What do ye do?"

"I was from Greece, but I travelled the world as a showman."

"A show man? Hmm... What did you show?"

"I performed simple tricks and sleights of hand. The illusions were meant to bring happiness," Luxor said, rolling his wooden coin across his knuckles.

"And precious metals I'm sure," Runi smirked.

"Yes, we made a decent go of it."

"You and yer brudder eh?"

"That's right. We always had one another. I'm not sure if he still cares about me though. Our first life ended badly."

Runi rocked back and forth as his mount hobbled across the plains. He frowned, staring forward and Luxor could almost see the memories that were surfacing in the man's mind.

"De mortal world was a merciless lady. She often took more den she gave. You'll like it here, little man."

"Tell me of your clan. What is your profession?"

"Oh I's a hunter. Nuttin I can't hit with a good bow. Meh brothers and I keep to the old traditions. We live free, no fancy rules from no kings."

No governing body?

Luxor and his brother had found freedom on the road but were ever answerable to authority. Taxed unfairly and detained on a regular basis simply for being different. True freedom was hard to come by. The prospect had a definite allure.

The sun finally began to move and as it did the bright orb sank far too quickly. It was as if the light of day was created by some artificial power. By the time it had disappeared, Luxor saw the outline of fires ahead.

"Welcome to Valhalla, little man." Runi said with a grin.

Luxor caught sight of large wooden structures in the darkening sky. Torches and bonfires cast shadows about the fine woodwork. The conglomeration of dwellings was crowned by a long tall building constructed of thick tree trunks.

Where did they find trees?

Following the large man into his town, Luxor felt almost naked. Not simply for the fact that he actually was almost naked, but also because everyone was looking at him. Large husky men and women craned their necks to get a glance. Runi greeted some and paid little mind to him as he followed meekly behind.

Finally, Runi dismounted and Luxor watched him hug the bear before tying it to a post and coming back over.

"Follow me, little man. We'll get some mead in ye."

Luxor didn't argue and soon Runi ducked into a medium-sized structure which smelled of roasted meats and other alien delights. He passed through a fur doorway which hung in strips to allow for easier passage. Once inside his eye stung from the smoke hanging in the air.

Moving forward, Luxor coughed several times and that made the room fall silent. Looking up, he appraised the people staring back at him. There were four in total including Runi. Three men and one woman. All of them seemed to be twice his size.

"Did you find that out on the plains today, Runi? The woman asked, smirking and leaning in to sniff him. Luxor stepped back, caught off guard by her pale blue eyes and golden hair which was braided behind her in two parts. She shuddered and slunk away after catching a whiff.

"I did, little sister. Smelled him before I saw him," Runi said. The room erupted in laughter.

Luxor remained silent, embarrassed by the state of his hygiene.

"Don't listen to them, little brother. We all passed over in much the same state," said the biggest of them, he had a shiny bald head like Runi but wore a thick goatee much more well-kept that his guide's beard.

"This little man's name is Luxor and he is looking for his brother..."

"Meredox," Luxor finished for him.

Luxor watched Runi nod and take a seat. He drew some dark liquid from a big wooden barrel in the corner of the room. It filled a horn that he had pulled from his belt and he drained the contents in a matter of seconds.

"Hail, Luxor. My name is Brock." The biggest man said.

"I be Dagur," a skinny man said. He had darker hair and seemed different than the others somehow. Unlike the others who had a drink in their hand, he sat on a barrel sharpening a dagger.

"And I'm Eerika. You best mind your hands if you'd like to keep them," she said smiling at him with a wink.

"Runi, get your guest a drink, man!" Brock bellowed, tossing his own drink horn toward the man who was draining his second cup.

Runi growled at Brock but filled up his horn a third time. Then, he offered it to Luxor who took it apprehensively.

"Thank you," Luxor said, taking a seat on a long wooden bench next to Eerika. He sniffed the liquid in the horn and it gave him a shiver. Despite its sweet smell it was clearly some fermentation. Likely stronger than any wine he ever drank.

Not wanting to be rude, Luxor took a drink and regretted having swigged so much. He shuddered at first but then a sweet taste of honey took over and he exhaled loudly.

The others erupted into laughter. Luxor huffed and took another swig. This time he held it together and the group cheered him. Despite their fearsome appearance they seemed to be a merry bunch.

Luxor soon found his head spinning. The northerners bantered with one another for a while, some telling him stories about themselves.

Suddenly, a great crash interrupted the merrymaking and they all dropped their cups and listened. Outside the dwelling they heard a strange voice cry. "Bardagi!"

Brock rose and reached into the corner of the room producing a large hammer. Luxor couldn't possibly imagine hefting it himself. Eerika fell off the bench and grabbed for a sword which lay on the floor behind her.

"It's a fight, little man! Hehe!" Runi yelled, finishing his horn full of drink and pulled an unstrung bow from a quiver on his back.

"Join us!" Brock yelled, a large smile on his face.

"I have no weapon, no armor," Luxor said.

I don't know how to fight either.

"Hehe, find a rock!" Dagur replied jumping through the fur doorway out into the night.

Luxor tried to refuse but Runi and Brock pulled him along as he stood in shock. The darkness outside seemed feeble as the world was blanketed in silver moonlight. An identical sphere seemed to hang in the same spot the sun had earlier that day.

Frantically, Luxor tried to pry his arm loose from Brock's thick sausage sized fingers. As he did, he was nearly bowled over by several men and women running toward where the commotion was coming from.

As he fought to keep his feet beneath him, the river of bodies carried him ever closer to the sound of metal banging against metal. Grunts and battle cries issued forth throughout the night.

Focus, Luxor!

Trying to maintain balance, Luxor felt a wide warrior bump into him. The man had a dagger in his belt, and reflexively, he lifted it without the man noticing. The dagger was large and seemed almost a short sword to him as he held it with two hands.

Soon, he was swept into a sort of clearing or courtyard which was filled with the snarls of men and women brawling with one another. A short but thick man spotted him and with wide dark eyes the man charged.

Luxor held up the short sword to block the man's stout cudgel but something impacted against the back of his head. The world spun and he sprawled on the ground in a heap the fight around him slowly darkening.

CHAPTER EIGHTEEN
Leaps in Intellect

Socrates hadn't met with the guild since they gathered on the farm. The Archon's lesson had fascinated him so much that he sought to find this power within himself. The ability to form things from pure energy would change this world. The possibilities could be limitless.

Calmly, Socrates focused. He had been sitting rather still for the better part of a week. Sighing out, he grumbled unable to find this energy that the Archon had described. There was no telling where the origin of this power was or how he could unlock it.

A knock came at Socrates' door and he gave up his long academic session. His legs screamed as he got to his feet. Sitting for so long was not a good idea.

I'll have to make a note of that.

Lumbering slowly to the door, Socrates massaged his left knee a bit. Sometimes it still ached like it had in his former life and he wondered why. Finally, he opened the door to his private quarters.

"Hello, old friend." Socrates said, letting the door swing in.

"They told me you wouldn't answer," Achilles replied, calmly.

"Oh it was time for me to take a break."

"I'm glad you decided to speak with me. I have some things that I believe you and your guild will be interested in seeing."

"You do? And what might that be?"

Achilles strode over towards his desk but Socrates cut him off. He trusted very few people with his private notes. The warrior raised an eyebrow towards him but didn't sue for answers to his reaction.

"I've made tremendous leaps in my physical prowess."

"Congratulations, how might this interest the guild?" Socrates asked walking with him back towards the door.

"Come and see for yourself. Bring your notepad."

Socrates followed the ancient warrior down the corridor which led out into the front of his humble estate. He didn't see any other guild members about and briefly desired to call for others to assess Achilles' feats. But the man was moving fast. Far too fast for him to keep up even though he seemed to be walking.

Catching up with Achilles by a large rock, Socrates evened out his breath and rested his hands on his knees. Before he could ask Achilles what he had come to show him the man leapt into the air.

A rush of wind shook Socrates as he watched Achilles soar through the air in a wide arc. He came to rest at least three hundred cubits away with a loud thud which echoed off the nearby plateau.

Socrates eyes went wide in surprise. Achilles returned in another bound his feet leaving a small hole in the soft dirt where he landed with a tremendous thump. Before he could put together his first question, Achilles walked over to the large stone nearby and picked it up with one hand.

That rock must weight thirty talents.

Scribbling on his notepad, Socrates eagerly described what he had just seen, noting the subject's muscles hadn't grown at all since he had last seen him. Achilles tossed the giant stone like it was nothing and it came to rest less than a hundred cubits away.

"My friend, how did you unlock these abilities?" Socrates asked.

"With great difficulty. But I simply decided that the forces of weight and gravity were no longer real in this world. Much like our artificial sun, or the unnaturally long days," Achilles said, brushing some white dust off his hands that the stone left behind.

"You are proposing that gravity and weight are manifestations of the physical universe that we came from. Rules that we no longer have to live by."

"I'm not sure, but I'm getting stronger every day."

"This is truly incredible, Achilles. I should like the rest of the guild to see this."

"News has reached me about what the Archon said to you all. He wishes to see a government put in place," Achilles replied.

Socrates shifted uncomfortably. The subject was not something he wanted to talk about, especially with a warrior such as this.

"The Archon meddles with our affairs. I suppose a governing body is inevitable, but we must do better than we did in the previous world. Corruption and greed spread too easily."

"This governing body will need a military to maintain order," Achilles said.

Crossing his arms, Socrates studied the man. He was a student of war and conflict from the age he could hold a sword that much was clear. Even he heard tales of the greatness of Achilles. The last thing that this world needed was war, however.

"Achilles, I pray that this world never knows war. With no needs like that of our human bodies, there should be no conflict."

"There have already been wars in this world. Zeus speaks of the formation of Archonia. The war of the Archons which left this land split in two..."

"Achilles, I will not condone the formation of an army unless the people demand it. For their safety, not to rule through fear."

Socrates felt his heart flutter. The man before him could do as he liked if he wanted. There was now nobody strong enough to stop him. Achilles simply nodded and walked away at incredible speed.

The subject is unnaturally fast and strong. The rules of the physical world no longer bind him.

Finishing his scribbles, Socrates retreated home to continue his study of this strange energy which supposedly surrounded him. As he walked he worried. He knew that Achilles already had a standing force of fighters that he trained with. They were not causing any trouble so nobody stopped them.

Socrates also worried that Achilles was right about needing an army. Despite his objections and desires for peace. There were clans in Archonia who relished fighting and did so for sport and out of tradition. Such pastimes did not simply disappear when they crossed over into this world.

As Socrates walked back through the narrow corridors of his home an idea formed in his mind. The prospect could satisfy everyone. Instead of retiring back to his private quarters he turned down another corridor towards where Aristotle made his home.

The bare stone walls guided him to his friend who was busy mixing some sort of concoction which smelled of citrus and sandalwood.

"Hello there, friend. We have not seen you for..."

"Too long," Socrates finished for him. "I'm afraid I was lost. In search of these powers the Archon explained to us. But I am here now. I think we should gather the guild. I'd like to propose something to them."

"Whatever might that be?" Aristotle asked peering over two thick cylinders of glass which seemed to magnify his eyes to a comically large proportion.

"I'd like to propose the creation of a battalion of peacekeepers. Virtuous sentinels who will help uphold the laws of a governing body."

CHAPTER NINTEEN
Posthumously

Yeshua listened intently to two of his former followers as they talked to one another along the road to Emmaus. Cleopas and another person that he did not recognized bickered about the events of his brother's death at the hands of the Sanhedrin.

Having been following them for several miles, Yeshua was just now catching up to them. So far he had not made himself known, curious to see what the gossips were saying.

"I'm telling you, Judas betrayed him. Kissed him on the cheek and handed him over to the guards," Cleopas said.

"That could very well be but Peter didn't stand for him either. They all let him suffer at the stake," the other man said.

"All I know is that he is dead and we need to be careful about who we talk about this to," Cleopas said now looking over his shoulder and spotting Yeshua.

Yeshua had his hood up and made sure not to appear too conspicuous at first. People's reactions could be irrational and even dangerous if a dead man was spotted walking down the road.

"I heard that death could not hold Yeshua. That by the grace of the lord he was resurrected after three days' time," Yeshua said, stepping up beside the two men.

"You old fool! I watched the legionnaires stab him with my own eyes and was there when they laid him to rest," Cleopas companion said, scoffing.

"Where have you heard this news traveler?" Cleopas asked, slowly.

"Cleopas, it is I, Yeshua. Do you not recognize me?" Yeshua asked lowering his hood.

Yeshua watched the man stumble and nearly fall as he stopped. Then, the man backed away as if afraid.

"Teacher?" Cleopas asked.

"Take heart, good Cleopas. I have risen. Go spread the word. Death does not keep me."

Yeshua continued across the countryside, greeting his followers wherever he met them, spreading the word of his resurrection. Finally, he caught up with a group of his disciples in Gazara. Peter and Simon had been hiding out there with a group of others and it had taken him some time to get this information from a local man.

After convincing him that he was indeed Yeshua of Nazareth the man showed him a secret door into the building they were hiding in. He found a group of nearly ten men dining and discussing a plan to escape to Galilee.

"The harbors will be watched. We need to secure good mounts and thick water skins," a man said.

"I say we stand against the Sanhedrin and continue our good work," another said.

"They crucified him and he had broken no laws! They will do the same to us," Simon exclaimed.

Yeshua sat down among them and lowered his hood. Only one man immediately recognized him and was too speechless to tell the others. He simply sat there gaping and pointing in alarm.

Smiling, he patted the man on the shoulder trying to recall his name but couldn't place it. Finally someone else spotted him and shouted.

"Ghost! It is the ghost of Yeshua!" he cried.

The room erupted in shouts of alarm but Yeshua waited patiently for them to calm themselves.

"Teacher is that you? Are you a ghost?" Peter asked.

"No, Peter, death could not hold me for my father is God and he has brought me back to life."

Yeshua let the silence in the room marinate for a few seconds before continuing.

"Have you lost faith already? Did you not know that my father would not let me die so easily?" Yeshua asked.

"We have seen you perform miracles before, teacher. But to return from death. We all saw you hanging on the cross..." Simon replied.

"Do not despair dear, Simon. I understand. But you have nothing to fear, for Almighty God is with us. Go from this place and tell the others that I have risen."

Before anyone could muster a protest or response, Yeshua got up and strode out the way he had come.

Yeshua watched the color drain from the face of his old friend. Standing over him, he waited for the man to say something. All of his old disciples had gathered after news had spread.

As Yeshua's father predicted, it hadn't taken long for his old followers to hear and flock back to him. Appraising the faces and eyes around him now, he could see fear, regret, and even sorrow.

Few of Yeshua's friends were in on the secret that he and his brother were twins. So only they might have figured out the great facade, but the momentum of his resurrection couldn't be stopped now. Gossips had spread far within the weeks following Joses' death.

Those that might have known acted as if Yeshua's return was a miracle every bit as much as the rest of them. Sitting down on a stone, he regarded his pale-faced friend Judas cowering before him.

"Teacher, I'm so sorry. I tried my best to lie to the Sanhedrin and their guard. Please forgive me. They are all calling me a betrayer," Judas plead.

"You know the truth of your actions in your own heart, Judas. I cannot and will not judge you for them. Only the Almighty can do such," Yeshua said.

Yeshua took note of his raggedy appearance and bruise covered body. Whoever accused him hadn't been kind. Based on what he saw in the garden the man was trying to establish a false identity for his brother.

"He took silver from the Sanhedrin in exchange for your betrayal!" Peter yelled.

"Please, Peter, do not let anger guide your words and actions. Be at peace. If Judas did betray it is not your place to persecute him," Yeshua said, holding up a hand.

"Yes teacher, I'm sorry. I'm just so overwhelmed at seeing you again," Peter said, his mouth tasting a lie. He was one of the few who knew.

"Teacher, now that you have returned we can continue on our path to spread the word and laws of God," James said, an awed look in his dark eyes.

"No, James, that work is done. It ends with my death and resurrection. You all know why I left before. The gospel was being twisted. Used by some of you for personal gain. The power was too tempting."

"How dare you!" Bartholomew exclaimed. "We have followed you until the death and even now return after your miraculous resurrection. Is this how your treat loyal followers? By shaming our actions?

"I do not say these words in shame. I am merely stating why I left and why this work must come to an end. I am proud of all of you for helping me spread the message."

Yeshua let the words rest in their minds for a moment. He expected some resistance and Bartholomew was one of the men he worried had gone too far with his actions in past months. The man's reaction didn't surprise him.

Looking out over the desert, Yeshua's heart panged with guilt, regret, and worry. He longed to leave this half-dead wasteland where men struggled to survive. The Promised Land was so close. But to get there he still had to endure tremendous pain.

"Enough of this! The work will continue," Thomas said, evenly. Then, standing up, Thomas grabbed Judas roughly by the hair and yanked him away from Yeshua's feet.

Yeshua watched, but didn't react. His worst fears were about to come true but it was necessary. They could do nothing to stop the spread of his word now. Any chances they had of twisting it would take centuries to undo.

Bartholomew jumped into action next, producing a rope tied into a slipknot. Wrapping it around Judas' neck they strung him up from a nearby tree. The rest of Yeshua's follows cried out but didn't move to stop them.

"This is not our teacher. He is a devil in disguise. Yeshua had a twin brother, Joses. We guarded this secret jealously but now the time has come for you all to know the truth," Peter said, walking forward.

"This false prophet, Joses seeks to destroy our good work. But he has only strengthened our message. Brothers! It is time for Joses to be reunited with his brother," Bartholomew said.

Yeshua waited patiently on his rock, watching the life slowly leave Judas while he dangled from the end of a crudely spun rope.

"The story will be written as follows. Judas Iscariot betrayed our lord and savior. In his shame, he hung himself. The glorious resurrection of our teacher has shown us the true miracles of the Almighty God but now his journey is over and he will take his place at the right hand of his father," Peter continued.

And so my legacy ends with lies and bloodshed.

Still not moving, Yeshua watched as Peter drew a long curved dagger from his robes and lunged at him. Even though he knew it was coming, he gasped. The cold metal bit into his stomach, once, twice, three times.

Each blow, brought with it pain and anguish. Yeshua's muscles flexed, trying to reject the cruel instrument, while his eyes remained fixed on Peter. His assailant could hardly look at him as he stabbed again and again.

CHAPTER TWENTY
The Other Side of the Coin

Meredox walked into a strange settlement dazed from his journey with the Archon. The buildings that comprised the majority of the town seemed very Greek in appearance.

Wiping sweat from his brow, Meredox noted the familiar limestone columns which held up the roofs of large structures towards the interior of the town. Stucco covered masonry made up the smaller dwellings.

Stopping for a moment, Meredox found that he had to catch his breath from the pace he had made on his approach to the town. So far as he had seen, This "Promised Land" was no different from that of the previous world. His muscles still ached and he felt just as hungry as he had in his former life.

Meredox's frantic approach to the only settlement in sight was due to the fact that he had arrived without his brother. He couldn't remember a time when he and Luxor had been separated. Ambling over the rolling fields of strange white grass alone had left him feeling naked and fearful that he had in fact been duped by the Golden-haired man.

After several minutes of wandering through the settlement, Meredox spotted other souls going about their business. The people were all young, clean, and astoundingly beautiful.

"Hello friend, have you only just arrived here in Archonia?" a man asked.

Meredox nearly jumped at the man's voice but held it together. "Yes, My brother and I. Have you seen another that looks just like me?"

"We have not, you are the only arrival today. Please wait here, I'll go find Mother Belladonna." The man said, placing a hand gently on his shoulder.

The hand was warm and heavy but calmed Meredox immediately. The strange feeling disappeared a few moments after the man did. He was left standing in the middle of the strangers who were all smiling at him as if they knew what he was going through. A handful of awkward minutes later, the man returned with a woman wrapped in a long white chitin.

"Greetings, my name is Belladonna."

"Hello, my lady, can you help me find my brother?"

"I will do my best, dear. I am trying to organize a group of people to aid those fresh souls that have only just arrived in Archonia. For now I will have to do," she said.

"Any help you can offer would be appreciated," Meredox replied.

"When did your brother pass? Was it long ago? I have access to the most up to date list of souls living here, I think," Belladonna said, wrinkling her nose.

"We passed at the same time. We were brought here at the same time by a being calling himself an Archon," Meredox said.

"Oh, that is strange. The Archon is an unusual being though. One never knows his intentions. I assure you if your brother is in Helios, we will find him."

"Is that the name of this civilization?"

"It is the name we have given this city."

"You mentioned Archonia as well?"

"Yes, that is the name of this world according to the oldest of us. Some still call it by other names."

Meredox walked with the woman who looked beyond lovely in her pure white gown. He eagerly took in her curves and his imagination whisked him away to a romantic scene where he held her close, kissing her plump lips.

Pain shot through Meredox's leg as his shin hit a post near the edge of the road. He stumbled nearly falling face first into the dirt as he hobbled around it. He felt the heat rise in his face while his shin throbbed in pain.

How embarrassing.

Thankfully, Belladonna didn't laugh at Meredox. Instead, she steadied him, her touch was as calming as the man's had been and he breathed out evenly as the pain in his shin subsided.

"You must be more careful...uh?" she said, fishing for his name.

"Meredox, miss, my name is Meredox."

"That is a strange name. I have never heard it before."

"I left my given name behind me along with my former life," Meredox said, coming to the realization then and there.

"Well even though it is strange, I like it," she replied, wrapping her arms around his and leading him further into the city.

Meredox walked in silence for a few minutes. She graciously let him take in the new sights. Eventually they entered a building of unremarkable size, its stonework more Roman in style.

"What do you do here in this life?" Meredox asked.

"Well, you can do anything you wish. There is little to no pain or strife. From what the Guild of Dokimazos has published so far, it seems that our souls do not need to eat, sleep, or even make water," she said, rolling her eyes a little.

"This guild of testers, you don't believe them?"

"I do, I mean these things have already been discovered. They are the first who are officially documenting things in this world. Trying to control it is all," she added at the end.

"Why is it that I feel hunger if I do not need to eat?"

"Well our souls are still able to experience the pleasures of life. Not to worry all of these things will be explained. I will educate you on the way of this world and if you so choose we can find you a profession. Just know that you could choose to leave and live anywhere in this world a free man, no longer bound by the constraints of your human body."

"What if I help you? I mean, help create your organization?" Meredox said.

Meredox froze, dumbfounded by her beauty as she smiled at him.

"I would like that very much," Belladonna said.

The next month of Meredox's second life was a whirlwind of events and a flood of knowledge. Luxor fell to the back of his mind. He decided that a break from his constant companion would be a good change of pace.

I need a break from you dear brother.

Walking regally with hands behind his back, Meredox passed tall marble columns on his way towards Helios' main amphitheater. The colossal structure sat at least one thousand people. He hadn't seen anything so magnificent outside of Rome.

Looking to his side, Meredox's cheeks puffed into a candid smile directed at Belladonna who had not only been his teacher for the past month but also somewhat of an authority figure. Despite their working relationship, Meredox was becoming enamored with her.

"Are you ready to present your proposal to the council?" She asked, smiling back at him.

"As ready as I will ever be I imagine. I think it is a sound proposal and you're the perfect candidate to run things," Meredox said, earnestly.

Meredox saw her cheeks turn rosy red for a moment even though she tried to hide it. Soon, he caught himself staring and nearly tripped over a small three step incline which led up to the main stage. Luckily, she didn't see him.

You fool.

Recomposing himself, he adjusted his fine white flax toga which was falling off his shoulder. Then, he proceeded on to the stage. Hundreds of souls sat in on the meeting. With there being no set governing body, the people decided things with a simple show of hands.

"Now, the lady Belladonna and her colleague Meredox will be proposing the creation of a group of people to aid with the new souls that arrive in Archonia daily," Aristotle shouted to the crowds.

Meredox couldn't hardly believe that it was thee Aristotle whose philosophies even in his time were taught and practiced. Supposedly he was also to see Socrates and Plato amongst this group. All great men of their time.

Breathing out, Meredox realized that his thoughts were all scrambled about in his head. Even though he was a practiced stage performer, he felt nervous, like it was his first show again.

"Thank you, good sir. As you know the souls that pass into this realm are often confused and lost when they arrive. There is never an exact location and some of these souls can go for days without finding others to show them the way," Belladonna began.

Meredox saw her turn and nod, giving him the lead.

"The lady Belladonna and I wish to propose the creation of a house of Matrons. This establishment will be created to train individuals on how to introduce new souls into this world once they are found," Meredox continued.

"These positions which we have dubbed Mámmi will be responsible for not only finding the new souls, but also for locating any ancestors that may have passed into this world before them," Belladonna said.

Meredox didn't continue. The crowd would need some time to consider their opening proposal. Belladonna whisked by him touching his arm and continued after she was looking at the opposite side of the crowd.

"These of course will be volunteer positions only. The particulars of their training will be forthcoming with the approval of this organization of course," Meredox added.

A man with simple brown robes stood up, he carried himself as though he had been in many of these meetings before.

"This sounds similar to your proposal for the saving of unborn souls that you described last month, my lady," the man said.

Meredox had not heard of this proposal and he found it slightly uncomfortable that she had withheld this information from him. But he dismissed the feeling. She, after all, was not answerable to him.

"Thank you for the reminder, Merideus. I see now that such a proposal was somewhat of an impossibility. I had hoped that this idea was more feasible than my last."

"I was lost when I arrived only weeks ago. Belladonna was there. Her skill with transitioning new souls needs to be taught," Meredox said.

Another man, sitting near the front looked at him thoughtfully and raised a hand. As he did, the whole theatre fell silent.

"You are new to this council. From what I have heard, you have a good education?" the man asked.

"Yes I was taught in the ways of Greek philosophies. I also partook in Roman culture and learned a great deal from firsthand experience," Meredox replied.

The group of men surrounding the one who had spoken began to chuckle. Meredox didn't understand why for a moment until he recognized the man who had spoken from his many stone depictions not only in mother Greece but in Rome as well.

"You are the great Socrates? Founder of the morale philosophies?" Meredox gasped.

"I'm not certain I can claim the title of "great" but I did offer the world some things to think about. It is good to see that I have reached so many generations," Socrates said.

"Nevertheless, it is an honor to be in your presence, teacher," Meredox said, offering a great nod of his head.

"Thank you, friend. Now, to the matter at hand. You have expressed your concerns about the fresh souls coming into this world. I too was lost when I first arrived. What would you say if I told you it was an enlightening time for me?”

Meredox thought for a moment. His aimless wandering didn't seem to benefit him in anyway. But this was a test, he had to dig deeper into Socrates' meaning.

“I do suppose that there can be a positive consequence to the mild suffering endured during ones transition here. It teaches us to appreciate what we have or what we come to have. But I think that this world could and very well should be the absence of suffering if possible,” Meredox said.

“Yes, we suffered enough in our past life!” Merideus exclaimed, the crowd rumbled their approval.

“Well it seems you have stated your case well. Let us vote,” Socrates said.

To his delight, a vast majority of the people voted in favor, and he grinned at Belladonna for a moment before realizing she looked at the crowd, frowning.

“Then it is settled. You may commission a building with the architects and begin signing volunteers,” Socrates said.

Meredox caught up to Belladonna who had already left the stage and was walking at a brisk pace back towards her home across town.

“Bella? What's wrong? We got the motion passed.”

“Only because of you,” she replied curtly.

“Many of the ideas were yours though. I can't take all the credit.”

"But they gave it to you anyway. Did you not hear them say it was *your* idea? They would not have passed the motion if a woman had come up with it," she sneered.

Slowing down, Meredox thought back to what had been said, and Socrates attributed the whole thing to him before the vote. He watched Belladonna walking away and decided that this would not stand. Running to catch up, he grabbed her gently but firmly by the arm, turning her to face him.

"This world will be different than the last. If I must I will make it my life's work to see that inequality is vanquished. This idea was yours and from now on I will see that you get the credit."

Slowly, Meredox watched her frown fade into a smile. Leaning into him, she stood up on her tiptoes and kissed him on the cheek. All thoughts left his head for a moment and he just enjoyed being so close to her. She winked at him and walked away leaving him standing in the thoroughfare holding his cheek.

CHAPTER TWENTY ONE
The Fray

Luxor lunged at a broad berserker who had flaming red hair. His cudgel struck the great oaf right in the nose and a burst of crimson sprayed from his nostrils. The giant man toppled to the ground, and he felt the vigor of battle rise up in him.

Months passed since that first fight, and Luxor was now as tough as the metal at the end of his weapon. When he had awoken from the first battle, miraculously healed by the Valkyrie, His new companions poked fun of him for days. He had never seen real combat in his former life only a handful of brawls and street fights. Despite this fact, Runi and Brock told him that a man should know how to fight no matter his profession.

Stepping lithely around a sweeping strike from a large spear, Luxor danced around the battlefield using his small stature and speed to his advantage. Sturdy warriors from all corners of history converged for The Fray. He learned early to wear deeply treaded shoes so that he didn't slip on the blood and bodies.

Ducking a blow, Luxor spotted Brock across the field handling three fighters at once as if it was a game to him. His too large hammer making great whooping noises as it swished through the air with ease. Making his way towards the half-giant, an arrow grazed his chest, glancing off a curved metal cuirass Runi fashioned for him.

"Another good fight!" Eerika shouted, jumping over a body and landing next to him.

"I might actually make it through this one!" Luxor exclaimed.

Just then, Eerika jerked Luxor low by the collar causing another berserker to narrowly avoid hitting him in the back of the head with an axe. She easily skewered the man with her sword who had lost balance over swinging to hit him.

"Thanks. Let's get to Brock. I always feel better with him at my side," Luxor said, parrying another blow and biting back with his cudgel.

Slowly but surely, Luxor and Eerika fought their way toward Brock. By the time they reached him, Runi and Dagur also formed up. As he approached, he heard Brock's loud laughter over the shouts and cries of pain and saw him fell another warrior with three skilled movements.

"Little brother! You still stand? This late in the fight? I guess Runi's lessons are working!" Brock exclaimed.

Luxor rolled his eyes but responded. "Yes, you giant oaf, and I'll be standing long after you've run out of energy swinging that hammer!"

Brock guffawed but they were both cut short as the Valkyrie began to descend. Bright white light shone down from the sky and winged horses fell bearing the clan's most beautiful women. The horns sounded, signaling the end of the fight and a great cheer went up amongst those that still stood.

Luxor felt Runi grip him in a headlock, and tried to wriggle free as the Valkyrie's light fell over the fallen. The wave of heat hit the man laying bloody just at his feet and his wounds slowly closed. Eventually his eyes popped back open and he sprung up from the ground. When he realized the battle was over he cursed his poor performance and headed off to the mead hall.

"Better luck next time, brother!" Brock called after him. Then the large man walked over and patted Luxor on the back.

"How about a drinking contest?" Luxor asked. His companions cheered and they all walked toward the great mead hall.

Just outside the main door, Luxor realized he was bleeding from his upper arm. The vigor of battle had worn off and he winced at the burning sensation emanating from the clean cut. He paused and headed towards the nearest Valkyrie.

"Where do ya think yer goin?" Eerika asked him.

"I thought I might have this healed, he said pointing to the deep gash."

"I can do it fer ya!" she yelled rushing over.

Luxor offered a disingenuous smile. He didn't like when she healed him. The wounds never closed the same and the pain lingered for longer. He would have much preferred a Valkyrie do it but he gave in, letting his friend practice.

Golden light sprung from her fingertips and showered over his arm. The warm energy coursed through his wound stitching the flesh back together. Soon he was rubbing smooth skin and he thanked her.

Then, Luxor headed into the mead hall finding that Brock, Runi, and Dagur had already saved them seats. Mead and wine splashed everywhere just like the blood had mere minutes ago. It was as if a whole new battle had begun but this time everyone was happy and songs filled the air instead of battle cries.

Before he reached the group the red-haired berserker he had dispatched earlier cut in front of him a tall frothy drink proffered in his hand.

"That was a right fine hit, lad. I'll see you next time!" he said, laughing.

Luxor took the beverage and slammed it into the Berserker's glass before draining it dry. Then, he made his way to his table where he found a bounty of pheasant, mutton, and beef, smoked and waiting to be eaten.

As he sat, Luxor heard the roar of the hall die down. Looking up, he already knew what was happening as he had seen it happen after every Fray. A statuesque man with a long well-combed beard mounted the table at the end of the hall and called out in a loud voice.

"Is there anyone who wishes to challenge me for the right to sit at the head of the table?"

A low rumble crossed over the room, and Runi jabbed Brock in the ribs with his elbow.

"You going to challenge him tonight, Brock?"

The large man shook his head. "I was foolish enough to try that once before, brother. Njord is too old and too strong for the likes of any of us," Brock said, grabbing a large chunk of meat and ripping it from the bone with his teeth.

The others began to eat as well but everyone's head perked up when someone shouted a challenge. The crowd hooted and hollered its approval of another good fight and the challenger jumped up on the other end of the table near the front.

"Oh sit down Raggjr ya fool!" Runi bellowed but the man couldn't hear him over the crowds.

A short but thick fighter with short grizzled hair bowed to the crowd swishing his axe around while Njord unclasped his cloak and took his own axe and shield from a maiden nearby. Finally, he slid on a tall helm that he had adorned with deer antlers to give him the menacing appearance of a devil.

Luxor chewed on a tough loaf of bread, finally dipping it in his mead to soften it up when he looked up, he nearly choked. The fight had begun and ended in a matter of four to five strikes.

Njord wasted no time in charging and battering his opponent with both axe and shield. Raggjr was overwhelmed in moments and Luxor watched the man's axe fly out into the crowd, hooked and pulled free by Njord's. Then the clan leader hit him with the edge of his shield to disorient him before twirling around and separating the man's head from his body.

Gasps rose from around the room before silence overtook it. Cups dropped and shattered to the floor as people realized what happened. Njord tossed his axe on the table next to the man's body and threw his shield towards the maiden nearby.

"You have all grown weak in your frivolity," Njord bellowed.

Luxor remained silent. Normally nobody died in these fights. The clan leader had clearly just shocked everyone.

"This sacred tradition is not a spectacle. Only the strongest among us should lead, this honor and burden should not be mocked by every puny man who wishes to try his hand!" Njord yelled.

There were some grumbles of approval but also people who remained silent and still.

"Everyone raise a glass to honor Raggjr. He fought bravely, but foolishly. Let his example be a lesson to you all," Njord said, then he picked up a large horn set before him and drained the contents.

"Brock, Runi. Will you do nothing? He killed that man in cold blood," Luxor said.

"These are old ways, little brother. If you wish to question the clan leader you must defeat him in battle. He speaks true, the rite of challenge is no joke or spectacle. Raggjr should have taken more care with his life. Though Njord has not finished them in many years, such a challenge is traditionally to the death," Brock said.

Luxor processed what had just happened. So far as he had seen and experienced nobody truly died. Even in the Frays the Valkyries always brought people back from the brink of death.

What happens if you die in this world?

The prospect of that question haunted Luxor for the rest of the night. He retired from the festivities early, heading back to the little shack he constructed with the help of his new friends. On his way he felt as if someone was following him.

Just before he reached his hut, he whipped around, cudgel in hand coming face to face with Eerika. She disarmed him in two movements and pressed her body up against his, smashing him against the hut.

"Eerika?" Luxor asked.

"Hey there, little man. I've been wanting to get you alone to myself," she said, smashing her mouth into his.

Luxor was shocked, but his loins did not protest. He hadn't been with a woman for a very long time and he was not about to deny himself the pleasures of this life. She was big but he picked her up from the ground by her hips all the same.

Stumbling inside his hut, Luxor banged into doorway while Eerika's legs wound around him. All the while their mouth's greedily sucked at one another. He flopped back onto his pile of furs and she ripped his armor free, tossing it into the corner.

In turn, Luxor tore her leather tunic off exposing her finely shaped breasts. She grabbed his hands and pulled them into her soft bosom and he thrust with his hips in response to the pleasure. She gyrated atop him as if it was the most basic and natural instinct.

Suddenly, she jumped up and slid down his trousers, exposing his manhood to her. She grabbed it gently but firmly and rubbed on it for several seconds before climbing back onto him. Luxor laid his head back, his eyes rolling into the back of his head as he slid inside of her.

Luxor thrust up several times as if his mind lost control of his body and something else was working his muscles. Sheer pleasure radiating from his loin, as Eerika bobbed up and down on him, moaning loudly with each impact.

In a matter of a minute, Luxor felt the pleasure reach its peak, and he released, almost growling as he gripped her luscious hips. She screamed into his shoulder, biting down on his naked flesh. And for a moment, they both simply shook in ecstasy.

After many moments of convulsing, the pleasure subsided, and they both began to breathe again. She collapsed on him before rolling over and panting pulling his hand over her eyes for some reason.

"For such a little man, you're sure not small!" Eerika said, laughing.

Luxor was still trying to catch his breath and didn't really know how to respond. Eventually he found some words as she covered herself in a fur and laced one of her legs between his.

"That was a surprise," Luxor said, exhaling deeply.

"Not te me. Been wanting to jump your bones since I first saw ya. I've had all the great oafs around ere but you are so handsome!" she said, kissing his neck.

"Thank you, that's very kind. You. Well, you are pleasing to the eyes as well," Luxor said.

She snuggled in closer to Luxor and he wrapped his arm around her awkwardly. He lay there until she went into the strange trance they called the reflection. Not sure what to do he remained still. It wasn't often that he had encountered the fairer sex in his former life. He found that it made him feel content and dare he say? Happy.

CHAPTER TWENTY TWO
Classifications

Socrates sat on the bank of a pleasantly round lake. The perfect shape satisfied his obsessive nature. A strange vibrant blue bird sang an unnaturally beautiful song as it sat amongst the branches of the tree which he had chosen to lean against.

Before him, his notepad was taunting him. He accumulated a wealth of information and now he was set to organizing and classifying the phenomena he witnessed.

The warrior Geirr was a conjurer. That was an easy classification because he created things out of thin air. Socrates looked over at his horse again appraising the fine craftsmanship of the beast. The detail was incredible. Right down to the way it smelled.

The woman Mahari and her abilities with fire were dangerous and powerful. Though fire wasn't the source it was the energy she pulled from like the archon had described.

Destructor? No. Projector.

Yes, Socrates thought to himself, she projected the energy from her body and it in turn, caused the blasts.

Socrates scribbled this down on his paper but was interrupted by the neighing of another horse. He looked over and found his apprentice Plato riding toward him. Stowing his notebook and charcoal, he rose from his shaded spot under the tree and hailed his old student.

"A fine day! Why did you wish to see me, teacher?" Plato asked.

"I wished to develop my abilities. I was hoping you could aid me," Socrates replied.

"I'd be happy to, sir. How can I assist?"

Socrates wasn't sure exactly how he could help because he wasn't completely certain how his gift would manifest.

"Just relax with me and I will try to concentrate."

Socrates noted the confused look on his student's face as he sat in the plush, green grass next to the lake. A light breeze swept over the area. Plato smiled at him with his dazzling, aqua colored eyes. He had to work hard not to let the man's gorgeous features distract him.

"What exactly do you think you can discern from me but watching me so intently? Teacher?"

Socrates didn't know but already he could feel that Plato was tense. Nervous almost. This sensation only came about when the two were alone together. He suspected that Plato knew about his affinity for men and wanted to keep his distance.

"Sometimes I feel as though I can determine the moods and even the intentions of others. In my meditations I've seen what I feel are the memories of others."

Socrates watched Plato's eyes grow wide and the man's unease grew visible in his bodily movements. He first closed off his posture, then he adjusted his toga.

Not letting these things bother him, Socrates continued to concentrate. Suddenly the unease in Plato's mind turned to terror but it was not from any action taking place in the present. He dived deeper and the terror took shape in his mind.

As if he were Plato, Socrates saw a large body standing over him, touching him and violating him against his will. The face took shape and the memory told him it was his father. The fiend had subjugated Plato to this pain and grief regularly. The images flashed so quickly he could hardly keep track but they were the only things that he could reach. They buried all his other memories.

"Teacher? Teacher!" Plato called.

Socrates felt his eyes come back into focus and he was sprawled out on his back, Plato standing over him.

"I'm so sorry that happened to you, my friend. I would never hurt you like your father did," he said.

Panic replaced the fear and concern clear upon Plato's face and Socrates felt his head hit the ground when his student recoiled.

"How do you... How did you?" Plato stammered.

"I don't know. I'm able to divine things from the minds of others. This ability is still in its infancy. But I promise I will not ever tell another soul."

CHAPTER TWENTY FOUR
Finally at Peace

Yeshua landed gently, his bare feet coming to rest in soft, black dirt. Gabriel stood beside him, his head hung low. He didn't much care for how his father felt. In his mind, Gabriel had failed him.

Appraising his attire, Yeshua realized the blood soaked garments he wore at the end of his mortal life were gone, replaced by fine silk dyed to match the color of the sea. His sandals still wrapped around his legs but they were fresh and new, the leather still smelled musky from the tanning process.

The air around was fresh with a scent he never smelled before. Trees, larger than any he ever saw, surrounded him. Their tall dark trunks rose their limbs and branches reaching into the clouds. Staring in wonder, Yeshua approached one, feeling the rough bark against his new hands. The holes he punctured in them were gone.

"Thank you, father. Goodbye," Yeshua said walking further into the trees.

"Please come with me, your brother needs you," Gabriel replied.

Yeshua stopped. Then, with a heavy sigh, he turned to follow the would-be god. Not conversing further, he trod through the forest, his senses experiencing a plethora of new sights and sounds. Still, he wasn't able to fully enjoy them as the worry in his heart peaked.

In a few short minutes, Yeshua made his way over a small mound of grass where he found a tiny dwelling. The structure was made from large round tree trunks. It had a stone pillar rising from the side where a plume of smoke wafted into the air.

"Joses is inside. I've planted some rather strong herbs in the garden nearby. They will help him deal with his anxieties. Dry them, and inhale the smoke," Gabriel said.

Without a word, Yeshua approached the house. There was translucent glass in places built into the side so that one could see in and out. A large square door appeared a dark green which seemed an unnatural color for the wood it was made of.

Moving to open the door, He began to hear sobbing from within. Without hesitation he pushed against the portal and it swung in. The sobs grew louder and he rushed through the entry and towards the sound coming from one of the many rooms.

"Joses?" Yeshua called.

"Brother!?"

Yeshua found his brother lying on a large square bed laden with finely crafted pillows and intricately woven blankets. He had never seen a bed so fine, nor would anyone outside of a king's palace. Joses lay curled up with his knees tucked to his chest. Tears streamed down his face.

Lunging forward, Yeshua met Joses halfway and they embraced. He felt the scraggly hair on his brother's chin rub against his, the salty taste of tears fell over his mouth as he pulled his brother's head in tighter.

Neither of them wasted words. Both knew of the horrors they just experienced. Yeshua let his brother sob for a time, just holding him. After what felt like an hour or more, Yeshua slipped out of his brother's grasp and let him lay down.

Yeshua seemed startled at first, seeing that Joses eyes were glazed over. He wasn't asleep though, just somehow gone as if in deep meditation.

Walking out into the main chamber of the home, he gaped at all the furnishings. Most of which he did not know what to do with. Plush cloth covered furniture dotted the corners. A finely carved wooden table and chairs sat near what he could only assume was a kitchen.

Yeshua noted the vast assortment of foods either jarred or hanging in a pantry adjacent. It was there he found bundles of dried herbs parceled out. Their Father had provided them with much to restart their lives.

Generosity of a guilty conscience.

He took down a bundle of the strange herb, his nostrils taking in the sweet, pleasant smell. The dried leaves crumbled easily and he was soon scooping up the makings and placing them on a small sheet of papyrus nearby. The thick paper rolled around the herb with some difficulty but eventually he was able to pick the roll up without any falling out.

Luckily, Yeshua found a candle burning nearby. He lit the end of the roll with the candle and let it smolder for a moment before returning to his brother.

"Joses, smoke this, it will help."

Yeshua shook his brother but he seemed unresponsive. His chest still rose and fell denoting the life still flowing through him so he decided to retire to the main room. Sitting on a long half bed-like piece of furniture, he sighed audibly as he sank into the cushioning.

Then, he put the herb to his lips and inhaled deeply. He had smoked before but never like this. Normally the smoke was filtered through water. He expected to cough as he had seen so many do when directly inhaling the smoke of herbs but the sweet fragrant taste went down and came out smoothly. He felt the effects immediately. His whole body relaxing, causing thoughts of pain or anguish to melt away.

He hunkered down further into his seat and let the remedy take him away. Soon he was adrift in a blissful memory of him and Joses as children. Their father was teaching them how to craft with wood. The pleasant dream comforted him as he sat quietly in his new home.

Yeshua stirred to find Joses standing over him. He rubbed his eyes which felt dry and sat up straighter in his seat. His brother's eyes were frantic and the reason soon became apparent as he heard the unmistakable rumble of a crowd outside.

Jumping to his feet, Yeshua grabbed his brother gently by the shoulders and led him back into his room.

"You don't need to see them, Joses. Just wait in here. I will see that they leave us in peace."

Then, Yeshua swiftly left, clicking the strange door shut behind him. Moving out to the front doorway, he heard someone knocking. Unafraid, he pulled the green door open and the light of the day fell in over his legs.

After his eyes adjusted. Yeshua was face to face with his cousin who had been killed long ago.

"John?" he asked.

His weathered cousin seemed much younger than when he had been killed at the hands of Herod but his wrinkled smiled was unmistakable. The man wrapped his arms around him and squeezed.

"Welcome home, cousin," John said.

Yeshua was bewildered but soon his mind caught up and he squeezed back, gripping his long lost cousin with love.

"It's been years. Is Joses with you? Your followers found me and told us that he had come. I didn't expect to see you here but your father just told us."

Yeshua looked out into the gathered crowd searching for Gabriel but he did not see him. He pulled away from John and offered him a wide smile.

"It's good to see you. I'm afraid Joses needs time to heal. He will not come out. I wish to be left alone for a while as well. We have led and surrounded ourselves with disciples for too long," Yeshua replied.

John frowned and nodded in understanding. "The people have come so far to see you. Will you at least address them?"

Yeshua sighed and walked out onto the smooth wooden porch. As he entered the light, his followers roared their approval. He gave a half-hearted wave and then motioned for them to calm themselves. He was practiced at controlling the masses.

"Yeshua! Our teacher! We are home!" a man shouted.

"Hello, brothers and sisters. It does me good to see you all. Thank you so much for following my teachings in life. I pray that you will find peace and happiness here in the Promised Land."

The crowd cheered again, and Yeshua receded as they got closer.

"Thank you for coming but please go now and live your lives. I have nothing more to teach you. I have given everything to you and now I ask a simple favor. Please leave me in peace."

Yeshua receded further as the people grew silent. Disappointment scoured their faces. Some grumbled in confusion, while others denied what they had heard and continued to shout for him.

"You heard him, people! Let us go. We know his words. We can spread his message still and practice his teachings. Come now," John said.

Yeshua leaned in as he passed John and whispered, "Feel free to come visit after a time. Preferably alone."

He watched John nod in understanding and then he ducked back inside and latched the door shut.

CHAPTER TWENTY FIVE
Inequality

Meredox sipped from a fine golden goblet. The rim was encrusted with precious stones and glimmered in the dull candlelight. The contents of his glass tasted of berries and honey. He was told that the mulled wine was a creation of a master artisan who had developed a special grape which could be found nowhere but in Archonia.

Draped in a regal tunic which was pinned at both shoulders, Meredox stood rather awkwardly in the corner of the hall. He had been invited to a gathering which closely resembled the excessive frivolity that he had witnessed in Alexandria. Though the people in attendance here were of a much higher caliber.

Meredox studied their raiment as well as their mannerisms so that he could attempt to fit in. In truth, he felt he would never be able to assimilate with such prestigious figures.

Draining his glass, he had nearly resigned to the fact that he was invisible to these people. Suddenly he heard his name coming from a man with a neatly trimmed crop of hair and a distinctly roman tunic, its iconic red made him shudder at the sight.

"Meredox isn't it? You proposed the creation of the house of Matrons." The man said.

Choking on his words he responded, his heart leaping against his breast. "Indeed, I am. I must give the credit to lady Belladonna however," he added after remembering his promise.

"Very kind of you to attribute such an idea to a woman. My name is Augustus, Perhaps you have heard of me?"

Meredox stared in a mix of horror and wonder at who he assumed was the first emperor of Rome.

"I daresay I have. You seem to have transitioned well between lives," Meredox replied, ignoring the quip about women.

"Not without difficulty. You can imagine my surprise when I came face to face with all of these accomplished souls. I was regarded as a child again. I still feel a commoner here at times," Augustus said.

Meredox offered a half smile, and waited expectantly for the man to either continue or bid him farewell. To his dismay, he continued.

"Come, you must meet some of my friends. We all like the idea of giving the women something to do to keep them busy," Augustus said, turning and tugging on the toga of a man nearby. The group parted and turned toward Meredox.

"Forgive me, sir, but I would appreciate it if you would not speak as if women were lesser than men," Meredox said.

He watched as Augustus' face soured. Then he smirked and elbowed his companion in the side playful. The group laughed together as if he had just finished a joke.

"Meredox, my good man. You are a funny soul. Surely the times have not changed so much since I left. There is an unspoken hierarchy…"

"That was the old world," Meredox said raising his voice.

The rumblings around the room stopped and soon everyone was looking at him. His discomfort faded and he felt a resolve forming even as he spoke.

"In my former life I was a pauper. A lowly stage performer, yet now I find myself surrounded by kings and philosophers. Nobody is who they were from their former lives here in this blissful world of Archonia. Yet I still see a despicable separation. A notion that women are inferior to men."

As more heads turned and the music which had been playing ceased, Meredox felt the unease creeping back up as if it was bile in his throat. Through the crowd, he spotted Belladonna, and as quickly as his anxiety had come, it receded.

"It was not my idea to create the house of matrons. That credit must go to the lady Belladonna. I helped, true enough. But it will be known that it is her creation. Furthermore I find it detestable that her original proposal for the preservation of unborn souls went unheeded. Surely there are people here absent of cowardice that could aid in this endeavor," Meredox said, confidence budding in every word.

Looking back towards the ex-emperor, Meredox watched as the man spat at his feet. A small fleck of saliva hit his toe but he didn't flinch.

"You are no friend of mine, Meredox of Archonia. There is and always will be a natural order. This world will soon catch up and the old ways will resume," Augustus said.

"Not if I have a say in the matter. Brothers, who will stand with me? Here and now I ask that you declare your intention. Who will fight the inequity of the old world and see a new order rise from our human mistakes?" Meredox declared.

Perspiration coated his forehead and he realized that he was balling his hand into a fist to avoid feeling them shake. He didn't have any idea if there were people in the crowd who felt as he did. He was so new to this world that such a declaration could very well be met with violence. Luckily, he had not seen any brutality in this life so far.

Almost immediately a calm, confident voice came forth. "I will stand with you, brother." Achilles said.

Meredox heard gasps from the rest of them. And he finally let out his breath which he had been holding in anticipation.

Thank the gods. You can always count on a fellow Greek.

"Such fierce words from one so young. It moves my heart. I face a similar inequality regarding my... sexual preference," Socrates said, rising from the chair he had been seated in.

This time raucous jeers and clear insults were flung as such a great philosopher revealed what must have been a precious secret. Meredox responded, shouting above the curses.

"Of course, teacher! We will fight it together. Everyone who wishes to stand with us, please come with me now. Show the rest of these people that we are strong and we are many," Meredox finished, then he strode forth towards the exit. Belladonna beamed at him as he passed.

Meredox stole a glance over his shoulder just before he passed the threshold of the door which led out into the night. The response was incredible. More than half of the people at the gathering were now marching out at his heels.

Can't believe it.

Meredox didn't know where he was going and began simply walking towards the center of Helios. Socrates must have realized this and caught up with him.

"This way, my friend. We must discuss this movement of yours. I know a great place to do so. Achilles, please gather those soldiers loyal to you. I imagine we will need to watch our backs," Socrates said.

Meredox now followed, thankful that he was not alone. Belladonna came up beside him and wrapped her arms around one of his as they walked. The philosopher took them to the other side of the city where they found a rather modest estate set against a hillside. At the top of the hill, a giant structure which resembled the famed Parthenon stood resolute against the horizon.

Eventually the group, which consisted of perhaps forty souls, made their ascent to the huge Greek style structure. Much of the masonry was unfinished in places but it was well into its construction.

"Welcome friends, to the University of Socrates. I hope that one day all Archonian's will study here at some point in their second lives. I've even been speaking with Lady Belladonna about a program which requires new souls to enroll for at least one cycle simply to learn the ways of this world," Socrates said.

"That would fit well with the house of Matron's functions," Belladonna replied.

"A fine plan, but what are we going to about the matter at hand?" Merideus asked.

The serious nature of the one-time politician, annoyed Meredox but he did not let the frustration get to him.

"This is my idea, but I need all of your help. I do not know the first thing about starting a movement. I was a simple stage performer in my former life."

"Illusions are as useful in politics as they are in your performances," Socrates said.

How did he know I did illusions?

Ignoring that nagging question, Meredox sank into the background and listened as the more prominent souls discussed concepts of a future for Archonia.

"This world *will* not be like the former. We think ourselves an intelligent species but can't seem to overcome the simple prejudices which separate us from one another," Aristotle said.

"As we saw, not everyone agrees with us. How will we institute this new regime?" Plato asked.

"It will come to bloodshed!" A giant man said, his large body easily a foot taller than the rest of the people around him.

"It does not have to, dear Zeus," Socrates said.

"A civilization ruled by fear is no civilization," said a strange looking man near the outskirts of the group.

Meredox regarded him with a peculiar look. His white eyes surprised him as they seemed to glow in the evening light. The man's gaze locked with his for a moment and suddenly torches burst alight as if through some sorcery. Nobody else seemed to notice which told him, despite his amazement, that this was commonplace.

"Fair words, but peace is not often found until the end of conflict. The two seem to go hand in hand," Merideus said.

"Nevertheless, we must strive for a peaceful transition. We cannot force others to think like us," Socrates said.

"First we must gather more support. Tomorrow we must all begin gathering allies. Travel in groups. I will not see the brutes of Augustus harm any of you without witnesses," Aristotle said.

"My men will ensure that none of you are harmed," Achilles cut in.

Meredox looked his way, astonished that he had already returned. Behind him stood a battalion of soldiers. They wore the armor of Greek Hoplites. Broad shields hid their bodies while long spears reached towards the ceiling.

How did he assemble them that fast?

"For protection only. I don't think that full combat gear will be necessary," Plato said.

"I agree, Achilles. You were instructed to create an order of peacekeepers not warriors," Socrates said, his eyes wary.

"My men will do as instructed by their superior. If peacekeeping is all that they need to do then so be it. But my sentinels will be here to safeguard from any level of threat. As we all know, our neighbors are extremely fond of warfare," Achilles added.

A grumble of agreement passed through the group. Meredox didn't have any idea that Helios had a neighboring colony. His mind raced, wondering if that is where his brother had been this whole time. Unfortunately he didn't get a chance to ask because the plans continued.

"Very well. We will meet here once a day at the same hour. Bring those you can sway to hear us and we can all discuss the future of Archonia. I would like the thank Meredox personally for standing up and saying what we were all thinking," Socrates said, then he began to clap.

The applause rose quickly and Meredox felt at odds with the sentiment. Merideus' words weighed heavily in his mind. Had he just started a conflict? Would it end in bloodshed? That was not what he wanted. He glanced at the shiny spear tips glistening in the torchlight and felt the pain in his chest. He didn't want to ever feel the tip of a spear again if he could help it. Nor did he wish it upon anyone else. Even his enemies.

CHAPTER TWENTY SIX
The Hunt

Luxor crouched low, holding his breath. He watched the delicate ears of his prey flick back and forth while the dark eyes looked in his direction. If he was unlucky, the beast had heard him. Peering through the brush, he noticed that Runi and Eerika had caught up.

Patiently, Luxor appreciated the animal. It stood on four legs, and bore two tremendous horns which protruded from its forehead one on top of the other. A thick mane of fur circled its neck sweeping down towards the ground where the end licked the earth much like a beard.

Waiting for his companions to get in position, Luxor fiddled with the fletching's on his arrow, eager to finally get a shot. Eerika nodded towards him and his mouth widened into a broad smile. Slowly he rose, leveling his bow. The string tightening against his pull.

Feeling the soft feathered fletching hit his cheek, Luxor looked down the arrow. The broad head tip lined up right under the beast's left shoulder. From there he pulled up ever so slightly to accommodate the drop and then, he released.

The arrow zipped through the air, and Luxor cursed as it stuck in the dirt just in front of his prey. The thump from the impact set the creature in motion. It sprang through the bushes, retreating from him.

Suddenly, Luxor spotted a figure rising across the field and another arrow arced quickly towards the target. This arrow found its mark. The projectile pierced all the way through the beast and came out the other side sticking into the soil beyond.

Luxor watched in annoyance as the animal slid across the ground, its lifeless body coming to a stop after a few cubits.

Ugh.

Emerging from cover, Luxor walked towards the fallen prey with the rest of his group. Brock wore a beaming smile as he met them from his position across the field.

"A fine shot, Brock," Luxor said, glowering.

"My thanks, little brother. I could not have hit him without you flushing him towards me."

Ugh.

Luxor waited until the laughter from his other two companions died down. This was not his first hunt but it was the first time they had let him try his hand at the kill shot. Slowly, he put his bow over his shoulder, the string pulling it tight to his body.

"You will get better with practice," Eerika said, striking him playfully on the upper arm with her fist.

Ruefully, Luxor went to work on the fallen beast. The group's rule was the man who misses guts the kill. He was used to this by now because the group's other rule was that if you had never fired a shot on a hunt you also had to clean the kill.

Kneeling down, Luxor pulled free his hunting knife, freshly cleaned and oiled. It sliced into the soft underbelly with ease. With gentle sawing motions he slide the knife parting the whole animal from tail to chin.

From there, Luxor sank his hands into the cavity which held the organs and pulled them free in several large bloody pilcs. Once there was nothing left inside the carcass, he slid his knife around the edge of the fur and worked the hide loose from the flesh. It peeled off nicely and soon he was able to flip the beast and pull it free completely.

Luxor didn't waste time and handed the fur to Brock who had earned the prize. Then he hefted the carcass up on his shoulder and began to march back towards Valhalla.

"Little brother, arm yourself!" Runi shouted.

Luxor looked back toward where Brock had been hiding and standing at the edge of the clearing was a group of five men. They wore metal armor and carried large shields and spears.

Dropping the meat, Luxor pulled his bow from over his shoulder and grabbed an arrow from the quiver dangling at his side. The others had brought their melee weapons but he had left home thinking that he would not need it for the hunt.

Fool.

"Hail, brothers. A fine day for a walk eh?" Brock yelled across the field.

The soldiers didn't reply but kept marching slowly towards them until they were less than twenty cubits away. Runi and Eerika stood ready for a fight.

"These lands belong to the city state of Helios. The beast that you have slain is our property. Surrender it, along with your arms and we will let you leave this place unharmed," one of the soldiers said.

"You hear dat, Eerika? Dees little bastards want a fight!" Runi shouted, his statement followed by hearty laughter.

"Calm yourself, Runi. There is no need for a fight," Brock said, shooting him a warning glance.

"What say you, barbarian?" the same soldier asked.

"Good sirs, we want no conflict with our fine neighbors. We revere fighting as a tradition in our clan but true war is to be considered carefully," Brock said.

"Brock, you're of Clan Bjorn. These weaklings have challenged us and honor dictates we must fight them," Eerika declared.

Oh no.

Luxor watched helplessly as Eerika charged, her sword in hand. Runi followed, roaring. Brock paused taking the time to turn his head and nod at him. Then, the brute leapt into the fray.

Quickly and decisively, the enemy soldiers closed ranks. Luxor saw their shields lock and their spears come level to the ground, but Runi and Eerika were already inside the line of spear tips.

Luxor pulled on his bow, an arrow nocked. The broad shields covered their entire torso however and with his allies in the way he had no shot at all.

Five curses.

Lowering his bow, Luxor ran, trying to flank the soldiers to get a clear shot. Meanwhile Eerika and Runi bashed into the shield wall, beating against the thick metal in a fruitless effort to break through. As he rounded the side of his foes, they dropped their spears and went for short swords sheathed at their side.

Luckily, Luxor had studied the famed Phalanx formation and even a single weak point would make the line break. He pulled back on the bow again and aimed for the back of one of the center fighters. His arrow head struck true sinking in the man's back sending him to his knees shouting in agony.

At the same time, Luxor spied Brock's large hammer come down hard on one of the end units and the man buckled under his blow collapsing to the ground. Runi and Eerika cut the remaining two to pieces in seconds.

Luxor ran in, dropping his bow and pulling his dagger back out. It bit into the man he had stuck with the arrow. The man's body jerked and Luxor felt the life leaving him. The limp corpse fell to the ground and he saw the man's eyes growing dark.

Oh gods!

Reeling back and falling to his backside, Luxor looked at his dagger in horror as it remained buried up to the handgrip in the man's chest. He had struck down plenty of men during the Fray's but there were always Valkyrie there to heal them. He had never before taken a life.

"Anyone injured?" Eerika asked.

"Nay, these men had little experience in true combat," Brock replied, stowing his hammer.

"Little brother? What's wrong?" Runi asked.

Luxor felt as though all the blood had left his body. He felt cold and sick, and something about him had changed. He had just killed a man. Without hesitation and without pity. A million emotions bubbled up all at once and he felt like they were tearing him apart.

"Luxor," Eerika said, kneeling beside him and grabbing him by the chin. She finished looking him over and then sighed. "He's not wounded. I remember this look. Saw it on my brother's face the first time he killed a man," she said.

"Ah I see," Brock said.

Without any further words, Brock scooped Luxor up and helped him walk back towards Valhalla. Runi had grabbed the carcass they had won because he still smelled it as they marched.

The walk seemed like a dream and Luxor kept reliving the moment when he felt the life leave the man's body. The image of his face seared into the back of his mind.

Would it ever go away?

Luxor vaguely registered that they had returned to the mead hall. The Fray that day was already over and everyone who had fought was already busy drinking and eating their fill. He watched Runi head over towards the fire and skewer their prize on a long iron pole before hefting it up over the fire. Eerika tossed a handful of weapons into a corner which could only have been from the soldiers they had just slain.

Plopping down on a wooden bench, Luxor slumped over on the table and remained quiet. Brock wore a look of concern but let him be. He watched his companion head over to the front of the table where Njord was sitting enjoying his meal.

Luxor saw them exchange some words, no doubt about their little encounter. Njord's face went from grim to angry. The Clan leader stood up slamming his hands on the table in front of him. He bellowed long and loud silencing the room.

"Clansmen. Warriors! Our pitiful neighbors to the east have drawn borders. They have armed themselves and mean to subjugate us. What say you?" Njord yelled.

The clan erupted in unison. Curses and war cries filled the room, followed by a steady pounding of horns and glasses on the tables.

"I say we are free men and we will do as we please!" Njord said.

Luxor was nearly deafened by the roar of his clansmen. He pressed his palms against his ears trying to drown out the sound. He just wanted to be alone.

"If any of you see those dainty bastards prancing about you give them a good lashing!" Njord continued.

Luxor jumped from his seat and ducked outside where in a few short minutes night had fallen. He had gotten used to the strange days, so the sudden change didn't bother him. What did bother him was that fact that he had killed a man and there seemed to be no consequences. The idea made him cringe. Was this the sort of life that he wanted? Or was he just trying to fit in with Brock and the others?

Soon, Luxor found himself on the outskirts of the town. The fields stretched out endlessly in front of him. With his body hardened and mind keen, he felt like a completely different person than when he had come to Archonia. He could probably run for miles without stopping if he wanted to. And so, he pointed east and did just that.

Jogging at first, Luxor's pace soon picked up and the only thought on his mind was that he wanted to see his brother and tell him about his horrible deed. If only he could tell him, perhaps everything would be alright.

The grass passed underfoot as Luxor swiftly ran across country. His thick leather boots gave him plenty of traction. His breath was frantic, and at times he could feel tears streaming down his cheeks, but still he ran.

Somehow he had gained an unnatural speed. The ground beneath him moving fast like he was riding on a chariot. His grief subsided and for a moment, he was free. He leapt into the sky and felt weightless.

"Halt!" a voice shouted.

Luxor came to stop and on instinct pulled his dagger free. In moments he spotted more hoplites converging on him from all sides. Far sooner than he realized he made it back to their territory.

"Drop your weapon."

Seeing that he was outnumbered six to one, Luxor obeyed. His steel clattering to the ground muffled by the thick blades of grass. Some part of his mind had already known that he would be stopped on approach to the neighboring city state.

"I surrender. I am searching for my brother," Luxor said.

The soldiers closed in and a few of them carried torches. Their faces, illuminated in the dark, looked serious.

"By the gods, he looks exactly like the Basileus!" one of the men said.

The prince? Meredox?

"Of course he does you fool, the Basileus has been looking for his brother since he got here. Luxor isn't it?" one of the hoplites asked.

"Indeed, why do you regard my brother as a prince?" Luxor asked.

"Just come with us and keep quiet. We don't know if this is some illusion. You may not be his brother at all," another of the soldiers said.

"Bind him!"

Luxor reacted too late and two men wrapped their hands around his wrists and arms. They forced him to the ground where he was bound with coarse rope which burn his skin as they tightened the knots. He tasted dirt until they lifted him from the ground, then they led him off into the night.

CHAPTER TWENTY SEVEN

The World's Greatest Warrior

Achilles knelt before his butchered men appraising the cut marks that had been left upon their bodies. They had been here a while judging by the dried state of the blood. Thankfully, bodies didn't rot in Archonia and there were no bloat flies. Calmly, he turned them over and recreated the fight in his mind. The careless brutality of the slash marks indicated that this was the work of their Barbarian neighbors.

Placing one of the body's hands over its chest as a sign of respect, Achilles rose. He turned back to the group of men he assembled to search for this lost scouting party. Their faces were fraught with anger. Each one thirsting for vengeance.

Achilles ignored their juvenile reactions and instead processed what might have happened and what it would mean. War with Clan Bjorn would certainly end in a bloody mess and he wasn't sure that his forces could even stand against them. He would be a fool to think that his one battalion of troops could overtake an entire clan which practiced live combat every day.

"Take the bodies back to the city to be burned. The funeral games will begin at nightfall," Achilles said.

"My lord? Does this mean war?" one of his men asked.

"Silence, soldier, we have a more pressing matter at this moment. The city state is in turmoil. Augustus is rallying fighters to his cause as quickly as we are. Things will soon boil over."

Achilles' men didn't object further and quickly saw to the corpses of his scouts. He looked west across the plains to where Clan Bjorn was undoubtedly mustering a fighting force as well. Whatever side had instigated the fight didn't matter. He knew that any sort of conflict would mean a challenge in their eyes. Somehow he would have to unite Helios against the barbarians.

In minutes, Achilles made it back to the city. His speed tripled since he had begun his unique training regimen. So far as he knew, his abilities were unmatched by any.

Sweeping through the streets, Achilles probably seemed a blur to those he passed. Smoke rose from the south and he leapt high into the air to gain a better view. Beyond the pillars of black smoke, Achilles saw a mob forming. They were moving towards Socrates' Parthenon.

Augustus.

Achilles feet hit the ground and didn't break stride. He quickly headed towards the university which they had been meeting at every day. Though they had gained support, the approaching mob would tear them to pieces. The movement was, after all, largely peaceful.

Climbing the hill at an incredible rate, Achilles came to a halt after sliding across the smooth marble floor.

"Achilles. Smoke rises from the southern part of the city. What is happening?" Plato asked with a panicked look.

"A mob is forming. Augustus must have rallied his own supporters. He is acting the only way he knows how. By trying to conquer those who oppose him."

"What shall we do? We are no fighters." Aristotle said.

"My men and I will take care of this. It would be best if you all remained here. I will be sending any civilians here as well."

Achilles looked over to the band of ten soldiers he posted here to guard the philosophers. They saluted and awaited his order.

"You will remain here. If any civilians turn hostile you will end them without hesitation," Achilles said.

"Achilles! War is not the answer. We want peace!" Socrates said.

"Peace is made through war, old man. Would you rather I let Augustus march up here so that you can talk with him peacefully?" he asked.

The hall was silent. Achilles knew just as they did that Augustus would march up here and slaughter any people who opposed him. He didn't waste any more words. These peaceful men were out of their depth. Diplomacy would come later.

Swiftly, Achilles exited the hall, diving from the hilltop in a long arc before landing in the main street. The heavily trodden dirt impacted as he hit. He stumbled for a moment before getting back up to full speed. Around him people were screaming and frantic, running from the approaching mob.

Soon, Achilles came upon a group of his men, they were standing on the corner where New Sparta met the courtyard of Athena. "Soldiers!" he shouted.

The men snapped to attention, some picking their weapons up from the ground.

"Prepare for combat. I need runners to recall the battalion. Tell all civilians that they should seek refuge at the Parthenon. Meet back here as quickly as you can. Go!" Achilles barked.

Then, like the wind, Achilles ran down the streets gathering what men he could and ordering the evacuation of the city. Visions of Troy flooded his mind. He would not let this be a repeat of that atrocity. Such a great Greek victory turned sour as his fellow soldiers pillaged and murdered the city's inhabitants.

"Get to the hill!" he shouted, pointing to Socrates massive structure.

"Sir! Orders?" shouted one of his officers, approaching with his unit in tow.

"To the courtyard of Athena. Form the phalanx and await my orders."

A handful of minutes later, Achilles made his way back. The plumes of smoke made progress and he guessed that the mob would soon reach his lines. He leapt to the building tops and skipped across them like rocks in a river bed. The people below flowing like the water towards safety.

Achilles faintly heard shouts of fear as people saw his incredible display of strength and speed. As he landed in the courtyard where the large statue of Athena stood, his men didn't flinch. They witnessed his incredible feats in their training.

"Form up!" Achilles shouted.

Quickly counting, Achilles estimated that around fifty of his men had gathered. Their armor clattered as the units formed together into one indomitable line. The shields played their song as they clanged together locking into place. He stood out front, unafraid of the danger ahead. Perhaps it was foolish, but his newfound strength made him feel invincible.

"Commander!" one of his officers shouted.

Turning, Achilles saw that the man was carrying his spear and shield. He took them and found his helm dangling inside. Untying it from the leather strap, he slid it over his head, the familiar smell of metal and dust greeting him. He checked that his short sword was loose in its sheath and then he glared south awaiting the mob.

Impatience ate at Achilles' mind while he watched the rioters approaching. Civilians still fled through their lines while more of his soldiers bolstered the defense. Soon, he was able to discern the enemy's weaponry.

The unarmored rabble grabbed anything they could. Pitchforks, wooden posts sharpened to spears, hammers, and other bludgeoning weapons made from an assortment of materials.

"Hold the line. Do not let their lack of armaments make you overconfident. You will not attack. Defend only. Disable if you can. If you can't, be sure that they die quickly. No suffering. Am I clear?" Achilles asked.

"Hooah!" his men replied.

Achilles was grateful that every single one of his men had been military during their former life. He had personally asked each one to serve him in this new army of Archonia. They had each jumped at the opportunity having heard of his own deeds of the past.

Among the men were heroes such has Hector of Troy who he personally killed. The man had not held a grudge. The fight was fair and glorious. Cadmus stood just to his unit's left. The founder of Thebes was a renowned warrior.

His eyes passed over Ajax who had fought alongside him at the battle of Troy and down the line stood the famed Theseus who was a close personal friend of his. Each great man should have struck fear in the hearts of this mob but so much time had passed that barely anyone recognized these warriors anymore.

Turning back to the on-coming storm, Achilles grabbed some dirt from the ground to dry his hands which were moist with perspiration. Rubbing them together, he began walking forward to meet them.

"Hold!" a voice shouted from the opposing force.

Then, Achilles saw the crowd part, making way for none other than Caesar Augustus and what must have been his personal guard. The peacock was dressed in far too many cubits of cloth to be functional in battle. His armor looked more decorative than anything. He had even put some eye shadow on in a feeble attempt to make himself appear more fearsome.

Achilles stuck his spear in the ground as a sign of truce and Augustus had one of his men do the same. They remained a fair distance apart but he knew that he could close the gap in seconds.

"The great Achilles! Son of a goddess, or so I've heard. You should not have gathered this force against me. We outnumber you four to one," Augustus said.

"My men are each worth ten of yours, so it is you who are outnumbered, Roman. Now disband this riot and surrender yourself for trial. You are responsible for any who have died today."

The man scoffed and Achilles felt his mouth tighten in annoyance.

Suddenly, Achilles heard a shrill whistle from one of Augustus' officers and a rhythmic clatter of weapons and armor erupted from both sides of the courtyard. Perfectly formed lines of soldiers enveloped his line, their tall square shields and spears forming a line similar to his Phalanx.

Then, looking ahead, Achilles heard a low rumble and the unruly mob began to part again, revealing some sort of large wooden machines. He had read about such siege engines but had never seen them used in combat. According to records they were devastating.

"What say you now, son of Peleus?" Augustus asked.

Achilles didn't waste time. They were outflanked and that artillery would shatter his line. He needed to strike. Stepping back, he grabbed his spear and with one swift movement launched it towards the group of soldiers that had flanked left.

The long sturdy spear shaft spun beautifully arcing towards the line. One of the soldiers held up his shield to block it, but the weapon pierced right through with such a force that it skewered three more men behind him.

Before the fourth man's body hit the ground, Achilles burst right, drawing his blade. With shield out in front, he battered into the other flanking force and sent a handful of men flying through the air. They screamed and were tossed like stones into the buildings around.

So far, the enemies were still trying to rationalize what had just happened. Everything around Achilles appeared in slow motion, his reactions much faster than those of the feeble men before him.

As the soldiers scattered in the wake of his strength, Achilles dove backwards through the air. Sailing high in a wide arc, he fell towards one of the strange siege engines, his blade crashing into the soft wood. The device splintered to pieces with a thunderous crack, then he dove towards the other putting a shoulder into it. The force tipped the artillery over, rendering it useless.

Finally, Achilles lurched through Augustus' guard and grabbed the man by the collar, kicking the inside of his knee which bent like a blade of grass with a sickening crack.

The whole maneuver had taken a total of ten seconds. Both flanks and the front line were in disarray and he had their leader incapacitated in his arms.

"What say *you?*" Achilles mocked, sliding his blade up to the man's throat.

"What in the name of the gods are you?" Augustus asked, groaning in pain.

"I am the law in this world. I am the answer to every act of evil. I am Archonia's guardian," Achilles said.

Achilles watched with some satisfaction as every single soul in the opposing force began to throw down their arms.

CHAPTER TWNETY EIGHT
Reunion

Meredox ran across the marble floor of the Parthenon. He nearly fell as he took enormous strides down the hillside. The southern part of the city still smoldered but he had been assured that it was safe. Word quickly spread of Achilles astounding victory.

Upon the man's return from the conflict, Achilles informed Meredox that his brother may have been found. Not standing on ceremony he had just enough time to learn where Luxor was being held before darting off.

Excitement and panic swept over him in alternating waves. His feet felt like they were barely touching the ground. Soon his body told him to slow, his chest rising and falling frantically.

Achilles' compound wasn't far and soon, Meredox was rushing up the front steps. Two guards caught him and brought him to a halt as he entered.

"This area is for Sentinels only."

"I am Meredox, you people have been calling me the Basileus, though I don't know why. I was told my brother is being held here as prisoner. I must see him!"

"Stand down men, Achilles has authorized this. I will see the civilian the rest of the way," Zeus said.

Meredox pushed past the guards and followed the man he had once thought was a god. It was not his first meeting with him but certainly the first time he had been in such close proximity. The giant soul stood two feet taller than he did at least.

"Thank you, Lord Zeus," Meredox stammered.

"Lord Zeus? I am no god, son. I realize you're Greek, but please," Zeus chuckled.

"Still you have a great name. And inspire many even today."

The large man didn't reply to the comment. Instead, he changed to the subject at hand. "The prisoner was captured crossing the border between Helios and Valhalla. Four of our soldiers were recently found slain by the barbarians. He claims to be your brother and looks just like you, however there are strange powers in this world and we are afraid it may be some sort of illusion."

"I don't know how or why the barbarians would want to impersonate my brother but I will know if it is him or not," Meredox said.

Following the huge soldier, Meredox descended into the earth. Crudely hewn stones were set into the wall around them and the temperature dropped sharply as they left the heat of the day behind.

The darkness of the dungeon was at odds with small candles that flickered silently as they hung on the walls. The melting wax rested in simple iron cups. The warm light flashed in his vision even after he looked away.

"Here we are," Zeus said unlatching a thick wooden door which locked from the outside.

Meredox peered into the dark cell beyond and saw a solitary figure bound to a stone bench with chains. As his eyes adjusted he could see that Luxor's hair had grown back out since he had last seen him. They looked like twins again.

"Brother!" Luxor exclaimed, his weary head rising.

Walking into the dingy cell, Meredox appraised the man before him. He wore leathers and furs crafted into fine armor which had seen plenty of use. Knicks and tears speckled the attire and he briefly wondered what his brother had been through.

"Check his pockets. If this is my brother he will have a small wooden coin on his person," Meredox whispered the Zeus.

The large figure unceremoniously patted down Luxor, who didn't fight it. Instead he realized what the giant was looking for.

"There is a small pocket on the inside of my belt, left side. The coin is there," he said.

Meredox smirked and moved in to greet his brother before Zeus produced the coin.

"Luxor where have you been?"

"I could ask you the same thing," he replied.

"Zeus, please release this man, he is truly my brother. We came here together and if he is a prisoner then so too should I be," Meredox said.

Zeus lumbered back into the hall and Meredox waited for him to return to unlock the chains binding Luxor to the cell. It only took moments and when they metal hit the floor, he embraced his brother.

"I've missed you. I should have looked for you but if I'm honest I needed a break. We spent our whole first lives together," Meredox whispered in his ear.

Luxor patted him on the back and replied "I felt the same way. The separation was good, but I needed to see you."

Meredox pulled away and looked back to where Zeus was still standing as if to guard from some treachery. He didn't wield any weapon but the thick plates of armor that wrapped around his strong frame made him seem intimidating all the same.

"Welcome, brother, to the city state of Helios. Like Athens or Sparta it is a place of beauty and higher learning. Though we have had our troubles lately."

"I saw the fires as they brought me here. What is going on?" Luxor asked.

"I'm afraid that we are experiencing civil unrest. I started a movement to banish the inequalities of the former world. There were many who resisted."

"You started this movement?"

"Yes. My followers have even taken to calling me the Basileus though I do not know why. I am no king."

"Such revolutions are how kings are born, brother. I'm afraid my own adventures have been far different. I found myself walking alone across a strange land. I was taken in by a group of warriors who, in the previous life, we may have called Northmen," Luxor said.

"Yes, I see that by your unusual attire. Here they are regarded as Barbarians."

"I assure you, many of them are misunderstood. They have strange traditions but many are intelligent and proud just as we are. They took me in and taught me their ways. I learned to fight, brother. Truly fight. Not like the scraps I would get in as a child. And.... I....."

"What is it, brother?"

"I've killed a man..."

Meredox took a step back, trying to process the statement. His brother still stood before him but now somehow something about him was different. It was as if the warmth and light he always felt around Luxor was somehow dimmer.

What has happened?

"I assure you, brother, I did it out of necessity. But I can't get his face out of my head," Luxor said.

"Was it you who killed Achilles men at the border!?" Zeus bellowed. As he did a tangible energy surrounded the man causing an unnatural wind to sweep through the dungeon.

"They attacked us, sir. My friend did his best to avert the confrontation," Luxor said, scowling.

Meredox watched in horror as Zeus lunged at his brother. He pushed himself between Luxor and the giant man's fist. The broad line of knuckles impacted hard across his whole face, and he lost all of his senses for a few moments.

A ringing sound clouded Meredox's hearing and it wasn't until nearly half a minute later that he was able to hear his brother's voice.

"Meredox. Meredox!" Luxor said.

Blinking his eyes, the world came back into view and he saw Zeus standing over his brother and Luxor at his side holding his head up.

"I'm fine," Meredox said, grasping his jaw which was throbbing in pain.

"I'm sorry, Meredox, you shouldn't have interceded," Zeus said.

"You should not have struck, sir. Surely there is always a peaceful way to settle these matters," Meredox said.

"If that was the case then the city would not still be smoldering. An apology to you is all I can give. I will not apologize for my actions. They were guided by duty and demanded by justice. I will have to report your brother to Achilles," Zeus said.

"Do what you must, my friend. But do so with the knowledge that I will always step between my brother and danger without hesitation. He is a part of me. As much a part of me as your mighty fist is a part of you," Meredox replied.

Meredox stood with the help of his brother a grimace on his face as he waited for the large man to respond. He could see the thoughts whirring about the man's head and finally all he offered was a low grumble.

"I can promise the people of Helios that my brother is no threat to them."

"How can you promise this?" Zeus asked.

"Because they have no money for him to steal," Meredox replied, chuckling.

Turning, Meredox saw his brother shake his head in annoyance but couldn't hide the grin forming on his face. Zeus didn't seem convinced and was certainly not privy to his brother's misadventures from their first life.

"Let me take Luxor before the others. They can question him. Perhaps Luxor can even foster a peace with the Barbarians," Meredox said.

"Very well. But I will be escorting you the whole way under armed supervision," Zeus said.

Walking down the chilled corridor of the dungeon, Luxor whispered low so Zeus could not overhear.

"Brother, the Northmen have good people living amongst them. Will you help me show the people in this place that they are much like the free people here?"

"I will do my best."

Meredox sat nervously amongst his new peers. He presented his brother and the situation to them as plainly and honestly as he could. He truly believed that transparency would be best.

To his dismay, Luxor was soon bound by chains again, and surrounded by Achilles' men. Meredox's eyes anxiously darted to and from the glimmering steel which hung at their belts. Incense burned in the brazier's dotting the Parthenon and the area was filled with not only Greeks, but Egyptians, Orientals, and Romans as well.

All the cultures showed up to be represented in the forming of the new republic. Meredox spied famous faces from every corner of history.

"Order! This meeting will come to order!" a statuesque man shouted. His short crop of dark hair lent to a fearsome appcarance.

The chatter slowly died out and Meredox was able to finally divert his attention to the proceedings.

"Thank you all for coming. As I'm sure everyone is aware we are at a very delicate period. The next weeks will decide the future of this incredible world in which we live. Even in this second life we have divided ourselves into groups. It is the hope of this movement to garner equality amongst people of every shape, size, denomination, sex, and whatever other traits that divide us.

"Having said this. We cannot have everyone give their opinions and state their needs for that would take a tremendous amount of time. As a rule, we have such time in this world, but not at the moment. There is a threat to the west of us that needs an answer. I ask that each group of people select an individual from amongst you to speak for your people. These speakers will then have a voice in creating the future laws of this realm," Socrates said.

Meredox noted a surge of approval as Socrates finished his statement. Through applause and other vocal cries it seemed that everyone was on the same page in this group. Several people already walked forward as if they had been predetermined and the old Greek welcomed them up onto the dais.

Many faces that strode forth were foreign to Meredox. He only recognized Anubis, from the Egyptian people's ranks. And Athena, from the Greek ranks. Suddenly, he smelled a wonderful aroma beside him and looked to see Belladonna, smiling at him from under a stiff cloth headdress.

"My lady," Meredox said taking her hand and pressing his lips against her soft knuckles.

"The great Basileus," she replied, jokingly, brushing her fingers over his arm.

"Please don't call me that. I didn't ask to be addressed as such."

"Don't be so humble, the title is an honor," she said.

"Perhaps. Are you pleased with our results?" Meredox asked.

Meredox waited eagerly for her approval. To his dismay, her face scrunched up as if she was frustrated.

"We are closer to equality but it seems that it is threatened now. These Barbarians will never allow themselves to be ruled by these laws. I just don't know what we are ever going to do." She said, hanging her head.

Meredox felt a surge of determination. Pride swelled within his chest and he felt duty-bound to reply with false assurances.

"We will fight. I will learn to fight if I must. I won't let what we are building fall into ruin," Meredox said, gently touching her upper arm.

"Meredox!" a voice bellowed over the crowds.

He realized that he hadn't been paying attention to what was going on at the front and felt slightly embarrassed. Standing tall he strode forth and hopped up onto the raised stone where the speakers were standing.

"There he is! The hero of Helios! The great Basileus!" Anubis said, a broad grin spreading over his face.

Meredox remained quiet as the cheers and applause took their course. He offered a kind smile but did not allow himself to be sucked into the uproar. Finally, it quieted again.

"Meredox, my good man. We are in a difficult situation but none more so than you. Your own brother has allied himself with the barbarians. From his own mouth he has admitted to killing a free Greek soldier. What do you say to this threat?"

Remaining silent for a time, Meredox looked at his brother who knelt with his hands bound nearby. Luxor stared back at him pleadingly. His head swiveled out into the crowd where he caught sight of Belladonna. Her gaze spoke as plainly as if she had said the words to him again. *We must fight.*

Her beauty clouded Meredox's mind momentarily before he snapped back into reality. His mind swam with possibilities but the crowd was awaiting a reply. In a knee jerk reaction he spoke.

"We have started something here that cannot be stopped. This world must have equality. This world must have peace. I had hoped that diplomacy could resolve our differences but the barbarians only understand the sword. I for one will fight!" He yelled, with vigor.

The crowd cheered so loudly Meredox couldn't continue speaking if he wanted to. He stared straight ahead and smiled at Lady Belladonna, admiring the perfect bone structure in her face.

CHAPTER TWENTY NINE
Brothers before Others

Luxor couldn't believe what he had just heard. The crowd before him roared their approval. As the applause ensued, he felt his chest tighten as he tried staring a hole through the back of his brother's head. The man he had spent his entire life with had just betrayed him.

The sound of voices from the meeting became an annoying buzz in the back of Luxor's mind as all the memories he shared with Meredox rushed through his head. Flashes of his childhood played out before him as his heart tore in two. One of their most sacred teachings was that family should be put before anyone else. And up to this point, they had both remained true.

Luxor jerked, trying to free himself from the bindings which held him but they were too strong.

"Thank you, good people. Now go. Your elected delegates will lay our plans for the future. If you wish to join in the great army to defend Helios please see Achilles at the west end of the structure," The dark-haired man with the loud mouth said.

Luxor waited patiently for the crowds to disperse. The roar died down and a handful of people were left standing around including his brother.

"Bastard!" Luxor shouted.

The outcry echoed across the stone around and slowly Meredox turned his head. Luxor could see in his eyes that he knew that he had addressed him.

"Soldier, keep that prisoner silent," the dark-haired man said, then Luxor felt hard knuckles impact against his face.

The strike knocked his head towards the ground while two other soldiers help him upright.

"No! Stop!" Meredox shouted, running over. "This is my brother. He is no longer a Barbarian. He has decided to defect. He can tell us all about our new enemy."

Luxor seethed, feeling his saliva almost bubble out of his mouth in anger. Every word in that statement had been a lie constructed to free him and repair the damage that Meredox had just done in choosing his side. His brother looked at him sternly as if to convey that very sentiment to him without speaking.

Shaking his head, Luxor gave Meredox his answer. His brother gripped him hard and their non-verbal conversation came to a close as he jerked away from Meredox's grip.

"Well at least I hoped that he would," Meredox added.

"Basileus, your brother has chosen his side. We can keep him safe in our prison until the war is over. Then perhaps you can find reconciliation," a strange man said, who Luxor could swear looked a lot like the famous philosopher Socrates.

Meredox walked away while Luxor struggled again against his bonds. There was no use, however. The chains which bound him were secure.

Perhaps I can take one of their weapons?

"Men, take the prisoner away. This tribunal has many things to discuss," the dark-haired man said, with a wave of his hand.

"Wait! Shouldn't we at least try to parley with the barbarians?" Mercdox asked.

"Brother? If we release you, could you talk sense into the leaders of the tribe?"

Luxor found his chance. Replying slowly so he didn't sound too eager. "I don't know if they will listen to me. But I can try. If it will save lives." Luxor lied.

The leaders of this city's people talked amongst themselves while Luxor sat with quiet anticipation. He sought this place and didn't find what he was hoping for. But he had something back in Valhalla. Something he needed to get back to. Eerika.

Suddenly, Luxor watched Meredox walk back over to him and give a hand motion. The soldiers beside him undid the chains wrapped about his wrists and he quickly pulled his arms in front of himself and massaged the tender skin.

Standing up, Luxor met his brother's gaze with a grimace. He didn't say anything, just waited.

"Brother, the tribunal is releasing you to send a message to the leader of your clan. Please help me foster peace between us. What we are building here is incredible. Safety and equality for everyone," Meredox pleaded.

Luxor didn't reply, he just stared ahead. Meredox sighed heavily and gave the order that the soldiers should escort him to the edge of the city. He began to walk with them and stopped, turning to say one last thing.

"Do you remember what father used to say to us when we were at each other's throats?" Luxor asked.

Meredox furrowed his brow for a moment then Luxor saw as the memory returned. "Brothers before others," he said.

Luxor nodded, and then walked away.

In under an hour, Luxor found himself at the edge of the city. Small yurts and dug outs were the only shelters this far out. A sense of hopelessness soon gave way to anger and a desire to break something.

Breaking into a jog, he left his escort behind him as he once again crossed the vast empty plains towards his new home. His feet carried him swiftly and he gave no heed to the fatigue which slowly built in his muscles. He longed for the rush of battle to take away his far off thoughts and replace them with the simple choices that fear fostered.

Luxor stopped momentarily to pull out a water-filled root from a long tendril of grass. The tuber pulled free from the soil with little effort. Sinking his teeth into the sweet bulb, He sucked the water in with a satisfying slurp.

His eyes moved back up to the horizon where he saw dark dots moving towards him in a line. By the time he was done drinking they were close enough to see. Clothed in furs he quickly recognized his clansmen. Each one sat atop a mount and quickly surrounded him, trampling the grass in the vicinity.

"Hail, brother. You have been missed at the mead hall as of late. Njord will have words with you," said a green-eyed berserker riding a black bear.

"I have words to deliver to him regarding the neighboring city state of Helios," Luxor replied.

"Best clamber up here. Njord is not a patient man," the berserker replied.

Luxor agreed, and grabbed handfuls of fur, hoisting himself up behind the large man. He smelled horrible which made the trip an unpleasant one but the meeting ahead of him could very well be even more unpleasant.

The bear carried them swiftly over the hills and soon Luxor caught sight of the great mead hall once again. The sea of stout, wooden domiciles surrounding the hall felt homely and a small measure of relief passed over him as the beast trotted into the narrow mucky streets.

A handful of minutes later, Luxor dismounted before the great carved doors of the hall. His escort led him in but didn't follow as he approached the head of the long table where Njord sat alone.

Luxor came to a halt, not sure how to greet the clan leader. He was still new enough that he didn't know all the etiquettes. His guess was that there were few. Slowly, he looked Njord over. Several mink furs fell over his broad shoulders leading down to a studded leather tunic he wore as casual attire.

Only once had Luxor seen him in full battle gear during the fray. He wore a metal armor which covered his torso and underneath small rings of metal linked together closely to allow flexibility. The ensemble must have weighed heavily but the man could move as quickly as any warrior on the field.

"You are the man that came to Brock during the last moon cycle." Njord said, not looking up from what seemed to be a map of the area.

"I am, clan leader." Luxor replied.

"Then I will forgive any lapses in etiquette for now. You may address me as Jarl. Where have you been these past days?"

"I sought my brother after I killed my first man. I needed someone to speak with and I was afraid there was no one in Clan Bjorn who would listen."

"This is weakness. A frailty that members of the clan do not abide. As you are not a descendant of our culture this can be forgiven but once and only because you showed courage in the face of a true enemy and slew him in combat."

Luxor's heart jolted. He shifted uncomfortably still unable to catch the Jarl's eye. His gaze shifted to the map where he tried to discern what information was being portrayed but the paper quickly turned over and Njord finally looked up, staring him straight in the eyes.

"You were taken prisoner by our enemy. Tell me what you saw and what you heard. If it is helpful you may retain your position with the clan. If I deem you a traitor, you will be beheaded at dusk," Njord said, his face grim and unmoving.

"Yes, Jarl, I was imprisoned. The enemy clan has many trained soldiers. Far more than we thought. The group of warriors recently quelled a rebellion there and a new leadership is forming which will unite many other clans against us. They believe us to be unruly and barbaric. They mean to destroy our way of life."

Luxor watched Njord's stoic face which didn't reveal the slightest emotion. The man was deciding his fate right before his very eyes. He died horribly once but the prospect of dying again made bile bubble up into his throat. Despite his bodily reactions, he tried to remain as stoic and impassive as the great warrior before him.

"We march in the morning for war. I suggest you take some rest and equip yourself for a lengthy campaign. Leave me," Njord finished.

"Yes, my Jarl," Luxor replied, exiting the hall.

Stepping out of the stifling hall, Luxor released the contents of his stomach onto the ground. There wasn't much in there to begin with but what came out at least didn't cause him further nausea. Standing up, he wiped his face with a sleeve and walked back to his camp.

There, Luxor found his new friends busy at work, sharpening their blades and outfitting themselves with additional armor. They hardly seemed to notice him as he stopped in front of his hovel.

"Hope ye enjoyed yer trip, little brother. Best get ta sharpenin yer weapon. Brock der is fashioning ya some better armor," Runi said, flicking an arrow into the ground next to nearly a hundred others.

Just then, Luxor spotted Eerika burst out of her tent and tromp her way through the dirt over to him. He moved to greet and embrace her but instead he felt her knuckles impact against his face. Stumbling back, he held his jaw.

"Where the hell ya been?" she asked, her voice filled with anger.

"I had to see my brother. I don't think that's a crime," Luxor replied, shooting her a glare.

"Thought ya left us is all," she said hanging her head.

Luxor spat a bit of blood out and grabbed her head pulling it into his own. He pressed his lips against hers with a sort of passionate fury before pulling it away. The others hooted and cajoled but kept to their work. Eerika blushed a bit but stormed off to the archery range.

"What did you learn on your journey, little brother?" Brock asked, approaching him from behind.

Luxor swung around and felt the urge to tell the truth. Stuffing it down inside of himself he spoke. "I learned that even after a lifetime of loyalty even a brother can betray you."

"So you found him then?" Brock asked, frowning.

"I did. He seems to be regarded as a king amongst our enemies and they have declared war against us," Luxor said, sitting on a short barrel and resting his arms on his knees. He regarded Brock's reaction noting the peculiar grimace he bore.

Does he believe me?

Luxor waited but Brock only offered a halfhearted grunt in response. Then, the big brute went about his business of polishing his new armor. He appraised the metal plates which were padded with thick furs to absorb the shock of a melee attack. The dark metal felt heavy just looking at it. He had left his arms free at the shoulder for more mobility but the rest of him was encased in the strong mail.

"Come, little brother, I've a new outfit for you as well," brock said.

CHAPTER THIRTY
A Woman's Allure

Meredox thrust hard with his spear and the tip bit into the wooden training dummy before him. His arm burned as he repeated the motion over and over again. His opposite arm sagged under the weight of a broad shield which someone had provided him with.

Breathing heavily, he continued his assault all the while acutely aware that he was being outdone by an Egyptian woman next to him. He thought he heard someone call her Chione but wasn't certain. He took a short break and watched her strong methodical thrusts score large chunks from her dummy. Her mousy face was painted, accenting her already stunning beauty.

On the opposite side a lean roman named Scipio seemed to have his thrust honed as well. But even he was feeling the heat of the midday sun and droplets of sweat peppered the ground, falling from his long wavy black hair.

Finally, the horn blew, signaling that training was done, and Meredox's shield clattered to the ground. Falling to his knees, his chest heaved in and out. The past week had been the most physically demanding of either of his lives.

"Form up for small group unarmed combat!" their squad leader shouted.

Meredox struggled to his feet, his body dragging and begging him to stop. At least small group he would be able to rest between bouts. Still gasping for air, he picked up his shield and shuffled over to where the others were standing.

Embarrassingly, Meredox was the last one in formation. He fell in next to a Persian man named Ardashir who, like the rest of them, seemed to be years ahead of him in the art of soldiering. The lean muscular man was a head shorter than him but twice as fierce. His dark features lent to an already menacing grimace which he seemed to constantly wear.

Snapping his feet together with as much energy as he could, Meredox waited for their squad leader to give the order. The ancient Chinese man's given name was Sun Ce. Even shorter than Ardashir, the warrior was once a general of a great dynasty known as Zhou. Though he had never heard of this empire, it was clear they were a military culture who prided themselves on strength and discipline.

"Ardashir, Scipio, no weapons!" Sun Ce shouted briskly.

Meredox sighed out in relief still trying to even out his breaths. Leaning against his spear ever so slightly, he hoped that his squad leader wouldn't see. The two soldiers he called out dropped their weapons and headed out ahead of the group.

Around them, Meredox noted that the rest of the army had broken up into small groups as well. The field which they had unceremoniously decided to use as their training ground was much the same as the rest of the surrounding plains.

"If the lines are broken, which they better not on our end. You must be ready to knock the enemy prone. An enemy on his back is weak and vulnerable. Get them on their back and they can be dealt with quickly so the line can reform. You two, attack!" Sun Ce barked.

Meredox watched as Scipio and Ardashir sprang into action. The Roman, a full head taller than the squad leader swept his arm at Sun Ce with a closed fist. The Chinese warrior ducked the blow stepping inside the strike. Expertly he shoved his hip into the soldier and tossed him easily to the ground. Ardashir shot low in an attempt to wrap up Sun Ce's legs, but the squad leader pulled back grabbing him by the hair and yanking him fast first into the dirt.

"I expected better of you Scipio. Ardashir, you shame yourself. You must always keep your body centered and balanced. Never lunge or overextend. Your stance must be strong and firm. Meredox, come." Sun Ce said.

Meredox dropped his shield and spear and approached. His legs felt wobbly from the fatigue but he did his best not to show the rest of them.

"Come at me slowly, mimicking Scipio's attack."

Apprehensively, Meredox did as he was commanded. He approached at what felt like a snail's pace and swept a fist at one quarter speed at their squad leader's head.

"Now, I duck the blow and slide my leg inside their stance, pushing my hip right up against their body. Then I use their own momentum and body weight to my advantage."

Meredox felt the small man wrap his arms around his waist as he pivoted. Sun Ce cradled him to the ground setting him gently on his back.

"Now pair up." Sun Ce said, offering Meredox a hand up from the ground.

The rest of the squad paired up quickly leaving Meredox staring at the Egyptian woman Chione as he dusted off the dirt from his backside.

"I'm Meredox."

"I know who you are," she replied evenly.

Then, without warning she lurched at him. Meredox jumped but she had her arms around him in moments. Soon he was back on the ground. This landing was not nearly as gentle as Sun Ce had been. His breath left him for a moment and the world spun above.

"This maneuver is not an attack Chione. It is a defense. Wait for your opponent to come to you," Sun Ce said loudly for the whole group to hear.

Meredox slowly got up from the ground, Chione hadn't offered to help. Instead she waited for him arms crossed a few paces away. Her muscles bulged beneath two golden serpent circlets which wrapped around her upper arms.

Gritting his teeth, Meredox widened his stance, got low and waited for her. She seemed to be waiting for him as well and for a few seconds neither of them moved. Finally she gave in and lunged at him again.

Knowing that he couldn't beat her with strength he would have to use the same finesse that the squad leader had used. He had only moments but if he was good at one thing it was mimicking others. The handy trick had saved him many times on the run from the law.

Meredox didn't think, he just reacted. When she was close, he slid his leg in, keeping his center and getting low. Her arms swept over his head and he felt her strong arms slide against his hair but fail to grip. He lunged his hip into her body and with all his strength wrapped her in a hug at the waist and moved with her body.

Chione's weight was greater than Meredox's and though he managed the maneuver she pulled him down with. They hit the dirt in a tangle of body parts but he managed to gain the advantage pinning her arms to the ground.

"Good, Meredox. You see, even a larger opponent can be defeated with the proper training," Sun Ce said.

Meredox beamed at his squad leader but let up for just a moment and Chione tossed him off her with ease. His face met the dirt and grass and he coughed as the dust choked him.

"Not bad, little man." Chione said, a half smirk on her face.

"Thank you, my lady. That is high praise as you seem to be a challenging opponent," Meredox replied spitting some dusty saliva out of his mouth as he got to his knees.

This comment earned him a full-fledged smile from his fellow soldier before she walked away. He admired her backside for a moment before his squad leader dismissed them for the day. Shaking his head his thoughts almost immediately strayed to Belladonna.

Most days, Meredox's mind seemed to be devoted to thinking of her beautiful features. The way she touched his arms gently and blinked her long eye lashes at him. He couldn't get the image of her smooth skin out of his mind.

This sort of thing was bound to happen with the amount of time they had been spending together since Meredox's arrival in Archonia. He knew she seemed to feel the same way. So far, professional pursuits had interfered with what could only be a budding relationship. But now he was training for war and he didn't want to wait any longer to tell her how he felt.

As he walked back across town to his home, his muscles began locking up. He stopped several times to rest, once stopping for water at the fountain of Athena.

Eventually, Meredox made it back to the building which he made his home. Unlatching the tall wooden door, he gazed upon the enormous room and all the material possession he had been given in wonder. Never in his first life could he have pictured himself living in such finery. The movement he started was not without its perks.

Followers created splendid tapestries and rugs to adorn his home. Silver flatware was provided so he could eat like royalty and silk sheets topped a plush bed that was large enough for three people.

His aching body hungered for the feel of that bed but he had other plans. He needed a bath and in this magical place he didn't have to fetch pail after pail of water. Somehow the building itself or some other mystical force brought the water to him. He had but to turn a small nozzle and warm water flowed into his tub.

Resting his head against a soft towel he let his muscles relax in the heated water. There, he searched for the words he wanted to offer Belladonna.

I care for you? No. I love you? No, too much. I feel a strong connection to you?

Meredox argued with himself until the water became cold and finally he emerged feeling slightly refreshed. He donned his finest tunic and wrapped himself in a luxurious mantle trimmed with golden thread.

Walking gingerly on his still tired legs, Meredox then made his way out into the evening air. The town bustled with people. Some busy repairing the damage of the conflict while others seemed to be getting back to the enjoyments of this second life.

Music drifted on the air, faintly masking the dull roar of the crowds. Where in Meredox's former life the streets were filled with filth and smelled of rot. Here he could only smell the finest of foods cooking on the spit and exotic perfumes hanging in the air.

After several minutes of searching a market, Meredox found what he was looking for. Amidst the vendors was a petite woman selling beautiful sashes made from fine silk.

Stopping in front of her, she offered Meredox a kind smile. The wrinkles around her eyes suggested that she was on in years which was unusual for the people he had seen in this world who all seemed to be around the same age.

"Good evening, I'm looking for something special to give to a woman," Meredox said, his hands hidden behind his back.

"How nice, young man. What sort of complexion does she have?" the woman asked.

"Dark billowy hair, dark eyes, and smooth tanned skin."

Meredox waited as the woman rummaged through a pile of garments and pulled free a wine colored sash. Gemstones speckled the cloth, inlaid into the fabric with golden fasteners. Such a sash in his former life would only be reserved for royalty.

It's perfect.

"This piece is beautiful. I'm afraid I have nothing to offer in return," Meredox said, taking the garment and gently folding it.

"Pish posh, I have need of nothing. I only wish to create these things then be rid of them, she chuckled. I do hope your woman enjoys the sash. I'm sure I will see her wearing it tomorrow," the woman finished.

Meredox bowed to her and made his way out of the market all the while jealously guarding his prize. Somehow he felt as though it would disappear before he got to Belladonna's home. Whether out of excitement or anxiety the trip to her lavish domicile was swift.

She lived near the eastern part of town far from the markets, and therefore, the hustle and bustle of the evening. The only sound that filled the streets was the whistle of some unusual insect that remained unseen to Meredox.

Finally, Meredox stopped in front of Belladonna's door. He had been here many times when they were planning the creation of the house of matrons. He had grown accustomed to oddly round doorway painted bright red like the paint she put on her lips.

I think I'll tell her that I'm in love with her. Yes the truth is the best option.

Stepping in front of her door, Meredox moved to knock on the wooden portal when he suddenly heard a shriek from inside. His chest pinched like his heart had missed a beat. The beautiful sash dropped to the ground as he registered the shriek had come from Belladonna.

All rationale left Meredox and he burst through the door without a second thought. Another moan filled the entry hall and he lurched forward, his stiff legs numbed by his sense of fear and duty. He knew the home well and what little light there was spilled from her bed chamber.

In seconds Meredox was rounding the corner, his imagination bombarding him with the most horrific scenarios. A finely woven sheen tapestry was the only thing that separated the hallway from her bed chamber and he could see a male figure hovering over top of her.

Throwing the curtain open, Meredox made to shout at the man to stop but soon realized that both she and the man were nude. He was thrusting ravenously and she was not in pain, but pleasure. He froze as Belladonna looked his way and screamed. This cry was fundamentally different and he realized what a fool he was.

"Meredox! What in the name of Athena are you doing here?" Belladonna shouted, covering her breasts with a sheet.

The man standing over her and clearly inside of her scowled at Meredox. His head spun for a moment and his stomach curled. He remained rooted to the floor as all his hopes fell apart before him.

"Get out!" Belladonna shouted, snapping Meredox into motion. He swiftly exited the room, then her home, not stopping for the sash which lay in the dirt at her steps.

CHAPTER THIRTY ONE
Prelude to War

Luxor pinned Eerika's arms to the ground seeing the flesh and blood accumulated under her finger nails. He growled as his back stung but thrust inside of her even more vigorously. She snapped at him with her teeth, a crazed smile on her face.

"Gods, yes!" she screamed.

As the pleasure mounted Luxor's grip waned and Eerika wriggled free of his grasp. She then pulled his naked backside into her hard forcing him deeper. The warmth over her loins overwhelmed him and he released his seed in a long loud moan.

Flopping down on top of her, Luxor let the sweet release consume him while he caught his breath. Eerika still gripped him tightly, gently kissing his neck, not letting him pull away. They both laid, blissfully connected for nearly a minute before she finally shoved him off.

He turned over on his back and rested his head on his hands behind him admiring her curves as she rose from the floor. At some point they had fallen off the bed but it hadn't impeded their carnal encounter. Even as he did, the pleasure was soon replaced by pain as the rough floor irritated the claw marks on his back.

Wincing, Luxor quickly rose trying not to let Eerika see his pain and annoyance. She seemed to like maiming him when they made love. Somehow it heightened the sensation for her. He couldn't deny totally hating it during the act. But after, he always regretted the feeling.

"Ready to march now love?" Eerika asked donning her hide pants.

"I'd follow you anywhere," Luxor purred, pulling her into his body again, his hands exploring her skin once more.

Luxor felt her lean back into him and half-kiss half-bite his neck for a moment. Then he felt a gentle but firm slap against his face which shocked him out of his bliss as she pulled away.

"Now, now, we've had enuf o dat, love. We need to get ready to march," Eerika said, pulling a shirt over her head.

Luxor sat there holding his manhood as a shiver rocked his body. Then, he scooped up his clothes and donned them quickly before heading out into the camp. The leather strands that made his door slapped at his back as he exited and he became aware of his scratches again for a moment but ignored the feeling and moved to equip his armor.

Brock crafted a unique set of battle gear for Luxor. He was thankful that such a skilled artisan had been available to help him. It would've taken him years to learn how to craft something this fine.

Boiled leather had been stretched over thin plates of metal and padded with furs. These only protected the main parts of his body, allowing him plenty of movement to utilize speed. All the pieces connected with flexible straps of leather that were braided together instead of buckled.

After several minutes, Luxor donned the gear and hung his cudgel from the hook on his belt. He squatted up and down several times to loosen the leather up and let it mold to his body then he jumped up and down a few times to get his blood flowing.

"You look like a true warrior, little brother," Dagur said, stowing some knives in their sheaths at his chest.

"Do you have enough or those, Dagur?" Luxor replied, indicating the array of knives stowed all over the man's armor.

"I'll let you know when the war is over," he replied snickering.

To Luxor's right, Eerika was stringing her bow next to Runi who had already laden himself with no less than three quivers of arrows filled to the brim. Brock meanwhile was loosening up his arms by swinging his mighty hammer around in careful motions.

"What's the plan?" Luxor asked, crossing his arms.

"March across de plains until we find something ta kill, little brother," Runi said, chuckling.

Luxor's face twitched in annoyance. The philosophies of this culture were simple and crude. Hopefully their prowess in combat would make up for the lack of a serious plan. He had heard tales of the phalanx formation they would be fighting against. It could crush an unorganized opposition.

Dutifully, Luxor followed his clansmen toward the great mead hall. The sun shone particularly bright this morning as if the day was happy to greet them. Valhalla shimmered in its glow as the armies accumulated beneath.

Soon, Luxor and the rest of his group were shoulder to shoulder with hundreds of other warriors. Most they had fought with or against in the Fray. Some were new to them, having returned from abroad to heed the call of Clan Bjorn.

As the clanking of armor settled a lone voice rose over the din.

"Brothers! Sisters! Our neighbors to the east wish to make us bow down to their rules and so called laws. They wish to strip away from us the simple freedoms that we by right have inherited. I ask you now. Will you bend your knee before this rabble!?" Njord bellowed.

The whole army roared in unison a song of defiance. Growls and bellows of anger and hatred echoed against the wooden beams of Valhalla.

"Good! Low do I see before me my father, my sisters, and my brothers. All the way back to the beginning of my bloodline. Low they do beckon me to the Fray once more. For honor, and glory. But most of all for freedom!" Njord roared again.

The army barked a rhythmic response, each shout split Luxor's eardrums even as he tried to keep time with his own shouts.

"Now! March eastward, warriors and leave none alive!" Njord finished pointing his great axe to the east.

Leave none alive?

Meredox slammed his door behind him and slumped to the floor. The walk back from Belladonna's passed in a mix of horror and anguish. He could still picture the man. He had seen him at many of the meetings he had been to. His name was Merideus.

Falling over on his side, Meredox's arms felt numb. He was sure she had been sending him signals.

How could she be with that man?

Tears forced their way out of his face congealing with the snot from his nose as he sobbed uncontrollably on the floor. Suddenly the anguish turned to rage and he beat his fists against the smooth stone floor until his hands hurt.

Eventually, his body reminded him that he was exhausted and soon his tantrum subsided. He rested his head against the marble tile below and stared at the finely sculpted ceiling reliefs above.

For just a moment. I thought I'd found happiness.

His gut wrenched then as he thought of his brother. Luxor wouldn't be happy with him. He hadn't returned yet which told Meredox and the rest of Helios that he wasn't coming back.

Rolling onto his side and pushing himself up into a seated position, Meredox resigned to be miserable just as he had in his former life. Dragging himself up he had just enough energy to keel over onto the large bed. Then a strange meditative trance took him and his mind traveled to a far off place.

When Meredox's thoughts returned, he felt rejuvenated. His body felt stronger, his mind seemed keener if possible and his self-pity was gone. He rose with grace and walked silently over to the window. His meditation brought him clarity along with rest.

For too long Meredox cowered from the whims of others. In his former life when he had lied and fooled that officer it brought him a sense of control that he never felt before. Taking down Chione filled him with the same satisfaction. The hollow place in his chest where Belladonna figuratively ripped his heart out was now filled with a hunger. Not the traditional hunger for nourishment but another ominous feeling he couldn't quite pinpoint.

Walking over to the kitchen area in his home, Meredox found a small knife. He'd used it the previous day to cut up an apple. He picked up the blade which had been sharpened to an extreme edge for easy slicing. His sure fingers began to practice palming the blade and hiding it within his sleeve. Such a feat was a delicate process while trying to avoid cutting himself. In fact on his third attempt he felt the blade nick his arm and a familiar burning sensation bubbled up from the wound. He watched the blood drip to the wooden table below with little emotion. Then. He continued his practice getting better with each motion.

Suddenly a knock came at the door and Meredox left the knife hidden in his sleeve. The sound hadn't startled him but the prospect of having a knife hidden from view excited him and he found himself moving to the door quickly.

Meredox cracked open the thick wooden door to find Belladonna glowering at him, her lips drawn in a frown.

"What is it?" Meredox asked.

"Meredox, why were you at my home last night?"

"I was set on giving you a gift. Something for all the things you've done for me. I heard a shriek from within and thought the worst," he said, his voice monotone and emotionless.

"Oh, good heavens, I thought perhaps…"

"You have nothing to worry about, my lady. Good day."

"Meredox!" she shouted, putting her foot in the doorway as he tried to shut it.

Meredox sighed, opening the door back up, all the way this time. Then, stood there with his arms crossed in annoyance, he could feel the blade's cool metal against his wrist.

"A lady of my status could suffer greatly in reputation if people were to find out that I engage in such activities frivolously," she said.

"I am a discreet individual, Belladonna. You have nothing to fear from me."

"I see. Well, that's very good."

"You felt nothing for me, did you?" Meredox blurted suddenly.

Shame and embarrassment forced their way up and took the form of a lump in Meredox's throat. Despite this, he set his jaw and waited for her reply which came quickly.

"Of course I didn't. We worked splendidly together but that is all. I'm sorry if you felt that there was anything more."

"You used me. You knew what you were doing. I am an old student of performance and I should have seen a master at work. I turned the whole world upside down for you. I gave you exactly what you wanted and now that you no longer need me you just dump me to the side like refuse!" Meredox roared.

"I didn't force you to do anything. Just because I was kind to you doesn't mean that I'm required to belong to you! How dare you accuse me of such falsehoods," Belladonna said turning her nose up.

Meredox's temper was on the brink. He felt the knife slipping from its hiding place his body shook with anger. Suddenly it all came loose.

"I learned to fight and kill for you!" He bellowed then the knife fell into his hand.

Meredox watched with some satisfaction as Belladonna's eyes widened at the sight of the knife. She shrieked and stumbled back into the dirt and in one swift motion he drove the small blade in to the wooden door at his side, yelling loudly. Then he slammed it closed with all his might.

Splitting down the middle, the thick wood door settled into two pieces latched in place with a small thin crack between them. Meredox looked away and when his eyes flitted back to the crack Belladonna was gone. The rage pouring out of his body felt good. There was purpose and action behind it. Control.

CHAPTER THIRTY TWO
Clash of Ancients

Luxor tucked and rolled across the ground, diving just under a spear head which struck the soil behind him. He came out of the roll on his knee and the hardened iron head of his cudgel impacted into the abdomen of a Greek soldier.

The scout doubled back gripping his stomach, blood spattering his lips and Luxor watched has Eerika relieved the man of his head.

"Clear!" Brock shouted.

Rising to his feet, Luxor nodded to Eerika acknowledging their fine teamwork. The small skirmish lasted less than a minute. They stumbled upon the scouting party as they crested a hill and Runi laid into them with arrows cutting their numbers in two by the time they had armed themselves. The rest didn't put up much of a fight.

"Scouting party no doubt. Well done, boys," Dagur said, pulling two of his daggers free from a corpse.

"Eerika, report this," Brock said, slamming his hammer into the dirt so he could inspect the slain enemies.

Luxor waited while the large man inspected the weapons and armor. Brock even went so far as to sniff the leather tunics they wore under their breastplates. This made him chuckle silently to himself.

"This is fine armor and these weapons are sturdy. These men may not be the weaklings we supposed them to be," Brock offered.

"We diced dees fools up pretty quick," Runi replied scavenging for arrows.

"We took them by surprise. Besides when have you ever known a scout to be anything but fast, old friend?" Brock scoffed.

"Both Greek and Roman fighters are renowned for their prowess in combat. You should not be too quick to judge this paltry handful. Together, a Greek phalanx could prove impenetrable," Luxor interjected.

"You must tell me of this Phalanx you speak of. Any information could aid us in the fight," Brock replied.

Luxor squatted down next to their unofficial leader and acted as though he was inspecting the fallen along with him.

"Brock, what Njord said is troubling me. I pray that when he meant leave none alive that he intended for us to target combatants only?" Luxor asked.

Luxor waited while the corners of Brock's mouth turned down and his brow dropped to match his grim look.

"Nay, little brother. Many of the clansmen will ravage innocents as well. It was their way in times long past."

"Brock I will not be party to such savagery. I will fight and destroy our enemies but not innocents," Luxor said rising.

Luxor's companion rose standing two full heads taller than him. "I don't wish to be a part of it either. You best keep that to yourself. Your new woman wouldn't agree.

Luxor's gut wrenched and he looked off into the field where Eerika was still visible cresting a hill to deliver their report. Stowing his Cudgel, he heard the clamor of the army as it crossed the horizon. A sound which had grown all too familiar as they marched over the endless plains.

The mass of Northmen nearly reached them when horns trumpeted a song of battle through the air. Luxor and the others looked across the field where they now saw an equally large mass flowing over the hill across from them.

"Form up the ranks! Battle is upon us!" Brock shouted.

Luxor ran, frantically falling behind the front line. He was not big, or crazy, enough to be on the front line with Brock. Still he nestled in between a group of smelly Finnish hunters and pulled his weapon back out.

The two armies came to a halt across the field. The opposing Greek army stopped in perfect unison and knocked spear against shield twice in recognition of the halt. Luxor was embarrassed by the untidy formations on his side of the war. The general lack of discipline also made him worry.

Clan Bjorn responded to their enemies with a war chant. It was menacing but fruitless because the Army of Helios didn't as much as flinch. Suddenly Luxor felt someone grab his arm and found that Eerika had begun to drag him to the front of the line. As the chant died down he could finally hear what she was saying.

"Come, Njord has given us the honor of fighting beside him. We drew first and second blood in this war!" Eerika exclaimed. Dagur and Brock were already standing outside the ranks again.

Luxor noted the excitement on his companion's faces. Brock, however, looked towards the center, his brow heavy. He and the others then moved down the frontline, the white grass crunching beneath their boots. As he got closer, it appeared two small groups were beginning to form for a parley in the middle of the field.

Brock rushed forward, trotting ahead to make it before Njord and his guard advanced. Luxor followed, surprised.

A palpable tension could be felt as Luxor fell in with the leadership and guard of clan Bjorn. Njord rode atop a large bear with pure white fur. Its aqua eyes felt deep as he looked upon them. Ahead he spotted the leadership of the Greek army. Achilles rode out on a chariot pulled by black stallions his personal guard was clad in black as well. Their spear tips glinting in the light.

Luxor jumped as Eerika pinched his backside. She offered a wink as she settled beside him and the parley commenced.

"Good day, my name is Achilles. Over a week ago a group of your men incited hostilities against our city state of Helios. Killing four men. This is an act of war," Achilles said, his face calm.

"Your so called men tried to tell my people where they could and could not hunt. Honor demanded that they fight then the same as honor demands we fight today. Tell your men that they should prepare to die," Njord spat.

"There is no need for a fight. We could come to a peaceful arrang...."

"Shove it up your arse. I'll see every last one of you dead. Your women will be slaves ravaged at the mercy of my warriors!" Njord interrupted.

Luxor shook his head in dismay. Achilles' eyes narrowed a grimace replacing his calm demeanor.

"Njord! I won't have it! My men and I will not kill innocents." Brock bellowed, stepping up beside the clan leader.

The old Viking snarled, turning to meet Brock at eye level. The two monstrous men looked like giants from ancient legends.

"Your men!? Is that a challenge?" Njord bellowed.

Blades were drawn then, a clatter of armor parted the guard on Luxor's side and it seemed that people were already starting to take sides. He ducked over to Brock's side and instinctively reached for Eerika's hand but it wasn't there. He spotted her standing on Njord's side suddenly.

Oh no.

"Yes. That is a challenge. Single combat for the title of Jarl," Brock said reaching for his hammer.

Luxor felt the lump in his throat that he got when he didn't know what to do or say. He looked to the opposing army's leaders and many of them had smirks on their faces. He soon realized that Meredox was not among them.

He said he was going to fight? Where is...Oh no.

Scanning the enemy line, Luxor now spotted Meredox standing amidst the spearmen at the front of the enemy formation. His heart sank.

"So be it! The challenge has been issued!" Njord cried. Then he pulled his massive two handed axe free from behind his back and lunged at Brock. Luxor forced himself to keep his eyes open but winced as the large hunk of metal clanged against Brock's hammer.

A swoosh of wind pushed away from the impact point and caused most of the men surrounding to take a step back. Luxor took two steps back just to put more distance between himself and the fight.

Several more clashes rang out over the field while animal like growls followed each great swing. Amazingly Brock was matching the Jarl's ferocity and strength.

Then, like two massive bears fighting, Luxor watched them fall to the ground in a tangled mess of limbs and armor. At that point, with a motion of his hand, Achilles ordered his guard to pull back a bit as the outcome of the fight was decided.

Luxor's hope rose as Brock got the upper hand on the Jarl. He straddled the great man and bore down on him with heavy elbows again and again. It looked like the fight was about to be over when an arrow shot out of the crowd and stuck into Brock's upper chest. He growled in pain and Njord was able to push him off and pull him into submission.

Just as expected the arrow had broken the tension and both sides burst forward roaring in anger. Luxor followed suit too caught up in the moment to do anything else. He needed to get to Brock and help him win this fight.

Cudgel in hand, Luxor waded into the fray dodging and ducking blows waiting for the right time to strike. He felt a shield batter him from behind which his armor thankfully absorbed. Staggering forward from the hit, he gained his footing just in time to duck a blade which had cut across at his neck. Lunging forward with his momentum he took down the warrior and buried his cudgel in the man's face.

In a second he was up again and could see Brock lying on the ground with Njord his arm twisted backwards. He spotted the Jarl pull a dagger from his belt and move to jam it into his friend. Jumping to his feet, he flung his cudgel, catching the Jarl in the face. It wasn't a hard throw but did the job and in the next moment, Luxor had his body around Njord's dagger arm. He squeezed his thighs and arced his back twisting the man's arm at an unnatural angle. Brock wriggled free and found a spiked helm laying nearby. The spike descended on the Jarl three times crunching each time it did. Then, he felt the arm he was holding go limp.

Luxor rolled free gripping the Jarl's old dagger. He scrambled for his cudgel but the skirmish had ended with Njord's life.

"I claim the title of Jarl!" Brock shouted standing tall with Njord's axe in hand.

Luxor scoured the field looking for Eerika as the rest of them fell silent not sure what to do. He found her finishing off a lanky fighter with shabby leather armor. Her eyes soon found his and her face turned down in a furious sadness when she saw him standing next to Brock.

"I challenge your claim!" a warrior shouted rushing at Brock.

Luxor looked on as Njord's mighty axe split right through the haft of the challenger's pike cleaving into the man's head. Brock kicked it free and waited for another challenger but nobody else moved.

"If there are no more challengers then by right the title is mine! Valkyrie, I need healing," he barked, wiping some blood from his face which had sprayed out of the challenger's neck.

"Brock what happens now?" Luxor asked frantically.

"I will renegotiate terms with our neighbors," he said walking towards Achilles and his entourage.

"Hello, friend. My name is Brock and I now speak for Clan Bjorn."

"Will you surrender and quit this foolish war?" Achilles asked.

"Nay, not unless I have assurances that my people will still have certain freedoms," Brock replied, sternly.

"Why go through single combat to claim your title if you are looking for the same outcome?" Achilles asked.

"My argument with Njord only went as far as killing innocents. I am still a free man and will be treated as such," Brock said, spitting.

By then a tall Valkyrie clad all in white leather armor laid hands on Luxor's new Jarl and began the healing process. He watched Achilles' eyes focus on the miracle and a mild shock spread across his face. He had clearly never seen such a thing.

"We live as free men as well but are protected by laws. Laws which are put in place by the people and for the people," Achilles said.

There was a long silence and Luxor waited, his breath ruminating in his lungs for far too long. Brock seemed to be thinking because he looked to the ground for answers.

"If I may have say in the laws on behalf of my people then I will agree to retire today," Brock said.

"We will not bow to their laws!" Eerika shouted nocking her bow again.

Luxor realized that it was her who shot Brock, her former companion.

"Eerika, no!" Luxor shouted.

"Then you will be relieved of your head, woman!" Brock bellowed.

"Stop! There has to be another way!" Luxor roared jumping between the two.

"There is another option." Achilles chimed in.

Luxor's head swiveled his way as did everyone else's.

"Good Jarl, those who do not sway your allegiance could be banished to the underworld. There, they would be bound by no laws and left to live as they please."

"Underworld?" Brock asked, furrowing his brow.

"A place of cold darkness far to the south. It is known as Dichonia," Achilles replied.

"Ah yes, Hel. We Northmen regard it as a terrible place. Yes, that could be a solution.

"Eerika, if you will not follow me then you will be exiled to Hel," Brock said, sternly.

Then, turning to the army behind them, Luxor cringed as Brock roared aloud for all to hear.

"I am Jarl! Should you disagree with this, go now and seek out your new lives in Hel! Know that if you step foot back in Valhalla you will be killed!" he finished.

Everyone waited with bated looks as a handful of men and women sifted out of the lines and moved south. Luxor couldn't believe that anyone would wish to live in a place they treated as the underworld. This was in fact the first time he had heard of such a place.

Luxor saw Eerika trudge away. He looked back frantically at Brock, who stared at him waiting for him to make a choice. His large friend must have known the predicament he was in. His eyes grew somber.

"Eerika wait!" he shouted, jogging after her.

She stopped and looked back, her face brightening with some hope but falling back into a scowl to hide the emotion.

"You helped that oaf kill my Jarl why don't you go bow with him to your new owners," she snarled.

"Eerika I don't care about any of them. I don't care who the Jarl is. I only care about you. I'm coming with you."

Then he walked over to her and smashed his lips into hers. She tried to pull away for a moment but he gripped her harder and then she gave in and wrapped her arms around his sucking on his mouth eagerly.

"Luxor!" a far off shout came.

Turning to look, Luxor spotted a lone Greek soldier out of ranks. The figure ran frantically down the hill towards then and he realized it was Meredox. His officers shouted after him to fall back into formation but he kept coming. He quickly opened his stance and pulled his cudgel free not sure what to make of his brother's wild charge.

"Luxor no! I'm sorry. Please don't go to the underworld!" Meredox shouted slowing to a halt and stopping to catch his breath.

Appraising the man before him, Luxor could hardly believe it was his gentle brother clad in armor and wielding a long spear.

"I'm leaving this place with my woman, brother, don't try to stop me," Luxor replied.

"Brother, no. I've heard tales of the horrors that lie in the underworld. It is no place to live," he said gasping for air still.

"I don't care! And why do you? You betrayed me!" Luxor yelled.

"If you would have simply returned we could have lived our lives in luxury. I have a huge home with so much…"

"Your possessions mean nothing to me, Meredox. You betrayed me. You cast me out. I'm going with Eerika."

Luxor turned away as Greek soldiers closed in on Meredox and began to disarm him for breaking ranks. His brother struggled and shouted but it fell on deaf ears as he walked away at Eerika's side.

A large group congregated to the south and awaited them. Perhaps fifty souls ready to start a new life in this so called Hel. Luxor didn't look back as he headed away from the battlefield with his new clan.

End of Part Two

Part Three
Hunt for the Fallen

CHAPTER THIRTY THREE
The Keepers

Socrates leaned on his knees as he sat listening to the first Synod bicker at one another. Everyone wanted to have a say in the new world and its laws.

Amazingly enough, the Archon Gabriel was in attendance. His white eyes flickering from person to person at an unnatural rate. The only soul besides the Archon that gave him unease was the new addition to the group. The self-proclaimed Jarl of the barbarians.

Socrates was not the only one who was wary of this man but Achilles had made a pact with him to establish peace. He supposed that this was an acceptable outcome to avoid excess bloodshed. Despite his appearance, the great oaf seemed to own a surprising level of intelligence. The barbarian displayed this through an extensive vocabulary and a far more rational demeanor than his predecessor.

Sighing as the arguments continued, Socrates secretly wished that his fellow guildsman were here to back him up. They always lent strength to his perspectives by agreeing with him. But he was the only one burdened with the station of this unusual council.

Instead of wasting his breath in the endless jabbering, Socrates enjoyed the views of his finished Parthenon. The university's epicenter was complete. Sculptors and masons had done a magnificent job of detailing the columns and arches. A mix of Egyptian, Roman, and Greek themes comprised the main hall where they sat now.

Just then a shrill whistle pierced the air silencing the room and making most cringe. The sound had come from the Archon who effectively gathered the attention of everyone in the room.

"If this Synod is to get anything done then there must be order. I suggest you elect a speaker to control the flow of conversation and delegate who has the floor. I nominate Socrates," Gabriel said, his lips pulled flat as if he was trying to smile but couldn't quite mimic the genuine emotion.

Socrates nearly fell backwards off his bench as all eyes turned to him. His posture changed and he tried to sit up straight to look proper.

"This is a good idea. I second the motion," Anubis said, his heavily painted face surrounded by an elaborate headdress.

"I nominate, Yeshua," a young soul named Isaiah said.

"Isaiah, I am not here to lead. I came only to guide those that ask for my help," The humble man said, remaining seated.

"Men like you make the finest leaders, sir," Gabriel interjected.

Socrates agreed. The best leaders were the ones who didn't ask for their position but were lifted to the rank by those around them. He hadn't even realized that he could be such an icon.

"Then I suppose we should vote," Athena said, her long, beautiful, perfectly curly locks of hair framing her even face.

"Socrates of Helios," Anubis announced. Many hands raised more than half he could tell but the vote had to continue.

"Yeshua of Archonia," Athena said.

Socrates didn't hesitate and raised his own hand watching Isaiah and a few others follow suit. The vote was clear and all eyes turned to him in acknowledgment.

"I do not take this position lightly. Only because you have selected me. My first action as speaker is to ask our brother Yeshua if he will be my close advisor," Socrates said bowing towards the man who had only recently come to Archonia. Strangely, the man seemed to be held in higher esteem than many souls he encountered.

"I will do what I can from a distance. I was only asked to be here today to advise Isaiah," Yeshua replied, calmly.

Socrates didn't push the issue instead he thought that guiding this council slowly to their goals would be more productive.

"Good people of Archonia. We are at a crossroads. Each of us represents a great civilization from the world before. Each of these cultures had starkly unique differences. It's clear from the morning proceedings that we cannot agree on the large matters. I therefore suggest we begin with small things in which we all can agree. If we begin to find common ground then I'm sure we can grow to understand each other and make this world a peaceful place to live," Socrates said.

"What small matters?" Brock asked with an appraising look.

"Well for instance. Is anyone else at their wits end with the cycles of days and nights?" Socrates asked, with a half chuckle.

The Synod members all smirked, some chuckling as well.

"It is difficult to tell the time of day," Ibrahim said.

"I would enjoy seeing a proper sunset again," Athena added.

Socrates smiled and winked at her. Then he looked to the Archon. "Gabriel, do you think you could create a more Earth-like lunar cycle for us?"

"I am afraid I will have to deny that request. I imitate the sunrise as a courtesy but it consumes much of my capacity. I think it is time for your people to become more self-sufficient," Gabriel replied, evenly.

This statement took Socrates by surprise. The whole room seemed dumbfounded but nobody could argue with the strange being.

"Are you suggesting that someone learns to create a new sun and make it rise and set like that of Earth?" Socrates asked hesitantly.

"I am. As you have discovered in your guild findings someone could learn this process and it could be instituted in place of my illusion."

"What say you all?" Socrates asked looking out at the rest of them.

"There could be a soul who wants to devote his life to the rising and setting of the sun," Yeshua said, stroking his beard.

"The strain would be tremendous for a time. I suggest you seek out a different soul for each function you wish to change about this world," Gabriel said.

"Other functions?" Athena asked.

"The wind, the running of water, weather that imitates that of your physical world," Gabriel added.

"The waters that we have seen, run smoothly. You fabricate this as well?" Ibrahim asked.

"Yes, like I said, much of my capacity is wasted on these things and I would greatly appreciate getting it back. I hope you all agree that I am not being too selfish in this matter. I have after all sacrificed this portion of myself for numerous cycles."

"Of course, Gabriel, and we thank you. Yes, it is our duty to care for this world just like the previous one. We will find people to keep these things. I'm sure every soul here appreciates the life-like appearance of this construct you have made for us," Socrates said.

"I agree. I wish for it to feel more like home," Isaiah proclaimed.

"Better than Earth!" Athena chimed in.

"I concur, I would love to sail on the waves once again," Ibrahim added.

The rest of the group murmured their agreement and Socrates spotted Yeshua give him a slow nod of respect. They had agreed on something and that was a start.

"What will these keepers be called?"

"Why not just that? The Keepers?" Socrates asked.

The group rumbled their approval.

"Very well. So we will find someone to command the sun. Another the moon. A third person the stars," Ibrahim said.

"Someone the waters," Yeshua said, standing to pat Ibrahim on the shoulder.

"The wind, the rain," Athena added.

"Can we skip snow?" Brock asked.

Many people from the group had never seen the phenomena of snow. Socrates had only experienced it once on a trip far to the north.

"We don't need to perfectly mimic all the seasons of the Earth," Socrates assured him. Nobody seemed to argue. "Then it is settled. Congratulations, we have all agreed on our first act as a collective society. Shall we convene tomorrow to discuss free education?"

The group agreed and as quickly as they did, the Archon disappeared. Socrates furrowed his brow, pondering the being's purpose but quickly decided that he had spent enough time trying to figure Gabriel out.

Instead, he made his way home with a smile on his face.

CHAPTER THIRTY FOUR
A Chance at Redemption

Meredox shifted uncomfortably against one of the four stone walls surrounding him. The prison cell he had been thrown in was dark and damp. In a few short weeks he had gone from the most renowned figure in the equality movement to a prisoner of the military.

If Meredox had any idea of how dire a sentence he would receive for breaking ranks, he never would've run after his brother. Regret and shame plagued his thoughts. Embarrassment as well. He knew that he never should've joined the military in the first place. The whole reason he had was Belladonna and that was a lost cause.

Fool of a man.

Still, a small part of Meredox was relieved that he was no longer up on stage trying to act as though he was a great leader of some sort. Perhaps if he served his sentence quietly he could just live a peaceful life after being discharged from the military. This prospect comforted him.

A clatter startled Meredox as the slide on the door opened and a small bowl of gruel was pushed into the cell. He didn't move to eat it. He had stopped many days ago. It seemed his body didn't actually need the sustenance. Instead he focused on finding nourishment in the periods of meditation.

With all his spare time, Meredox also decided to keep up on his strength training. His drills in the military had caused his body to become addicted to the positive changes he was seeing. No longer the soft doughy showman that he had been in the previous world, his arms and legs boasted hard defined lines and thick protruding veins.

Kicking the bowl of gruel to the side Meredox swung his legs up over his head leaning them against the wall. With his body inverted he pressed the floor away again and again, his arms straining to lift himself with each movement. When he could take no more he flopped back down. Just then, he heard a commotion and the unlatching of his cell door.

Gracefully, Meredox rose, sweat dripping from his brow. The door swung in to reveal Zeus and Achilles.

"Come with us, soldier," Zeus said, his gruff voice reverberating down the stone hall outside.

Meredox didn't argue. He followed silently as the two great warriors led him out of the dungeon. Soon, he found himself in a small round room with an assortment of weapons hanging all over the walls. A small table and chair was set out and Achilles motioned that he should use it. They remained standing.

"Meredox we feel you've rotted in that cell long enough and we wanted to offer you a chance to shorten your sentence," Achilles said.

"We don't age in this world. Time is meaningless. What is the point of shortening my sentence?" Meredox chided, defiantly.

"You act tough, but the darkness and solitude will break you. I don't want to see that happen. There is another way," Achilles replied.

"What? A public lashing? Banishment?"

"Meredox, your brother has led a group of renegade souls to the land of darkness. The people are nothing more than ruthless murderers who intended to rape and pillage their way through our lands."

"That's not what I saw. They merely appeared to be stubborn men and women who wished to live without rule."

"Their old leader ordered them to ravage our people without mercy. They did not agree with the new one who fought with honor to prevent a war. There is no room for people of this nature to live. Freely or otherwise," Achilles nearly growled.

Meredox furrowed his brow, taken aback by Achilles first real display of emotion. The man clearly lived with hate in his heart. A new but consuming emotion that was plaguing his own life.

Is Luxor really like that? Would he have killed innocents?

Shifting in the uncomfortable wooden chair, Meredox thought about the fresh air outside the dungeon. He pondered at length his brother's actions of late. On the battlefield, he witnessed his brother kill a man after freely admitting in this very dungeon that he murdered a soldier.

Perhaps he is a killer now.

"What makes you think I would want to find my Brother? What makes you think I even could?"

"There are strange powers in this world. I've seen this manifest between people's souls. Family members able to divine the emotions or even the intentions of one another."

"And my brother and I, being twins, must share such a connection," Meredox snorted.

"That is my hope. If you cannot find, or forge, such a connection then we will be exploring other options that may possibly be available to us," Achilles said, his head swiveling towards Zeus.

Meredox observed Zeus, whose imposing figure took up a large part of the small room they were in. He hadn't offered any words beyond his order in the hallway. Suddenly, he spoke.

"I have a brother, perhaps as a Greek you have heard of him," Zeus said.

"What, Hades? Guardian of the underworld?" Meredox asked incredulously.

"Indeed and in the underworld I believe his soul lives on just as in the myths of our world. He was always a troubled soul. His actions as a mortal may have made his legend come true. There are times where I feel like I can sense him. His anger, his rage. Only the strong emotions, but they are there," Zeus added.

"So you will teach me this power if possible and then what?" Meredox asked.

"If you agree to aid us you will be released immediately where you will continue your training in the arts of war. We are putting together a team of soldiers to put an end to the fallen ones," Achilles said.

"The fallen ones," Meredox scoffed.

"This is a serious matter. Our borders will not be safe until they have been destroyed. I will not be worrying about my back at all hours of the day. I want peace and prosperity to flourish in Archonia. That cannot happen with these rampant souls running loose," Achilles said, his fist pounding the wooden table.

The force of the blow cracked the piece of furniture in half and Meredox jumped back in surprise. Rumor had spread of Achilles' amazing strength and speed. Seeing the inhuman feat with his own eyes excited him beyond words. Such abilities could provide him with the control that he sought in his life.

"I will agree on the condition that you reveal to me the secrets of your strength and speed," Meredox said, crossing his arms.

Waiting patiently, Meredox enjoyed the apprehension in the man's look. Firstly, Achilles narrowed his eyes, then the man closed off his posture much the same way Meredox had only moments ago.

"Very well. I am already training other soldiers to achieve this level of ability. After your combat unit exercises you will report to me for this specialized instruction," Achilles said.

A surge of excitement and satisfaction swept through Meredox and he rose to salute his commander.

"I will take you to your new home. A place for warriors to train away from the peaceful city of Helios," Zeus said.

Meredox followed, relieved to not be returning to the dank prison cell with the crusty bowl of gruel. As he walked, Zeus exited the building they deemed as the prison and justice building in Helios. He exited behind the tall figure and a bright sun nearly blinded him. The glowing sphere was not in its normal high noon position in the sky above. Instead, it floated just above the horizon, waning as if dusk was upon them.

"How long was I down in that dungeon?" Meredox asked.

"Nearly a month," Zeus replied.

A breeze tickled Meredox's neck and felt warm against his skin. That too was also new.

"I feel as though I'm back in the other world again," Meredox said.

"Yes, the order of Keepers have been working non-stop to give the people in Archonia a human experience again."

Meredox basked in the lovely feelings of air and light. His tattered tunic, still slashed where his fellow soldiers had ripped his armor off, fluttered in the wind. Walking slowly behind Zeus, he rounded the corner of the justice building to find a long wagon halted on the thoroughfare.

A group of soldiers were sitting in the back and Meredox quickly recognized his squad mates. Chione admired the sunset while the rest of them looked his way offering a mixture of indifference and annoyance on their faces.

I embarrassed them at the battle.

"Climb up, this wagon will take you to your destination," Zeus said.

Meredox did as he was told and as he climbed up his gaze met Sun Ce's. He lowered his head and tapped his chest with a half-hearted salute. The Squad leader responded by looking away and ignoring the gesture.

Taking a seat, next to Chione, Meredox leaned back glad to feel something besides stone under his backside. Several large beasts of burden pulled the wagon. He couldn't guess at what they were called because he had never seen anything like them before.

Short curved horns stuck out of the sides of their wooly heads. Their backs came up over their heads much like a camel's hump but their fur was black and dark brown. Their hooved feet reminded him of oxen. These were clearly a distant cousin.

The wagon jolted into motion and Meredox rested his elbows on his knees. The vehicle took them out onto the sightless grassy plains. He found himself wishing this world had some flavor to it. Perhaps it was just this area that seemed to be mundane. Hopefully there were other lands that remained unexplored with amazing new plants and animals. The thought made him happy.

"Where are we going?" Meredox asked finally, as Helios faded from view behind a hill.

"Be quiet, traitor," Scipio spat.

Traitor? Is that what they thought I was doing running after my brother?

"I'm no traitor. I was imprisoned for breaking ranks. Any of you would've done the same if it was your brother being banished to the underworld," Meredox said, in annoyance.

Meredox saw Scipio give Sun Ce a look. The squad leader nodded.

"It's true. I was just informed. Commander Zeus apologizes for not telling us sooner. You still broke ranks. You're an embarrassment to this squad," Sun Ce snapped.

"Be angry if you must. I don't care," Meredox said.

The rest of the trip was at least pleasant. With the fact that he wasn't a traitor out in the air people seemed to relax more. Soon, they were bantering about the almost-war and fantasizing about how it would've ended had they actually fought the battle.

"Our phalanx would've crushed them. Those fools would've come at us with their unruly tactics and been decimated," Scipio said.

"I didn't like the look of their mounts. Did you see the size of those bears?" Chione said, shaking her head.

"Nothing a spear couldn't handle," Ardashir chided.

Meredox kept quiet. It was clear to him that the others made their decision about him. The only thing he could do was focus on becoming the best. Perhaps then they would not be able to walk all over him.

"There it is!" Ardashir exclaimed, pointing west.

Turning his head, Meredox gasped as a tall structure jutted from the landscape. A broad wooden hall was in the middle of being stoned. Hundreds of souls speckled the sides on scaffolding. They hefted the rock with pulleys over what looked like a barbarian hold they had begun to form an even larger structure.

"Behold, the mythical mead hall of Valhalla," Scipio said.

"This was the barbarian's home?" Meredox asked.

"Yes. Their new king offered it to Achilles for the housing and continued training of Archonia's army," Sun Ce said, his thin eyes staring at it in wonder.

"Achilles wasn't worried that this was a trap? These savages could kill us all as we sleep and leave Helios defenseless," Chione said, her expression a terse scowl.

"Tensions may be high. Keep on your guard at all times," Sun Ce replied.

I'll end any barbarian who crosses me. Meredox thought as they rolled into the mucky streets of the town.

CHAPTER THIRTY FIVE
Hel

Luxor shivered, hunkering down under his fur and gripping Eerika tightly. Two days earlier the long white grass of Archonia had given way to barren, rocky ground. Around the same time the heat drained from the world. It happened all at once and everyone in the clan took notice.

Licking his cracked, chapped lips, Luxor tried to ignore the dire thirst he felt each waking moment. The growling in his belly was an afterthought now. They hadn't found any sources of food or water since the cold had taken them.

Coughs and grunts split the thin air, carried on the eerie winds which swept by in gales. Luxor pulled back his hood to chance a peak at the horizon. Sharp rock formations interrupted the largely empty area.

"I'm freezing, starving, and utterly miserable," Luxor said.

"Welcome home," Eerika replied, snuggling into him more.

"We should go back, plea for mercy. This is no place to live," Luxor said.

"Quit with dat shite. We'll find a good spot yet," Runi grumbled.

"We need a clan leader. Someone strong to lead us and set us on the right path," Dagur said.

"Well, ain no one gonna agree on who dat should be," Runi replied.

Suddenly, Luxor heard panicked cries echoing through the rocks. Craning his neck so see what was going on, he heard shrill screeches overtake the shouting.

"To arms!" someone shouted.

What in the name of Hades...

Jumping to his feet, Luxor fingered his Cudgel and squeezed his hands, trying to get the feeling to return. Now standing, he saw winged creatures falling onto his clansmen further down the line.

"Eerika get your bow strung!" Luxor shouted.

Luxor didn't have to ask twice and Eerika quickly bent her bow locking the string in place. While she worked, he moved closer examining the attacking creatures. From this distance they appeared almost reptilian in nature. Long necks connected with thin leathery wings. He had never seen anything like it before.

A twang startled Luxor as Eerika loosed an arrow. The shaft struck true and one of the creature's screeched, sagging for a moment. Then, it continued its assault upon their brethren below.

"Whatever they are, they're tough little bastards!" Eerika shouted.

The rest of the clan was up in arms now and arrows streaked through the air. Shouts and screams made it impossible to talk to one another. Luxor pushed through, but everyone wanted a crack at killing the beasts.

"Blasted fools, give me a shot!" Eerika said, unable to draw her bow again as bodies pressed in around her. Luxor sprang into action knocking some of his brothers out of the way to clear her line of sight. It was about the only thing he could do to help.

Luxor watched, satisfied as another arrow whistled over his head finding purchase in one of the creature's hides. Already stuck by several others, it finally fell, flapping and writhing while the axe men ripped into it.

By the time they reached the skirmish the rest of the creatures fled or fell. Eerika barked at the group of axe men for butchering her kill. Luxor walked up and squatted next to her. Inspecting the corpse, he held his breath to avoid a pungent odor radiating from the corpse. Tufts of fur covered the hide, not scales like he had originally thought.

"What in Hel is this thing?" Eerika asked.

"Some spawn of Hella," Runi barked, spitting on the corpse.

"Hey! Don't spew your filth on my kill. This is dinner I hope you realize?" Eerika said punching Runi in the arm.

"Valkyrie!" someone shouted.

Luxor's head swiveled in the direction and he amongst a group of others craned to see. Several warriors lay dead, their bodies clawed and mangled by the now dead creatures. He spotted their only Valkyrie Shiva rush over. She knelt by a woman squirming on the ground. Blood seeped between the victim's fingers as she pressed them against her own abdomen. Shiva threw her hands away and healing light fell over. After several seconds, the woman screamed again, then gurgled and quit moving.

Eyes widening, Luxor looked on as Shiva stumbled back looking at her hands. Her healing aura hadn't saved the woman. He rushed over and knelt next to the fallen warrior. The claw mark across her stomach was blackened and sizzling. This wound was different. Some type of poison or plague.

"Why didn't your healing work?" Runi barked.

"I....I do not know." Shiva replied shaking her head.

"Shite!" Runi yelled.

The cold set back in as Luxor watched Eerika cut a leg free from the kill. He counted seven dead clansmen for the four creatures they felled. That left seventy two mouths which still thought they needed food.

With no wood for fire, the men dug into the raw flesh of the fetid creatures. Luxor didn't deign to try to stomach something that smelled so rotten.

"Eerika I wouldn't..."

"I'm hungry and I killed it. Don't tell me..."

Suddenly one of the men suckling on the dark flesh gave a cry and began vomiting. Along with the chunks of chewed meat he spewed pitch black liquid which congealed in blobs on the ground below. Then, he fell face first into it and stopped moving.

Luxor watched Eerika drop the leg and stand back as a handful of others began to wretch as well. One red-haired berserker rose, shouting and cursing. His eyes turned black and his skin streaked with purple as his veins pushed outward. After a few seconds he picked up an axe and lashed out at one of his friends standing near. The weapon opened the man's chest and two others leapt in cutting the berserker down in response.

What devilry is this?

The rest of the clan looked on in horror. Nobody knew what to do. Six more people dead just like that. Luxor amended his count to sixty six with no food to feed anyone.

"This is truly the underworld." Luxor said.

"You regret your choice," Eerika replied, stalking off.

In truth, Luxor did regret coming to the underworld, but he didn't regret choosing her. He watched her leave the perimeter, apparently to be alone, so he didn't follow. Dagur came up beside him, his heavy footfalls scraping the stone and breaking up the sound of wind whistling across the area.

"Scouts came back. They found some sort of brambles to the south. Might be useable for fire. We're all moving there shortly," Dagur said.

"Good, perhaps some warmth will make everything feel a little better," Luxor replied.

In a few short minutes the entire clan was on the move. Luxor caught up to Eerika and explained what they had found. She didn't answer but fell in with the rest of the group.

The cold made Luxor's joints ache as they trudged along the uneven ground. Grey clouds masked the feeble light trying to pierce through. After several hours of hiking he spied the outline of large vine-like tendrils winding amongst one another.

As they got closer, the vines appeared as thick as tree trunks. The creeping limbs were laden with thorns the size of a short sword. These growths must have been what the scouts had found. Some of the clan members eagerly picked up their pace at the prospect of a warm fire or even shelter. Precious wood could provide both.

By the time Luxor and Eerika got to the edge of the forest of brambles many of the men had already began chopping at the dark chestnut colored vines.

"Get some big fires started. Burn the bodies of our brothers," Eerika shouted above the din.

Suddenly, Luxor heard screaming again.

Oh gods, what now?

Eerika was already on the move and Luxor followed. He pulled free his cudgel once again twirling it to loosen up his cold, stiff wrist. Ahead, one of the woodcutters dangled in the air, his body being tossed around by a long slender vine.

Rushing forward, Luxor found the source of the vine and hammered down hard against it. The slender limb seemed much more flexible than the larger ones because it slumped under the impact but didn't seem affected. Cursing loudly, he heard a great groaning and cried aloud as a huge spiked vine descended from above.

Luxor dove out of the way, falling face first into the coarse dirt. The tree-like vine crashed down next to him pounding a divot into the ground. Scrambling to his feet, he moved into the tree line which was the only direction he could go.

Looking at his cudgel for a moment, Luxor realized it was useless in this fight. He needed a blade. Quickly scanning the area, he spotted a clansmen being crushed by one of the brambles. The man's body rose into the air impaled by the large spikes but his sword fell to the ground as his grasp failed.

Wasting no time, Luxor sprinted for the weapon. He ducked another vine which swiped at him, and skidded to a halt grabbing the sword. A crack sounded next to him and he stumbled back, his side in pain. One of the slender vines must've whipped him. His armor had held but his ribs felt bruised.

The vine whipped again but Luxor brought the sword to bear. The dark tendril struck itself against the sharp edge and was severed in the process. Moving to cut into it again, he didn't see the large limb come from behind.

Luxor's torso slid between two giant thorns. Luck, the only thing separating him from a gruesome death. The tree-like vine however knocked the wind out of him and he flew through the air farther into the forest.

Landing hard, Luxor lost his grip on the sword. Pain radiated from somewhere in his back Shooting down his leg and even up through his shoulder. The thrill of the fight surged through him and he pushed the injuries to the back of his mind.

Pushing himself up, Luxor realized that he had been tossed a fair distance from the fight. He picked up the sword again gripping with two hands due to the weight. Then tried to put together another plan of attack. A storm of brambles were separating him from the rest of his clan. Through the chaos he couldn't spot Eerika.

Hades be damned!

Thoughts raced through Luxor's mind, He needed to think of a way to get out of this mess. His gut twisted into knots as he saw arrows tipped with fire plunking against the wooden vines. The alien brambles caught fire quickly and in seconds, he was feeling the heat.

Luxor pushed forward trying to find a gap in the flailing vines but in addition to the thorns, many of them were now covered in patches of fire. He decided the only way to survive would be to push deeper into the forest. The mess of Brambles beyond didn't seem to be moving or aggressive.

Ducking and dodging between thorns, Luxor moved into the forest acutely aware that he was alone. He knew his chances of survival were slim facing the unknowns of this world. But something kept driving him forward.

Without warning he ran into a large bulbous object of sorts. The surface felt strange but he didn't take too long to think about that fact because the fire was right at his heels. He hopped up on to the object and moved to scoot across. That is when it moved.

What in Hel have I found now?

A terrifying growl rumbled from the bulbous object and the dirt around shifted. Luxor watched in horror as the ground began to move on all sides. Whatever he had stumbled upon was coiled up like a snake.

The hard surface beneath his hands were thick plates of armor like scales. Bone spikes protruded at the edges of the wide back plates. It seemed like a giant insect but a snake at the same time. One thing was certain, it was dangerous.

Luxor rolled to get off the creature but the body lurched forward right into the fire. He threatened to roll off into the burning underbrush below and instinctively he buried his sword between the gaps in its armor. The beast let out a screeching roar of pain and dived deeper into the fiery mess.

Gripping with all his might, Luxor closed his eyes. The heat bit at his skin singing it in the places where it was exposed. Thankfully in moments, the creature burst forth from the forest. Cold hit him and his eyes went wide. Shouts from his fellow clan members resurged and he saw them staring, terrified by the sight of the massive creature he was riding.

"Wyrm! Tis a Fire Wyrm!" someone shouted.

"Bring it down!"

"Flee!" others shouted.

Luxor pulled himself closer to his sword and continued to hold on. He lost all sense of orientation as the Wyrm tossed him around.

Better to be on its back than in its mouth!

The spinning and jerking soon got to Luxor and he felt his stomach begin to turn. Though he had nothing in his stomach to expel his body still wanted him to wretch. Thankfully there was a momentary lapse and he reaffirmed his grip on the sword putting almost all his body weight on the hilt. The blade sank deeper into the creature and he slid off the side as it jerked in response. Still gripping the hilt, his body sagged and pulled at the blade. The sharp edge cut down as he hung there and soon his feet hit the ground.

Above Luxor, a viscous liquid ran down over top of him from the wound his sword had inflicted. This time, he doubled over and wretched uncontrollably. Behind him the creature let out a cry of agony and then flopped to the ground.

"He's done it! He's felled the Fire Wyrm!" Runi shouted.

"Finish the beast. Make sure it's dead!" Eerika cried.

Luxor felt strong arms roll him over and a gloved hand pawing to clean the gore off his face. The sludge burned his eyes but he could see Eerika peering down at him, her eyes frantic.

"Stupid man. Where did you find that thing?" Eerika shouted.

Pointing was the only thing Luxor could manage. The motion made his hand hurt and he realized that his palms were red and blistered weather from the heat of the fire or rubbing against the cross guard.

"Looks like we found ourselves a clan leader," Runi said hoisting him up against his will.

Some of the clansmen were still hacking at the fallen Wyrm while others began to gather around him. Eerika wore a bit of a smirk and Runi held his hand aloft.

"All hail Jarl Luxor! Slayer of the Fire Wyrm!" Runi shouted.

CHAPTER THIRTY SIX
The Impure

Socrates' head drooped as the hour grew late. He and the other Synod members had been in delegation nearly all day long.

With so many different groups of people coming together. All their various beliefs and opinions made deciding on anything an arduous task. Though his first idea had been a successful one the subsequent policies were a fight every step of the way.

The Archon Gabriel attended every one of their meetings. Always ready to offer his opinion to steer the conversations where he wanted them to go. His thoughtful white irises infuriated Socrates and he didn't know why.

The air in the room was moist and smelled of rain. The keeper of the weather must have created a cleansing shower for them. Socrates secretly wished he could walk around the streets as it fell. Anything would be better than being here a moment longer.

"The question shouldn't be about who comes to this world from the previous one, but are they allowed to live here amongst us." Athena said, tersely.

"All should be allowed to live in the Promised Land. If they were welcomed here, then they walked the path of righteousness!" Isaiah shouted.

"Socrates, did you not execute a rapist some time ago? Do we want that sort of righteous person to live amongst us in this peaceful world?"

"I did not personally execute him, I did however witness his confession. While I want to agree with Isaiah, I think Athena is correct. Not all the souls that are coming to Archonia are good souls," Socrates grumbled.

"Well how can we tell if someone has goodness in their heart or not? Such a thing is impossible. Therefore..."

"Ahem..." Gabriel interrupted.

Socrates rolled his eyes. The rest of the Synod seemed to hold this being's opinion in high regard. He himself kept a careful skepticism at all times but there was little he could do to rid himself of this man.

"Forgive me, but it is not impossible. I could teach you all to see one's soul for what it really is. Based on their past deeds of course. Going forward it would be impossible to tell what a human soul will choose to do," Gabriel said.

"Please teach us." Athena said.

The group looked to Isaiah who they expected to argue with her. "It was taught that a higher power would judge us for our actions on earth. Perhaps we could be that higher power," he said.

Socrates frowned. Such statements were slippery. That amount of power could easily be misused.

"Making snap judgements about someone based on what they have done in the past? I very well might be cast out of Helios then. I have made many foolish mistakes in my life," Socrates said.

"Did you ever intentionally hurt anyone in this or the previous life?" Gabriel asked?

"Yes, I'm sure that I did." Socrates said stretching his mind to think.

"I can safely say that you have not. Your Archonian essence, or soul as you all seem to be fixated on calling it, is quite intact," Gabriel replied.

"What exactly do you mean by that?" Athena asked, her lush, red lips terse, almost worried.

"Any action that our minds understand to be inherently wrong are reflected in the make-up of one's essence. For example I'm sure all of you understand that striking someone inflicts pain. If you intentionally strike someone, knowing that it will cause them pain this act affects your essence. Degrades it if you will," Gabriel said.

"You mean to tell me that we punish ourselves with our wicked acts?" Isaiah asked.

"That is certainly a valid perspective. Ultimately these acts cause a breakdown in the bonds which hold our essence together," Gabriel said.

Suddenly Socrates jumped because the Archon appeared beside him. The being was so close that he could feel the heat emanating from his skin. Gabriel was terribly beautiful and to be so close to him was intoxicating.

"Look at your companion, Athena. Look closely. Don't study her skin but look deeper. There is more that your eyes can show you. Reach out with your feelings and you will begin to see," Gabriel whispered and in the same instance he was back across the room.

Socrates' eyes darted from person to person curious to see if they had noticed Gabriel's movement. Nobody acted as if they had witnessed the event and he found himself staring at Athena. Immediately he could see fleeting images of distant memories. He was getting more used to that now when looking at people. But now he could see something more.

He looked at some of the other people in the room to make sure his eyes weren't tricking him. They all appeared normal to him but Athena seemed a shade darker than everyone. Alternatively, Isaiah seemed brighter and more colorful if possible. All at once everyone in the room looked different aside from the Archon.

Sitting up a little straighter in his chair, Socrates sat for a moment, dumbfounded as his companions' souls were revealed to him in shades of grey and white. He caught sight of the Archon who betrayed a small grin of satisfaction.

"The Archon speaks the truth. I... I can see it." Socrates said.

"Truly!?" Isaiah blurted.

"Then I say we judge people on this measure. If they have done wicked things in their previous life then they do not deserve to live amongst us in peace and harmony," Anubis said, rising with a fist in the air.

There was a rumble of agreement and Socrates didn't know if he liked this idea. He looked to Yeshua who sat silently behind Isaiah and his face didn't hint at what he was thinking. The Judean's soul was clear. More pristine than anyone in the room.

"If this is to be the way of things, then nobody will be exempt. If we judge people, then we ourselves should be the first ones to be judged," Socrates proclaimed.

This brought a swift silence to the chatter. Socrates saw Yeshua give him the familiar nod of approval.

CHAPTER THIRTY SEVEN
Archonian Strength

Meredox stood in line at attention. Sun Ce walked in front of them inspecting his new recruits. Ten more souls had been added to their unit and the strange faces seemed grim in the morning light.

In the distance the great mead hall known as Valhalla grew ever larger into what would be the military complex for all Archonia. The old wooden exterior now boasted a thick layer of perfectly cut stones, stacked and mortared. High walls and Roman-style turrets encompassed the greater area surrounding. Tidy lines of barracks were slowly replacing the disorganized huts the barbarians once called home.

Meredox caught a look of appreciation from his superior when Sun Ce inspected his shield and spear. He had given the man no excuse to disparage him, by following the rules to the tiniest of details. Unfortunately this was beginning to make some of the other, less detail oriented members of their unit, look bad.

In truth, Meredox didn't much care about the others. He only cared about his promised training with the legendary Achilles. So far he had been here two weeks and had not so much as seen the great warrior. He was beginning to worry that the man had lied.

Standing there anxiously, Meredox's eyes darted amongst the others in his unit as they were each inspected. Sun Ce found several minor infractions that could have been overlooked but instead, he highlighted them.

"Ardashir, you have a chip in your spear point. Sharpen it down lest it break off. Chione, your uniform is a disgrace. Don't you wash?" Sun Ce asked.

Meredox shifted from one leg to another impatiently, only straightening up when the squad leader looked his way. His eyes betrayed him though and suddenly Sun Ce made for him.

"Meredox, the rebel. Can't you stand at attention for a few minutes without my having to keep you in line!?" Ardashir barked.

"Yes, Sir!" He replied.

"You think you're better than the rest of us? That you deserve special treatment!?"

"No, Sir!"

"That's not the orders I've been given! Listen up, grunts. Your fellow soldier here struck a bargain with our glorious leader. He is to receive special training from Achilles himself."

Clenching his jaw, Meredox caught the rest of the unit glaring at him. Any work he had done to mend the broken bonds between him and his fellow soldiers just shattered.

"Get out of my sight, grunt. Report to Achilles unit to the north. Good luck getting there in time," Sun Ce finished turning away.

Meredox furrowed his brow in confusion but looked to the sky where the sun was rising from the south. He headed the opposite direction, north, looking back over his shoulder where his unit was falling in for drills. Shaking his head he began to jog briskly. The comment about him not being there in time was troubling and he didn't want to be later than he already was.

After several minutes of jogging he reached the northern most part of the training grounds. So far he had not seen Achilles or his unit. He swiveled around on his heels and looked back to ensure he hadn't missed them. Hundreds of men and women skirmished and drilled, exercising their bodies and honing their muscles. The dark blue tunics they wore all made them run together. To his dismay, Achilles was nowhere to be found.

He looked north out into the fields away from the training grounds. They must be further out, training separately from the main army.

Blast it all.

Worried about the repercussions of being late, Meredox took off, running out into the plains. His legs were stiff from all the training but his body was getting used to it by now. After a handful of minutes his chest began to rise and fall harder. Behind him, the training ground faded and ahead the endless fields rolled onward.

Soon, he began to worry he made a mistake by continuing north. He wondered if his squad leader had lied to him about where his training would take place.

Stopping for a moment to catch his breath, Meredox was sure he had ran at least two miles. He decided to head back and look through the training grounds more. He clearly made a mistake.

Suddenly, Meredox heard a loud crack. The sound shot across the open field and his head snapped to the direction it had come. Squinting, he could just make out some figures far off in the distance.

That has to be them.

Meredox jumped back into motion. His strides long and powerful. Putting at least another mile behind him he began to see the group take shape ahead of him. Men were jumping into the air far higher than they should be able to. Their black outfits stuck out amongst the golden white grasslands.

Another crack threatened to make Meredox trip as he flinched from the incredibly loud sound. His legs began to burn causing him to slow his pace. The speed he had been running was far too fast to sustain for long. A shrill whistle let out moments later and all the figures who had been jumping around or sparring ceased.

In the next minute Meredox came upon the group of soldiers. He recognized many from Achilles original guard. Each one a legend from the history of Mother Greece. Bending over he placed his hands on his knees and gasped for air. Craning his neck, he spied Achilles waiting for him.

"My lord, I apologize if I am late. I was only just told that I was to begin my training," Meredox said, still sucking in huge breathes.

"You *are* late, recruit. I instructed Sun Ce exactly when to release you from duty this morning. You have been given ample time to get here. You will run faster next time. Until you can get here on time, your punishment for being late will be to hold the atlas," Achilles said, motioning to his left.

There, Meredox gazed upon a large spherical stone. Its diameter was as long as he was. The chunk of rock must weigh 30 talents.

"Forgive me, sir, but I do not believe that any man could lift that stone, much less hold it," Meredox said, finally standing at attention.

Meredox watched Achilles walk over to the stone, and with quick practiced motions, hefted the impossibly large rock off the ground. Then the Greek warrior set it on the curve of his back and squatted into a resting position. It was as if, he was staring at the spitting image of the Greek god, Atlas.

Meredox's eyebrows raised in wonder. He would soon be learning this strength. Apparently it was also his job to learn inhuman speed as well.

"Your task today will be to lift that stone and hold it. Until you can do so, you will not be able to train with the rest of my Myrmidons," Achilles said and then whistled.

The Myrmidons leapt back into motion. Some skirmishing while others lifted other incredibly heavy objects. Meredox did as he was ordered and approached the atlas ball. He placed a hand on the rough stone and leaned into it with his weight. As he figured, the rock didn't move.

Placing his back against the stone and squatting down, he tried to leverage the ball to at least roll a bit. Again the stone didn't move. He strained and pushed with all his might but there was simply no moving such a heavy rock.

After many long minutes, Achilles approached. Meredox had slumped to the ground, sweat beginning to bead upon his forehead.

"Your mind still thinks it is in the mortal world. Where that rock weighs more than ten times your own weight. But we are no longer in the mortal world. Tell yourself that the stone does not weight that much. Convince yourself that it weighs as much as a blade of this grass," Achilles said.

"Is this how you achieved such power? Simply believing that there are new rules in this world?"

"It was not a simple matter, but yes. Now I can run a stadion in the time it takes you to blink your eyes."

Meredox stood once again and continued. This time he grabbed a blade of grass and tugged it free from the ground. The water-filled tuber in the roots dripped and he sucked it dry before tearing the roots off. The grass, of course, nearly floated in his hand because of its miniscule mass. He held it up between his body and the Atlas.

Letting it lay in his hand so he could get the feeling for how light it was.

Then, after several moments, Meredox reached out his hand to push the Atlas. The stone felt different as his skin came into the contact with the surface again. His heart fluttered and he smiled as he pushed on the large rock. The smiled instantly faded as the rock didn't move.

Growling, he tossed the blade of grass to the side and shoved his shoulder into the mass ahead of him. His growl turned into a roar as he struggled and pushed to no avail.

The next morning, Meredox broke from ranks as soon as Sun Ce released him. He was past the edge of the training ground in a matter of a minute and his legs were soon submerged in the grass.

Trying to ignore the pain, Meredox pushed his body to its limit. After some time, it felt like his body was threatening to quit on him. His rubbery legs wobbled while his out of control chest pinched as it tried to expand farther and farther to get more air in.

The last stretch was brutal and he fell onto his hands and knees as he passed into the small training area the Myrmidons had been using. It was little more than trampled grass but it grew spacious from the intense activity that took place there.

"Late again," Achilles said, indicating the Atlas.

Meredox nodded and after a minute struggled to his feet. There, he leaned against the large stone until his breathing evened out.

Finally, he pushed against the rock, trying to make it wiggle but he nearly fell over backwards as he merely pushed himself away from it.

Curse this stone.

Meredox jumped as Sun Ce barked at him to stand at attention. His eyes were from sheer fatigue. For a week he ran drills with his squad and then trying to be on time to Achilles training. His body felt near the breaking point. Even a full night of meditating hadn't completely restored him.

Straightening his back, he felt his eyelids peel back, revealing the morning light. Despite his struggle, He noticed a considerable increase in both his speed and his strength. This of course could be attributed to the hard work he was putting in, but the progress seemed exaggerated. Like he was gaining much faster than he could have in the previous world.

Skidding to a halt, his labored breathes pained him but he ignored the steady jab at his ribs and stood at attention.

"Congratulations, recruit. You are on time for training," Achilles said. The rest of the Myrmidons smirked as they stood in formation. Meredox wondered why but dismissed the thought as excitement washed over him. Now that he was on time perhaps he could start other forms of training.

"Now that you can make it here on time you will have more of the day to complete your first task as a recruit...Lifting and holding the atlas ball above your head," Achilles finished, his arms crossed.

Meredox's head slumped to his chest while the Myrmidons chuckled at him. They must have all understood his plight because some of them offered words of encouragement as he stalked off to the stone sphere.

CHAPTER THIRTY EIGHT
Warlord of Hel

Luxor Held Eerika close while she coughed. He didn't like the depth that each cough shook her. She was not the only one suffering from the cold, desolate wasteland of Hel. Many of the others were falling ill as well. Most of them couldn't remember the last time they had been stricken by disease.

The Valkyrie did what she could but Luxor knew her powers were dwindling due to lack of rest and nourishment. He released his grip on Eerika and tossed his cloak over her to help against the wind. Then he walked across to where they were stacking the bodies. Four had died due to the plague which had broken out.

"Cold, Disease, famine. Yer de worst Jarl we've ere had and tis not even yer fault," Runi said, sniffling as he sat nearby.

"We should go back. Plead with Achilles to let us surrender. Perhaps my brother could…"

"You keep dat shite to yerself, little man. Dees folks'll skewer ya fer surrendin.'"

Luxor gritted his teeth but didn't reply. The man was right. These stubborn fools would die rather than admit defeat. The only other option was to keep moving until they found some sort of refuge.

So far, the only respite they found was near a great chasm two days prior. A clansmen found heat rising from the depths, ushered by a feint orange glow. The heat wasn't significant however and the exposure to wind nullified the life-giving warmth. He chose to have them move on.

Nobody could tell how far they had come, nor in what direction they were travelling. An ever hanging blanket of clouds shrouded the sky adding to the bleakness and misery.

"Get everyone moving. Leave the bodies, we have nothing to burn them with anyway," Luxor said.

Walking away, he let Runi be the bad guy ordering everyone up for the march. He then returned to help Eerika up. She hacked more as she rose. Soon, he was leading the column of souls deeper into the underworld.

After the brambles and the wyrm plus the four gone to disease, his little clan now numbered fifty two. It was difficult to believe that they could perish again. He wondered if there was anything after this life.

Probably not.

Hours passed in misery, and Luxor felt blisters squishing inside of his boots. His fine hide greaves were caked in the unusual ash-like dust which seemed to accumulate on the ground. With that clinging to him and the dried filth from the Wyrm encounter, He was sure he looked like a vagabond.

Luxor thought of the Wyrm and gripped his new sword in response. He checked on his blade a little too often now. The act comforted him. Knowing it was close at hand was like a warm blanket. His fingers then dug into the pouch at his belt and he began to fiddle with his wooden coin.

Has your luck run out?

The wind picked up and Luxor felt Eerika grip him tighter. The gale beat against them and he felt as though someone was scraping rocks over his ears and nose. He cringed looking to the horizon where he spotted another patch of the deadly brambles they encountered.

"Move for cover!" Luxor shouted.

"And die in the wake of those horrible moving trees?" Eerika choked.

"They may let us be if we don't harm them. I'll take anything over freezing to death in this place."

A few others agreed and began to follow him. Eerika had little choice for he had won the title of Jarl. The appointment dumbfounded him. He had, by accident, slain the Wyrm merely trying to hold on for his life.

Luxor's legs groaned in protest to every step. The closer they got to the wall of brambles the harder the wind seemed to push across them. Finally, He stumbled across the threshold of the wicked vines and led Eerika over to a rock formation helping her to sit.

The wind ceased and relief took them both for a moment. The basked in it with their eyes closed while feeling came back to their exposed skin.

"We're going to die here," Eerika said.

"It is possible. But we must keep going until that time comes. Rub your hands and legs together. Keep moving around. It will help," he said.

Rising again, he left her to make sure the rest of the clan made it. Thankfully, his hunch about leaving the vines alone seemed to be right. So far they weren't moving and nobody was screaming.

"Don't touch the Vines. Don't as much as lean against them!" He shouted.

Just then, Movement to his left caused his head to jerk. Twisted amongst the thick underbrush he saw a pair of yellowed eyes glowing amongst the thorns and twigs.

What in the name of Hades is that?

His sword sung as it came free of its sheath. Upon hearing the sound several other men produced weapons of their own.

"What is it?" Runi asked, rushing up beside him.

"In the tree line, just there. Yellow eyes," Luxor replied his voice nearly a whisper.

"We see ye! Show yerself, creature!" Runi bellowed.

The eyes went wide for a moment but then disappeared a moment later. Runi made to lunge for the bush but Luxor grabbed him by the fur at his shoulder and held him back.

"Leave it. It's gone. We must have scared it off. No sense in chasing and running into something that isn't afraid of us."

The thick wooden vines creaked around Luxor and he, along with everyone else, jumped in surprise. But it was merely the wind beating against them causing them to shift. His clansmen huddled together and hunkered down for a rest. He snuggled in next to Eerika and his legs rejoiced for a moment.

Luxor came to and his heart jolted from the sound of a loud horn. He must have fallen into the strange meditative trance that took them at night. The horn sounded again and he jerked upright his whole body protesting.

A shrill battle cry let out, reverberating amongst the brambles. It sounded like a small animal. Several of his clansmen were on their feet at the ready as he was still scrambling to his feet.

Luxor pulled his sword free just in time to see a flock of small black creatures skittering out of the tree line. They walked upright on two legs but didn't appear to be human. The short twisted little men swung clubs and lunged with crooked spears as they fell into the clan.

"To arms! Defend yourselves!" Luxor roared.

As he yelled this, a huge figure burst through the bushes. It looked like the others only bigger. Its vast thick arms went to the ground like tree trunks as he hobbled towards them.

Unlike the small ones, the large one stopped short of the fight which had already escalated into a full battle. Luxor lunged, stabbing out at the nearest monster. His sword skewered it striking the ground behind its small form.

Quickly, Luxor kicked at the body, pulling his blade free from the sinew. With a swish he deflected a gnarled wooden club that threatened to strike his knee.

With three violent movements he hacked the little creature to death before moving forward to the next. Another wave of the monsters fell over him however and two grabbed at him forcing a short retreat. A small flat-faced monster leapt at his sword arm stabbing wildly. Luckily the makeshift shank he was wielding didn't find purchase in his thick leather bracer.

"Cease!" the large monster shouted.

Luxor missed his mark as the monster he was targeting dove backwards out of harm's way. Some small scuffling ensued until the attackers fell back far enough for a parley. He remembered that he was the Jarl and would need to speak on behalf of his people.

"Who are you and why have you assaulted my Clan?" Luxor called.

The enormous beast-like man lumbered forward. His yellowed eyes narrowed.

"I am Kavin, overlord of these lands. You are trespassing strangers. In this world that is an act of war."

"We are not from this world. We do not know its laws," Luxor said, motioning that his men should form up behind him.

"I see that now. You are from far to the north where things grow. The land of light," Kavin replied.

"We were banished to this land for desiring to live free. I was told we could find freedom here. So far we have found only death," Luxor said, sullenly.

A rumbling of footsteps interrupted the dialogue and Luxor looked over his shoulder to find that another large group of the twisted little monsters flanked them. The parley must have been a strategic maneuver. The group behind cut off any hope of retreat.

Curses!

"Stand fast, men!" Luxor shouted.

"Lower your arms, Clan leader. Surrender to me and your men and women will live freely and with plenty under my rule," Kavin said.

Hope filled Luxor's heart for a moment but he quickly remembered the creed of Clan Bjorn.

"Clan Bjorn does not bow to anyone!" Eerika shouted next to him.

Luxor cringed, wishing that it wasn't so. Could he remake the rules as Jarl? Would anyone follow him?

"My companion speaks true. No member of Clan Bjorn will bow to anyone, at any time," Luxor said.

"Then how is it that you rule them?" Kavin asked.

"My rule is dependent upon their freedom. At any time my clan members could challenge me for the right."

"Then I challenge you!" Kavin bellowed, rearing back and beating his chest with his two enormous arms.

Oh gods...

Luxor's throat, though already dry, felt as though it would shrivel away. Heat rose in his face and his insides squirmed. He spotted Eerika looking at him, her face screwed up with a mix of fear and determination.

Hand shaking, Luxor held aloft his blade, aware that a fight was inevitable. He moved forward one slow step at a time mustering the courage to accept the challenge. Just as he was about to speak Eerika shouted.

"No outsider will be my Jarl!" Then, she lunged forward towards the enemies. The rest of his clan roared and followed, passing him in moments. Even the enemy overlord was taken off guard and reared back to gain footing.

Luxor jumped into action again as well, watching Clan Bjorn break apart the enemy line in moments. Unfortunately, Kavin gained his balance and struck back. A huge swipe sent four clansmen flying through the air screaming. With another mighty fist, the great creature pounded a man into the ground with a crunch.

"Take him down!" Luxor yelled cutting down two little monsters while making his way towards their leader.

A thin sheen of hope flickered in his mind and a thrill rose up in him as the battle commenced. He urged his men onward looking away for only a moment. When he looked back, Kavin was standing over him and a large hair covered forearm connected with his upper body, sending him flying end over end until he crashed to the ground.

CHAPTER THIRTY NINE
The Order of Justice

Socrates paced around the room, admiring the fine marble tiling which grew richer and more detailed every day after the artisans left. By now the Synod chamber was the finest in all the world.

Rubbing his low back, Socrates sat back down in his seat while the council deliberated. He found better ways of dealing with the rigors of the Synod chamber and his body was becoming accustomed.

Though the list of issues seemed to be growing longer instead of shorter, Socrates and the rest of them were finally finding common ground. Decisions were being made faster.

Leaning back in his seat, Socrates spotted one of Achilles men entering the room. The unexpected surprise stopped the discussion on labor requirements in its tracks.

Clearly a soldier, the man strode in with fine leather armor studded with metal discs. His heavy greaves clattered against the fine stone while a purple belt drew the eye to his short sword.

"Forgive me for interrupting, Great Synod. My name is Hector. I am the Sentinel Captain stationed in Helios while the commander trains his armies."

"We know of you, sir. What is the meaning of this intrusion? I trust it is important?" Socrates asked sitting up a little straighter.

"It is. There are many souls stubbornly fighting the order to be judged. Crimes are being committed which include theft, vandalism, and assault. My men simply aren't enough to police the streets. In addition there is no process by which to bring these criminals to trial."

Socrates, stroked the stubble of whiskers on his chin. Looking to the others in the room they wore looks of concern.

"This will be addressed immediately. Dispatch a message to Achilles urging him to send more troops to aid you. He must have some recruits ready by now. We will decide on how the justice system will work. In the meantime detain all those who have committed offenses," Socrates finished.

Then, he stood walking toward the middle of the room.

"Socrates, we must get a court system in place. We cannot detain these people without the promise of a trial," Athena said, her crimson gown piling up at the foot of her chair.

"Do we want to do things the old way? Trials were held in the former life and we know that corruption and bribery could easily run rampant in such a system."

"I agree. These men who are judging the souls of our people. They have shown aptitude at determining the truth by simply looking at someone," Anubis said.

"You're suggesting they simply judge everyone on the spot? How would we prevent them from becoming corrupt?" Isaiah shot back.

"I once bore witness to a strange people who could change someone's beliefs through the application of radical physical and emotional stress. Those who underwent this process would emerge as zealots completely devoted to whatever ideal they had been arranged to pursue," Socrates said.

"That sounds barbaric," Athena said.

"Indeed, but I suggest we create an order of soldier. Through rigorous training we could purge their minds of all self-interest. They will be strong enough that nobody could threaten their safety, they will be wise enough that nobody could outwit them. They would be consumed by the idea of justice and therefore infallible in their judgements. Such a soldier could adjudicate any offenses on the spot without need for witnesses or a trial," Socrates finished.

"It could work, but we cannot force anyone to undergo such a demanding induction. They would have to volunteer. We would need checks and balances just in case their training failed," Annubis said.

"We don't even know if anyone has the skill to train this type of zealot," Isaiah butted in.

"I will train the first, the rest will be born of them" Gabriel cut in, appearing beside Socrates.

Socrates couldn't help the reaction and jumped as the Archon spoke.

Blasted Archon.

"Gabriel, you interrupt our meeting yet again. Why is it that you continue to...Help us?" Athena asked.

"The answer is simple. You were born of my brother Prometheus and I see you as family. I would have you live in harmony here in Archonia and if there is anything that I can do to aid you I will," Gabriel replied.

"And what exactly will you be doing to train this first soul?" Socrates asked.

"I have abilities that far exceed anything that you could possibly imagine. Her training will be swift and painless. I cannot promise that of those who follow," Gabriel said running his hand over the finely carved heading of Socrates' chair.

"Her?" Isaiah asked, instinctively looking back to where Yeshua usually sat. His eyes returned to the Archon, his face scrunched in annoyance because his teacher wasn't there.

Socrates thought for a moment and it didn't take him long to realize who the Archon was talking about. Of course she was the obvious choice. She would jump at the chance to undergo this change.

"You speak of Themis." Socrates said.

"Themis? Mother of Prometheus?" Athena asked.

"Daughter and mother of Prometheus. She was the first of us to cross over into this world. The first being touched by an Archon. She then bore his child who had the gift of an Archonian essence. The child took his name.

The room fell silent and Socrates noted that everyone seemed to turn inward for a moment, contemplating the situation. None of them liked the Archon meddling in their affairs but so far he hadn't led them astray.

"Very well, we shall ask her, but I will be there when you make the change," Socrates said.

Socrates shifted uncomfortably at the sight of Themis standing alone in the center of the dark chamber. Despite her thin frame, she stood tall and unafraid, her fine ivory skin exposed to the darkness. He guessed that any other man would relish her nude form. Her feminine curves did nothing for him but make him feel cold.

"Gabriel, my brother," Themis said, moving to embrace the Archon as he strode into the room.

"It does me good to see you, little sister," Gabriel replied.

Stroking the stout whiskers on his chin, Socrates tried to understand the nature of their relationship. There were several instances in Greek history where a god supposedly mated with a mortal to create a demigod but those stories were always born of embellishment. Themis was the only human to have ever lay with an Archon.

Socrates interviewed Themis at length, hoping to discover the origins of Archonia. Though people called her the daughter of the Archon Prometheus, she divulged to him that they were actually lovers.

"Are you ready to become the embodiment of justice?" Gabriel asked.

"I am. And in doing so, I will fulfill my final purpose in this life. Once I complete this task you will show me how to move on?" She asked.

Move on?

"I will sister, you will be with my brother once again," Gabriel said.

Be with Prometheus?

"Was Prometheus not destroyed by your brother Lucifer? How is it that Themis will be with him again?" Socrates blurted.

Nearly stumbling over on his backside, Socrates felt the world spinning. He tried to maintain his balance but the Archon was gazing at him with those piercing white eyes. The god-like being was doing something to him that much was clear. Soon, the struggle was over and he toppled to the ground in a delirium.

CHAPTER FORTY
Out of Control

Meredox's foot shifted, sliding across the gritty pebbles of the sparring circle. Across from him stood the broad form of Ajax, whose long beard was braided tightly in front of him.

Keeping his body loose and fluid, Meredox fought the voice in his head desperately searching for control. Stepping lithely, he hopped around the circle waiting for his opponent to strike.

When he did, Meredox was ready and ducked under Ajax's wild swing. Then, grabbing him from behind he clasped his hands around the large man and tried to fling him backwards over his head. Ajax broke free however and with practiced motions countered with an elbow to his face.

Meredox hit the dirt hard, colors blurring his vision. He rolled what he hoped was away from the fight, and regained his feet fast, but Achilles called the match with a shrill whistle.

Growling, Meredox cursed the commander under his breathe. As he watched Ajax recede from the circle he realized his face was in a tremendous amount of pain.

"You're done for the day, soldier. Get healed and report back to your unit. I expect you here tomorrow on time. Lift the atlas ten times and you may join us again," Achilles said, motioning that two others should enter the sparring circle.

Begrudgingly, Meredox exited the ring, making his way over to a dark-skinned barbarian who was known only as Valkyrie. There were many others like her but Achilles had chosen her to be a myrmidon.

"My goodness look what he did to your face," Valkyrie said.

"I would have had him if Achilles would just let me…"

"You have made a great deal of progress, little man. You only just found the strength to make the run and hold the stone," Valkyrie replied.

"I need to be better. I need to be stronger. I'm tired of being weak. Letting others rule me," Meredox said.

Warm light gushed over Meredox's face for a moment and he felt relief from the throbbing, burning pain. When she was finished, he turned on heel without another word and took off running toward Valhalla.

The trip now took Meredox mere minutes. He was gaining speed and strength at a satisfying rate. As he skidded to a halt in front of his squad he was met with faces full of surprise and wonder.

"Meredox, Achilles has let you go early again today. You must not be able to cut it in his squad," Chione chided.

"Be silent, you braying donkey," Meredox replied.

"What did you say to me!?" Chione yelled. The rest of the squad stopped what they were doing and watched as she lunged at Meredox.

Meredox felt his mouth tighten into a half grin while he watched her slowly move. His reactions were improving too and it was all too easy to toss her aside as she lunged at him.

"Enough! Fall in line, soldiers!" Sun Ce bellowed.

Rolling his eyes, Meredox moved to his position, adjusting his loose flaxen training tunic.

"Meredox you seem to think yourself above us now. Perhaps you would care to spar against me," Sun Ce goaded.

Despite his recent confidence boost, the idea of fighting his superior made him uneasy. The man was a great warrior who had devoted his first and second life to combat. Still, he was tired of being beaten down by everyone and never before had they been given the opportunity to fight him.

"I accept your challenge."

Meredox enjoyed the look on his squad leader's face after his reply. It was one of anger mixed with surprise.

"So be it, soldier! Enter the circle!" Sun Ce said, fuming.

Without a second thought, Meredox strode into the sparring circle for the second time in one day. He was still loose from his training with Achilles and not tired in the least.

Watching Sun Ce enter the circle, Meredox appraised the man's stature. Ajax was twice his size. The difference boosted his morale and washed away any doubt in his mind.

"Scipio, call the match," Sun Ce ordered.

Meredox's eyes darted quickly to the Roman who nodded and gave the whistle. Immediately, Sun Ce lurched into motion. He was stunned by the quick assault but not totally caught off guard.

Deftly, Meredox dodged away to his left as a high heel kick swooshed by his face. A backwards fist swung wildly, following up the perfectly executed spin out of the kick. He ducked the blow and backed up to get his position.

The next assault was upon Meredox instantly but this time he imagined the stone and its incredible weight melting away as he lifted it above his head for the first time so many days ago. The sense of control it had given him flooded his mind. Euphoria enveloped him and he reacted as Sun Ce's powerful leg swept in again.

This time, Meredox caught it, gripping Sun Ce's ankle in one strong hand. Then, grabbing him by the throat with the other hand, he savored the surprise in the man's eyes as he took him to the ground.

With a strong hand, squeezing his opponent's windpipe, Meredox bore down with his opposite fist, letting go of the leg that he stopped. He smiled as Sun Ce struggled with every technique he knew to break his grip but Meredox's new strength overwhelmed him. His squad leader's face was like clay mashing under his mighty fist. In that moment he let go. All his rage, all his feeling of insecurity and inadequacy.

Meredox hadn't even registered the whistle but soon several sets of arms were wrapping around him and pulling him off. Crazed shouts filled his ears as his anger seemed to subside. It took four men to pull him off and even they had struggled. He backed up, not taking his eyes off his mangled squad leader as he sputtered up blood.

"Valkyrie!" Scipio shouted.

"You madman!" Chione yelled.

Wiping the blood off his knuckles, Meredox noticed that everyone stopped their drills and were converging upon the scene. He had nowhere to go. There was no hiding from this.

Thankfully, Meredox spotted a Valkyrie rushing over, her healing aura swept over Sun Ce's bloodied visage and in moments the bones began to realign and the lacerations healed.

"Explain yourself, solider," Zeus bellowed, his shadow casting a long cold silhouette over Meredox.

"The Squad leader challenged me to a duel. I accepted," Meredox replied evenly.

"Is this true?" Zeus asked.

"Yes, commander, but he continued to pummel the man after I had ended the fight," Scipio said, eyes narrowed in anger.

"Recruit, for your excessive force. And for the fact that you didn't cease the fight when instructed. You will spend one month in prison. Consider yourself lucky that we were able to save your squad leader in time," Zeus said.

For a moment, Meredox contemplated his options. He didn't want to be locked back up again. A month would go by in no time and he could train while inside, but he found himself considering other options.

Could I defeat Zeus?

Then, Meredox realized even if he could, Achilles and his Myrmidons would put him down with no trouble. He had to bide his time. Become stronger than them. Then he would have nothing to fear.

Without a word, Meredox led his escort of soldiers towards the ever growing stronghold of Valhalla. Zeus stayed right by his side. It didn't take a learned man to see that the Greek god didn't trust him. Oddly, this notion gave him a sense of importance and power.

Meredox was soon walking through a new part of the stronghold. The passages were lit by torchlight and led down into the bowels of the foundations where he guessed they had created the prison. It was far roomier than the dungeon in Helios, even his personal cell had a stone slab for him to keep off the filthy ground.

"Consider your actions, soldier. Also, I would make it a priority to find your brother. Once Achilles hears what you've done now he may banish you to Dichonia altogether," Zeus said latching the door behind him.

Meredox didn't reply. Instead, he strolled to the back of the cell and laid down on the stone slab. A square of light shone down through a vent which ran to the surface. He could see bars studded in the tiny window making escape improbable.

Suddenly, he noticed that he wasn't alone and sat up straight, his heart pounding from the surprise. A lone figure slunk in the shadows. The man stood so still he could have been confused for a statue.

"Gods you gave me a start," Meredox said, exhaling loudly.

"That was not my intention," the man said, receding even further into the darkness if it was possible.

"Who are you? Come out of the shadows so I can see you."

Meredox noted the state of the man's clothing as he stepped into the light. They were soiled to the point of being rags and hung loosely on his thin decrepit frame. A long scraggly beard covered his face, while his unkempt hair hung about his brow. The greying hair almost covered his peculiar white eyes.

"I am a prisoner who has lost his name. They have kept me down here for longer than I can remember," the prisoner said.

"What did you do to deserve such a sentence?"

"I have done plenty to deserve my plight. The stories are not worth telling. The better question is, why are you here?"

"I overstepped my boundaries in a duel," Meredox said, rolling his eyes and leaning back against the stone wall behind him.

"Overstepped, or succumbed to rage?" the prisoner said, evenly.

Meredox sat back up, his eyes narrowed, studying the prisoner before him.

How did he know? A lucky guess?

"How did you guess that?" Meredox asked.

"It was no guess. I can see it in you. An unbridled force which you have very rarely let out during your two lives. Instead you have pushed it deep down within yourself until it erupts uncontrollably," the prisoner said.

"Get out of my head, old man," Meredox said, rising to stand face to face with the stranger.

"I can give this emotion focus. I can make you stronger," the man said, his voice now almost a whisper.

Stronger?

"Show me," Meredox said.

Without warning, the prisoner's frail hand snapped out and grabbed his. The bony fingers were much stronger than they appeared. Then, he felt weak. His knees buckled as the room began to spin.

"What in the name of the gods are you..." but Meredox was cut short before he could finish and a clarity came over him. Suddenly he knew things. Wisdom that he had not had before. It seemed alien to his mind but comfortable at the same time. Like it was meant to be there.

Meredox squeezed his fist shut and felt a surge of energy. He didn't know how or why, but he knew that if he wanted to he could break down the thick wooden door before him and walk right out of the room.

"It's incredible…" Meredox started to say to the prisoner, but the room around him was empty.

Rushing to the corner of the room he felt around in the darkness but there was no one. A shudder ran the length of his back and he turned in a full circle to ensure he was alone.

What just happened? Did I imagine that whole conversation?

Shaking with the same thrill he felt when facing off against Ajax, Meredox slowly sat down on the stone slab once more. All at once he felt tired. Not the normal fatigue that one would feel after a hard day of labor but something infinitely deeper. He could barely raise his limbs. After some effort, he pulled his legs up crossing them so he could get comfortable and then let his mind slip away into a meditative state.

A clamor shook Meredox out of his trance and as his eyes fluttered open he saw Achilles and Zeus standing before him. He didn't speak. Instead, he waited.

"Have you had time to think on what you did last week, recruit?" Achilles asked.

Last week?

Meredox looked to the floor near the doorway and spotted several plates filled with gruel that had been knocked aside as his commanders entered.

Was I meditating for a week?

"Do you have an answer, soldier!? Zeus barked.

Meredox calmly stood, his eyes rising to meet the great men before him.

"Yes," he replied.

"I hope you have. Your quest still lies before you. Despite your...mistakes," Achilles said, crossing his arms.

"What is to become of me after I have served my purpose? Will you cast me aside? Execute me?" Meredox asked.

Calmly, Meredox waited while the two exchanged glances. Zeus stooped down and whispered into Achilles ear. Somehow Meredox could hear every stifled whisper.

"He could be purged by Themis."

"Who is Themis?" Meredox asked.

The look of shock that crossed Zeus' face almost forced a smiled from Meredox's lips but he held firm.

"Themis has become the embodiment of truth and justice in this world. She is training an order of soldier to follow in her footsteps. The process has not been tested on anyone yet but it is our understanding that the volunteer's mind is essentially purged," Achilles said, not a hint of surprise on his face.

"But I would not be a volunteer. You would make me walk this path," Meredox replied.

"No you would not be. It is either that or we imprison you upon your return for an undetermined amount of time," Achilles said.

Almost without hesitation Meredox replied. "I accept these terms. When does my quest begin?"

Meredox watched patiently as the two commanders exchanged glances one again. Zeus shrugged and Achilles nodded.

"You can leave tonight. You will lead two squads to the underworld. There you will find the rogue members of the former Clan Bjorn and report their location to us," Achilles said.

"Meet on the training grounds in one hours' time. I will muster the scouting party," Zeus added.

Meredox followed silently as they exited Valhalla's dungeon. He parted with the two warriors at his Barracks to gather what few belongings he had. His armor was still safely stowed in a chest at the foot of his bed. He donned the leather tunic and metallic greaves in record time. Everything he did seemed to be faster, as if exaggerated. For a moment it was difficult not to fumble things. By accident his bed crumbled under the force of his arm as he leaned against the frame.

He had leapt in strength and speed. Doing his best to hide this fact, he exited the barracks, sliding a short sword into the sheath at his side.

CHAPTER FORTY ONE
A Slave or Worse

Luxor coughed, choking on a foul taste in his mouth. He tried to put his hand against his lips to wipe away what he assumed was blood, but his hands were bound behind him with a scratchy rope.

Lying face down with his head craned to the side, Luxor pushed his shoulder into the dirt and rolled so that he could get a better look at what was going on.

The rest of the battle had been a blur after Kavin sent him flying across the field. His whole body ached and each movement seemed painful as he struggled to grasp his situation.

Luxor managed to catch sight of several little monsters skittering around him. They appeared to be tying up some of the other survivors. Moans and cries of pain could be heard between the moments of cold silence.

The fight had been lost, that much was clear. Clan Bjorn was broken. Luxor tried to wiggle up to a seated position but his back ached and began to cramp. He growled in pain and flopped back down.

"Bring him to me," Kavin's grisly voice rumbled.

Luxor felt a dozen tiny hands grabbing at his armor and clothing. They dragged him across the dirt across rocks and lumps. Eventually he was released but not before two large hands righted him so that he was on his knees before their master.

"You have been bested, warlord. I own you now and what is left of your clan. I thank you for the fine weaponry you brought us. These instruments will make us strong," Kavin said.

"How many of my clansmen still live?" Luxor sputtered on the already drying blood in his mouth.

"Only a handful. Perhaps twenty or less. You need not be concerned. They are mine now," Kavin replied.

"Eerika!" Luxor shouted, trying to look behind him, his neck was so tight he couldn't fully turn.

There was no response and Luxor felt a stab in his chest like someone skewered his heart with a pike. Panic took him and he began to shout her name wildly, his cries echoing off the shambled vines around him.

"Be silent, slave. Your woman still lives. She is a strong fighter. I subdued her without harm," Kavin said.

Luxor fell over, in a mix of pain and relief clouding his thoughts. He couldn't continue a conversation and things became a blur once more. The tiny hands wrapped something around his neck and something began to pull him.

The thing around his neck choked him and he had to move with it to avoid the awful feelings. Somehow, he managed to find his feet and stumbled in the direction he was being pulled. Time seemed to run together as his parched throat screamed for water, and his empty stomach groaned for food. But the worst feeling was the coarse rope rubbing against his wrists every moment of the hike.

After what seemed like hours of torture, Luxor felt a warmth spreading across his back. Someone laid a hand on him and after only a few seconds he realized it was Shiva. The tightness in his neck relaxed. The throbbing in his chest ceased, and thankfully, the blisters about his wrists sealed up and his wits returned.

"Thank you, Shiva," he said.

"What is your plan, my Jarl?" she replied sternly.

"Shiva, there is no plan. Clan Bjorn is gone," Luxor replied looking at the area around.

They were back in the wilderness, the chilled wind licked at his body. A great crevice loomed to their left glowing with a sinister light.

"We still have Dagur, Runi, and Eerika. If we can defeat this Kavin creature we would rule his underlings," she said in a hushed whisper.

"They took our weapons."

"A bear does not need weapons," Eerika butted in.

"Eerika!" Luxor said, changing his gaze and moving to embrace her.

To Luxor's dismay, Eerika recoiled. He hung his head. He had been defeated. The ultimate shame for a Jarl of clan Bjorn.

"So it was not love between us then?"

"It never was, little man," Eerika said.

Luxor felt like he was going to throw up. Everything was ruined. There was no point in continuing on. He was about to stop then and there and figured that they would start to drag him, but the rope around his neck went slack. The army of twisted monsters stopped.

A warm wind swept up over the edge of the crevice nearby. Luxor looked to Shiva who wore a grim look. Runi and Dagur walked up and huddled next to them.

"There are so few of us left," Dagur said.

"Line them up!" Kavin roared, his call rising above the winds.

The black humanoid monsters all began to chatter and bark at them, lunging out with their own weapons. In moments Luxor and his companions were backed up to the edge of the chasm. A foul odor like rotten eggs emanated from below and the heated winds rising from below were riddled with ash.

Luxor coughed as he breathed it in. He looked at Eerika. Her stern yet beautiful azure eyes stared straight ahead. It was as if he no longer existed to her. This was appropriate then. He had lost everything in the former life and now he was losing everything in this life. He must be ready to die again.

"The time has come to make a choice. The choice is simple, live or die. I am a benevolent leader. If you serve me, I will provide safety, security, and all the pleasures you could ever imagine," Kavin said, his large body standing tall as he rested on his arms in front of him.

"We won't serve anyone!" Dagur shouted, and many of the remaining clan members hooted in agreement.

Luxor remained silent, noting that Eerika had done the same. Shiva scooted in close to him however and her face twitched like she had something to say.

"I will serve you, monster. This is not how my story ends," Eerika said stepping forth.

The mighty Kavin bellowed a deep chuckle and waved her over. She strode forth and stood next to him staring back at her former brothers and sisters. Though the idea of servitude went against everything she stood for, Luxor knew that ultimately she was a survivor.

"Eerika, ye bloody coward. How can ye kneel before such a creature? How can ye give up yer freedom?" Runi asked.

"Clan Bjorn is gone, its traditions mean nothing. I will live. If I must serve for a while I will," she replied turning away in shame.

"Anyone else?" Kavin asked, surveying the paltry few before him.

Luxor didn't move or speak as he had resigned to his fate. He almost wanted to die again. It would be easier than continuing. He had failed his beloved brother on Earth time and again. Now he was failing those he cared for in this life.

A few former clan members fell to their knees, bowing in servitude and Luxor quickly counted fourteen souls standing tall and awaiting their deaths, including Runi, Dagur, and Shiva next to him.

"Push them over!" Kavin bellowed, pounding a large fist into the dirt.

All at once, the spears and swords lunged at them and it was either a bloody death being poked full of holes or a fall to their death in the pit below. Luxor had no chance to make a choice because Shiva grabbed him by the collar and yanked him over the edge with her.

The ash filled air engulfed him and Luxor's insides twisted as he fell. He looked above and his clansmen began to fall over the edge after him, their screams reverberating off the orange chasm walls. Then he closed his eyes and let himself go.

Sweet release.

Luxor gasped suddenly as he was jerked out of the fall. His leather cuirass rode up under his arms and he stopped dropping altogether. He looked above and Shiva floated in midair above him.

Of course! The Valkyrie can fly!

Struggling to not slip out of his armor, Luxor felt another jerk as Shiva dragged him through the air. He collided with something and realized it was Dagur who had leapt off the cliff just after them. He wrapped his arms around his fellow clansmen and held tightly.

Luxor looked up and saw Runi falling above them. He must have tried to fight his way through the beasts. A trail of blood followed him as he fell but Shiva moved to intercept anyway because he was still cursing loudly while he spiraled downward.

Luxor and Dagur stretched and nearly missed their large friend as he passed but caught him at the last moment pulling him in. Shiva sank under his weight and began to descend slowly. Only now did he realize that it was much hotter than it had been on the plain above.

Looking down, Luxor winced against the sulfurous clouds billowing forth and his eyes squinted at the bright orange glow of molten rock stirring beneath. He had seen volcanic activity before but never in such close proximity.

"Catch him!" Shiva shouted above the chaos as another clansmen fell nearby.

Someone must have grabbed him because they sank lower and their fall became faster.

"You can't hold anymore!" Dagur shouted.

"Just need to get there!" Shiva yelled motioning with her head to a small out cropping of rock against the cliffside.

Two more bodies rushed by as Luxor clung to his clansmen. They fell into the magma below screaming and shouting. Only then did he realize they were not the only ones writhing in the superheated rock. Countless black specks screamed with flailing arms reaching out.

Where did they all come from?

Luxor had no more time to contemplate this because he felt another tug as they caught their fifth man. Shiva was now in a steady drop and she was straining to keep afloat at all.

"We're not going to make it!"

Luxor heard Shiva roar, and saw the veins in her face begin to bulge. All at once he and the group of six people desperately clinging to one another hit the cliff wall. Runi dangled over the edge and Luxor gripped him with one hand.

"Don't let go little man!" Runi pleaded looking for footing.

Slipping slowly towards the edge, Luxor felt as though his arm was being tugged from his body. Despite this he held firm. Just before he himself slid over the edge many hands grabbed him and pulled him back up. Runi clambered over the edge moments later and everyone flopped down with a sigh of relief.

I'm still alive.

Luxor watched Dagur roll over and hug Shiva.

"Bless you, woman. Bless you," Dagur said.

"Get off me. We need to get out of here!" she responded wrestling free of his grasp.

"It's hot down here," Luxor said, gasping on the thick air.

"Too hot for us to stay," Shiva said.

"Can you carry us one by one back to the surface?" Dagur asked.

Luxor knew that couldn't work, the temperature was already becoming unbearable. He thought the cold was bad on the surface, but this heat was fire against his skin.

"We don't have time. We will perish down here if we wait.

One of the other clansmen that they saved yelled loudly and a bright flash of light blew away from him. Luxor toppled onto his back but the heat disappeared.

"What devilry is this, Geirr?" Runi asked the man.

"I bend my energy. It will protect us for a short time but we must hurry!" He yelled his voice strained.

Wasting no time, Luxor rose and helped Runi to his feet. There was little room on the small precipice. He quickly jumped into Shiva's arms and she took off into the sky. The heat enveloped him once more but soon disappeared as they rose back to the surface.

"When you get to the top, hide, they may still be on the other side," Shiva said.

Luxor didn't have to be told twice and when she tossed him up over the edge, he fell onto his belly, crawling across the ground and rolling behind a boulder nearby.

A minute passed and Luxor dared to look over the boulder. Across the chasm he saw Kavin and his Army lumbering away. The sight made him sigh and sit down against the stone. In seconds Runi was crawling toward him, then Dagur, and finally Geirr and Shiva.

Seeing Geirr made Luxor Wince, the man's body was covered in burns. He must not have been able to hold the barrier he created for long. Despite this, he saved them all.

"Where did you come by these abilities? I thought only the Valkyrie were blessed with strange magic" Luxor said.

"It is not magic. We have developed gifts in this world," Shiva said laying hands on the man's burns.

When he was healed, Luxor moved in close.

"Geirr is it? Thank you. And thank you, Shiva. We owe the both of you our lives," he said.

"Aye can' believe little Eerika would stoop so low," Runi said, shaking his head.

"Forget her, we are leaving this place. There are plenty of corners in the land of light that we can get lost in," Shiva said, peeking over the rocks to watch the enemy's recession.

Suddenly, a screech issued forth from the skies, and they heard the vicious flapping of wings. Luxor looked up while keeping his body low and pressed against the rock. He was running from one danger to another without end. Only now they were unarmed, fatigued, with nowhere to go

CHAPTER FORTY TWO
Adjudicator

Socrates scribbled notes in his journal as he watched the Purge commence. It was a laborious process that he could only watch in short intervals. He couldn't imagine what the subject was going through.

The chosen soul was a strong one however and Merideus knelt before Themis with reverence despite his suffering.

Hmm, did Themis shave their heads?

Scrawling in journal, Socrates noted the subject's heavy breathing and wild perspiration. Across the room an orb hung in midair. The sphere moved like a cloud displaying scenes of a horrific nature. These graven images, produced by Themis were being experienced by Merideus to the tiniest detail.

This part of the process, called The Suffering, caused the mind to be broken down so that it can be remolded. Socrates wanted to stop the madness taking place before him several times now. He had to remind himself that the man had chosen this and everything had been explained to him before the purge had begun.

Socrates shook as Merideus erupted in a scream of agony. He watched helplessly as the man fell over onto his side and fought against an unforeseen force which seemed to be torturing him. The cries of pain and anguish caused his insides to churn. Soon he could take no more of it and went running from the room.

Several weeks passed and Socrates couldn't bring himself to return to The Suffering. Achilles continued his relentless training of new soldiers. The Synod its endless debates. All the while Helios boomed not only in population but also in its grandeur. The abilities of the few souls who had shown aptitude were quickly teaching others. The power to create and destroy things using one's inner energy resulted in a tremendous boom in creation. Buildings, art, even foods which had never before been seen or eaten.

Socrates walked the street with some of his guild members glad to be free for the moment from the Synod's troubles. Aristotle walked beside him, regaling him with the new facts and discoveries which his old group had chronicled recently.

"Soon the new capitol building will be completed and you won't have to use the space in your university to hold your meetings," Aristotle said.

"Hmmm. Yes that will be very good. We need to educate the people and quickly before they begin to regress to the old ways of thinking," Socrates said thoughtfully.

"My lord! My lord!" a voice cried above the crowd's hustle.

Socrates turned, his hands behind his back to see who the man might be addressing. He was shocked to find that a young soul was rushing through the crowd to address him.

"Young man, I am no lord to you. I am a representative of the people. I humbly serve you. Now, what can I help you with?" Socrates asked.

"Sir, your presence is requested at an emergency meeting of the Synod. The new soldier is to be tested," The man said, bowing low and retreating as quickly as he had come.

Blasted meetings. Will they ever end?

Socrates bade farewell to Aristotle and made his way through the streets to his university. Upon arrival he noted that not all the Synod members were in attendance. They likely travelled far away to their homes during their recess.

Strolling slowly into the all too familiar chamber, Socrates appraised Merideus who stood tall and still in the center of the room. Just outside the circle, Themis stood quietly, her head down.

"Welcome, Socrates," Annubis said.

"Thank you, old friend. As always it is a pleasure to see you. How can I help the people of Archonia this day?" Socrates asked.

"Merideus has been training for weeks and we think he is ready to be tested," Anubis replied, a smile on his face.

"We think?" Socrates said, scratching the whiskers on his chin. "And what does his teacher think?"

Socrates turned to Themis who looked up and shook her head. "He is nowhere near ready, we have only just begun the second phase, The Indoctrination," Themis said.

"We need these soldiers now. Achilles' men are already falling to corruption. Why just yesterday we raided an underground gambling arena, several of our own soldiers were found in attendance," Isaiah said.

"If he is not ready, he is not ready," Socrates said.

"When will he be ready?" Anubis demanded.

"I have only just begun to reshape his broken down mind. There are still several more steps to his training which include combat training so that he cannot be defeated or challenged in his decisions.

"Commander Achilles is to help you with this correct?" Socrates asked.

"Indeed, The Forging will take the longest," Themis said.

"Could he possibly make his judgements sooner, with soldiers to back his decisions and protect him?" Socrates asked, trying to please both sides.

"Fear of reprisal is a powerful tool that evil men use. He must be devoid of this fear. Only confidence of strength and ability can do this," Themis said.

Socrates shrugged to the rest of the Synod that had shown up and tried to make it clear that he had tried to find a compromise. He did agree that more and more people were slipping away from the ideals they instituted.

"The Suffering, the Indoctrination, the Forging. These are the three steps in your process?" Anubis asked.

"Indeed, but a continued education is required. Constant accountability from peers and of course from outside of the order. If you wish this to be a success you need to send more pupils to me. The Suffering did not take long for this one but it could take years for others to break. I should begin training more now," Themis said.

"We will have more volunteers sent to you as soon as we are able. One volunteer, Meredox is on a mission to the underworld," Isaiah said.

"Thank you, in the interim, I can find time to see to your city's problems. Make an announcement of my coming. In three days' time I will descend upon Helios and deliver my justice. You can consider me the first of this order of Adjudicators. I have written out a recommended Hierarchy for this order and will be selecting students for these positions once they are ready," Themis finished handing Socrates a heavy scroll.

Unrolling, the fine paper from its golden bar, Socrates watched Themis recede from the room along with her pupil. Then, he looked down to review the proposal.

Order of Adjudicator

Ranks

Grand Justicar

To be the deciding vote on the council and report to the Synod.

Justicar

Eight of these to make up the council of Adjudicators.

Judge

As many as needed, assigned to teams to undergo continued training from the Justicars

Sentinel

These footmen already in training will cede control of any situation and aid the judges in their work.

Socrates finished reading the parchment and it seemed to be simple enough.

Themis must be Grand Justicar?

"Themis seems to have things well in hand. Let us make our announcement that justice will be enforced as of tomorrow. And let us pray that we have done the right thing," Socrates said, rubbing his forehead with concern.

CHAPTER FORTY THREE
Following Orders

Meredox smiled to himself as the others slunk away from him or avoided his looks. It was Sun Ce's squad and one other of equal rank that made up this scouting party. With his other squad mates they numbered ten in total. The small group was meant to cover a vast distance at great speed.

Upon his return to their squad, Meredox hadn't heard a single jibe, not even a whisper. Even Sun Ce seemed to be genuinely afraid of him. He basked in the feeling. He was no longer the weak little showman who would buckle under the pressure of conflict.

The scouting party had headed out two days ago and Meredox took the lead. The underworld was an easy place to find according to most. He simply began by heading south. Somehow they magically expected him to find his brother and the rogue group of barbarians who hadn't pledged to Achilles' allegiance.

Meredox trotted at a brisk pace and despite how slow it felt to him his companions strained to keep up.

Often, he found himself stopping so that they could catch up.

On one such occasion, Meredox appraised his companions as they ran. Scipio ran at in the lead next to their squad leader. His incessant saluting bothered everyone. Chione carried extra provisions on her back. She was trying to prove that she was strong. Ardashir was the negative one. His near constant complaining and spitting was getting on everyone's nerves.

Bunch of fools.

Meredox was glad to have them steer clear of them. He was supposed to trust them with his life but they mostly annoyed him.

When the sun got low in the sky, Meredox stopped as he neared a small lake sitting in the middle of the sea of grass. The others seemed to agree that it was a good spot to camp and halted upon their arrival as well.

"Get a fire going," Scipio demanded as if he was the squad leader.

Walking to the edge of the lake, Meredox took off his dust ridden greaves and dipped his toes in the water. The cool liquid felt incredible as his body relaxed. Suddenly he felt a presence approaching beside him. It was like a tingle in his brain.

What is that?

"Meredox, may I speak with you?" Sun Ce asked.

Looking his way, Meredox furrowed his brow but nodded. Then he splashed some cool water on his neck as well.

"I wanted to apologize for my behavior these past weeks. It was wrong of me to ridicule you the way I did," Sun Ce said.

Meredox felt the surprise not only in his mind but in his face as he took a second look at his squad leader. Then, running his fingers through his hair, he rose from the ground to look him in the eye. In that moment he could sense the man's life force. The feeling had seemed so alien to him but now it clicked. The strange man in the prison had given him abilities or shown him how to use them. Even as he watched Sun Ce stand there awaiting his reply a soft glow emanated from the man's body.

"Well, I just wanted to tell you that. I guess I'll...

"I apologize too. For the excess force I used in our match," Meredox said hoping simply to keep him there a bit longer. The discovery fascinated him.

"I deserved what I got. I challenged a stronger fighter and I lost," Sun Ce replied.

Meredox ignored the comment and focused on memorizing the man's unique signature. He wondered if he could sense him from far away.

Could this be how I find Luxor?

A long pause followed, and Meredox didn't seem to realize. After an awkward moment, Sun Ce stalked off without another word. He followed the man with his eyes taking in the fluctuations in his body that before were not apparent to him.

Finally, Meredox absorbed the fact that the man apologized to him. His tense shoulders relaxed a bit, relieved at the prospect of mending the bonds between him and his fellow soldiers. Perhaps if he did so with the others they could be true comrades again.

But not tonight.

Walking around the lake until he was a fair distance away, Meredox plopped down on a soft tuft of grass and crossed his legs. He needed to meditate on this new power and develop it further.

Already, Meredox lost track of his squad leader. They had a roaring fire going and from the smell, something was cooking on the spit. The glow made the figures of his companions blurry which would be perfect for his testing.

Trying to imagine the feeling he had gotten when Sun Ce was near, he reached out looking for it in the night. After many minutes of failing, he was beginning to get frustrated. Suddenly his thoughts strayed away from Sun Ce and drifted to Luxor.

His lost brother, who had refused to stay with him in Archonia. The same brother who had gotten him killed in his first life because of reckless thievery. Before that he ruined his shows in Rome, and he was constantly picking on him when they grew up.

Meredox suddenly saw Luxor standing right in front of him and he fell backwards out of his seated position and scrambled to stand. By the time he did, Luxor was gone but a feeling remained.

Luxor.

Turning wildly, Meredox pinpointed the aura immediately. He had been in tune with it his whole existence. His twin brother's presence which had brought him a near constant anxiety during his mortal days. His heart pounded as the feeling gave him a sense of dread.

Are you afraid, brother? Are you dying?

The feeling seemed unmistakable because he felt it before when he had been nailed to the stake in Jerusalem. The horrible hollow feeling. Just wanting the pain and sorrow to come to an end.

Meredox's meditation that night was fraught with emotion. Old memories from his former life bombarded his mind until he felt like he was suffocating. When he came out of his trance, and was yelling and Chione stopped in her tracks as she approached him.

"Sorry, bad dream," he lied.

"The others would like to go," she replied retreating quickly.

Rising and donning his greaves again, Meredox took off south east. The grass under his feet gave way as he plowed a path for the others through the unmolested terrain. His direction was clear now. The feeling of dread from the previous night lingered but had grown less intense. He worried that his connection was breaking but decided that he would worry about that when and if it happened.

"Meredox!" Scipio shouted.

Looking back, Meredox realized he had put several hundred yards between him and his companions. As they caught up they stared at him in wonder.

"How in the name of the gods can you travel that fast by foot?" Sun Ce asked, panting as he caught up with the others.

"I have learned a great deal about this world from Achilles and his men."

"Can you teach us this speed?" Chione asked, her eyes betraying her enthusiasm.

"Perhaps one day. For now we have a mission, and I have a bearing," Meredox said.

"You've found a connection with your brother? Gods be praised we can get this done quickly and return home just as swift," Ardashir said, spitting.

Meredox jolted back into action, this time taking things slow like he had the previous day. His squad leader's aura lit up in his mind and he could sense the man's fear and uncertainty. Chione's body soon attuned with his mind as well and he could feel her insecurities bubbling up from within her every move. The facade she put on each day was a mask meant to convince others that she was not weakling.

One by One, Meredox began to sense them all. The other squad leader known only as Cal was wise. Every move he made was calculated and sure. His men were utterly loyal and would die for him in a heartbeat.

Meredox hadn't bothered to learn the names of his subordinates. This didn't stop him from feeling their fears, and anxieties.

At around midday, Meredox slowed along with the others as the long white grasses of Archonia gave way to hard crusty ground. He stepped over the threshold as he skidded to a halt and almost immediately a chill rushed over his skin. His breath puffed like smoke in front of him as the temperature dropped sharply.

Looking back, Meredox noted the perfect line of grass pushing up against some unseen border. They had crossed it and the weather had changed. The strange phenomena was unnerving but not entirely surprising in this world.

"We have arrived, the stories are true. Dichonia is a frozen wasteland. Let us be wary," Cal said.

"Where are the renegades? Can you still sense them, soldier?" Sun Ce asked.

Despite the cold, Meredox got caught up in the view ahead of him. Vast emptiness stretched out as far as he could see and a sense of peace fell over him. He could get lost here and nobody could ever order him again.

"Soldier?" Cal barked.

"Yes, sir. I can still sense him. They are not far now. A few hours away if I'm not mistaken.

Without further debate the whole group jumped back into motion. Meredox had no real way of telling how far away his brother was but the connection seemed to be getting stronger with each step and it was only a matter of time before it felt as strong as he sensed the rest of his group.

The dust on the ground clung to Meredox's leg armor with each footfall, accumulating like a second skin. None of his fellow men had heavy clothes and with each gust of wind the rest of them shivered. For some reason the cold wasn't bothering him much. He guessed it was the energy burning inside of him waiting to explode at the first sign of a fight.

After some time, the clouds above them began to churn menacingly. Streaks of light forked across the sky as a storm formed with each passing moment. The thunder vibrated the ground underfoot. Just as some of the soldiers began to call for cover, Meredox stopped and motioned with a hand that they should as well.

Ducking down, Meredox crawled up an incline of stone and peaked over the ridge before him. A flash caused him to wince and then thunder crashed deafeningly as he spotted five lone figures rushing across the field below them towards a cavern to the west.

"Who are they?" Sun Ce asked.

"That, squad leader, is what is left of the great Clan Bjorn," Meredox said.

"It looked like they will be taking refuge in that cavern during this storm. We should head back and make our report," Scipio added.

"We do not know if that is the last of them. But if we capture and interrogate them then we can surely find out," Cal butted in, his voice rising over a gale of wind.

"Our mission was to report their location only. We have found them and they are clearly no longer a threat. Even if these aren't the only ones, the clan has clearly broken up," Sun Ce replied.

"Commander Achilles has given me leave to alter the plan as needed. We move in now. Trap them in that cave as the storm hits and take them prisoner to be questioned," Cal said, tossing a small scroll to Sun Ce.

Meredox felt his face tighten and eyes narrow as his squad leader unfurled the message. The man struggled to hang onto the parchment as the wind assaulted him but he managed to read the orders because he soon threw them aside.

"Our orders are clear, men. Capture or kill." Sun Ce said, scrambling to his feet and motioning for them to follow.

CHAPTER FORTY FOUR
Twin Fates

Luxor's legs felt shaky and each stride wobbled as he ran with everything he had towards the cavern ahead. Beside him, Shiva kept pace followed closely by the others.

"This storm looks bad," Shiva said, aloud.

"If it was anything like the other one we experienced then we need to get to that cave," Luxor yelled over the rumbling thunder.

"What if a beast lies within? Rarely da caverns such as dis go uninhabited," Runi bellowed.

Slowing down, Luxor hoped the man was wrong but more often than not when it came to animals and beasts, Runi was the expert.

"Aye and I've nothing to trap it with," Dagur said.

"We kill whatever is inside," Gierr said, running ahead and pulling his axe free as he got to the cavern's shadow.

Luxor drew his sword which felt freezing against his palm. He gritted his teeth and squeezed the hilt to get some blood flowing. Then, he moved to follow Gierr into the cavern. He only had a glimpse of the man as a light burst from his hand then the giant figure of a Wyrm fell over him crushing him in an instant.

"Wyrm!" Shiva cried, as the beast writhed wickedly towards them.

Meredox's legs carried him at inhuman speed down the rocky hill. He was about to overtake Sun Ce but felt his squad leader's arm cross his chest. The man's feeble arm couldn't have held him if he really wanted to pass but he slowed to his pace for a moment.

"We should stay together," Sun Ce said.

"Nobody touches my brother. I will have words with him. Do you understand me?" Meredox replied.

Meredox acknowledged the grimace Sun Ce returned and the quick glance towards Cal who was the one determined to carry out these rash orders.

"We will capture them," Sun Ce replied.

Thunder rumbling across the open field pushed Meredox and the others to move faster and suddenly another sound broke through the din. A horrible screech made his head swivel back to the figures ahead who had now reached the cavern. To his surprise a terrifying silhouette moved in the mouth of the cave. It crushed one of their number and he burst forward without thinking.

Luxor is in danger.

Meredox's innate reaction didn't register right away but by the time it did he had already committed to the assault. In a flurry of strides he had closed the tremendous gap and was now very close to the new threat.

To the side, Meredox quickly noticed his brother who seemed to be running from the beast. The creature twisted overhead, with a long snake-like body covered in spikes. Using his momentum, he hurled his spear at the creature. The throw was wobbly but powerful and stuck into the side of the giant snake piercing into his armored hide.

Meredox's sword whirled out of its home at his side as the beast screeched and recoiled at the bite of his spear. Now that he stood before the creature it loomed over him rising to the top of the cavern some twenty cubits high. It was much larger than he thought at first and he began to doubt whether his new strength would best this snake.

Before Meredox could decide its long coiling body snapped out towards him like a hammer. He reacted by simply pointing his sword to the ceiling.

I am stone. My body will not be moved.

Flexing every muscle and yelling loudly, Meredox felt a great rush of wind which carried a foul stench from the snake as it drew closer. The creature's body covered him like a squishy blanket and he watched his sword disappear along with his arms as it drove inside the snake's hide.

Despite his willpower, Meredox fell backwards. The snake had committed its full weight to the blow and the force was just too much. With his arms trapped inside he couldn't dive or twist away and the spikes all over its skin trapped him like a cage. The incredible mass bore down on him crushing him in darkness.

Luxor was frozen as his mind caught up with the scene before him. He had just witnessed his brother being crushed by the Wyrm.

How or why is he here!?

"Meredox!" he shouted, rushing wildly at the Wyrm.

Diving at the beast, Luxor drove his sword towards the creature which was wriggling around slowly as it screeched and roared. He stabbed over and over but his sword wasn't penetrating the hardened scales.

All at once, the Wyrm began to rise from the cavern floor. Luxor moved back, his sword at the ready. To his amazement, Meredox was lifting a section of the beast from the ground. The rest of the body was beginning to grow limp. His brother tossed the mass of spikes and scales to the side and yanked a gleaming sword free from inside its belly.

Then with a fury-filled cry, Luxor watched Meredox plunge the weapon back in several times. Eventually the Wyrm ceased to move and the cavern grew quiet for a moment. He gazed at his brother in confusion, watching a sticky yellowish goo drip from his brother's body.

"Meredox!" Luxor said, rushing over to embrace his brother. As he did, Meredox pointed his sword right at him and he nearly impaled himself upon it. The tip brushed his throat and he stopped with arms splayed out in the air.

"Luxor! They've come for us!" Shiva exclaimed.

To Luxor's left at the mouth of the cavern, a handful of figures stood with weapons drawn. Their line closed off any chance of escape. Across from him Runi drew his bow and Dagur climbed on top of the wrym's body to gain high ground.

"What in the name of Zeus is this?" Luxor demanded.

A stranger strode forth wearing the hoplite style armor of his ancestors. His helm sank low over his face giving him a serious visage.

"Members of the renegade Clan Bjorn you are hereby under arrest. Drop your weapons and we need not spill your blood," the man said.

"Meredox? Have you come to kill me, brother?"

Luxor studied the filthy face that he had known since birth. His brother's eyebrows were pointed down sharply lending a ferocity to his eyes which had somehow changed. The good hearted showman he had always loved seemed to have drained away. The anger and rage which very rarely escaped him was now present in his demeanor.

"We cannot lay down our arms. It is against our beliefs! You know this!" Shiva spat.

"Then you will die," the strange man said, charging in.

An arrow zipped by Meredox's head and Ardashir fell to the ground dead, the shaft sticking out of his eye. The other soldiers rushed in and soon a full-blown skirmish had erupted in the cavern.

Meredox stood still dropping his sword to his side as his brother retreated to form with his clansmen. A man with two daggers leapt from the top of the snake carcass and one of Cal's soldiers fell. The man's daggers were no match for long spears however and he was immediately skewered by three of them.

A bright light sprang from the woman blasting out violently against the sides of the cave. Meredox squinted in response as another of Cal's men fell to the ground, his head completely scorched off. The sorceress put up a fight against Scipio but she was outnumbered and his fellow soldier's blade pierced her chest.

Still not moving, Meredox heard another twang from the fat man's bow and Chione took it in the throat. The large bearded clansmen blocked a blow with his bow which broke in two. Spinning he produced a long dagger but three men were already on him filling him with holes.

Meredox's heart jumped as he realized that Luxor was the last one and his head jerked to him in a panic. Thankfully, Sun Ce had subdued him as promised. His brother knelt with hands on his head towards the back of the cavern.

Meredox lurched into motion as he spotted Cal moving towards them.

"Your clansmen are dead, barbarian. Tell us where the rest of you are hiding," Cal said putting a dagger to Luxor's throat.

"They are all dead. This land is merciless," Luxor said, his head hanging in shame.

"Liar! Tell us where they are or I will cut your throat!" Cal said nearly spitting on Luxor.

Clenching his fists, Meredox moved slowly towards them, He hated his brother wanted him to hurt but something about seeing Cal threaten him made his skin crawl.

Only I am allowed to hurt my brother.

With two swift movements Meredox lunged at Cal and sent him flying against the cavern wall with a crash. Everyone stepped back all at once brandishing their weapons.

"Meredox, No! I promised you we would capture him and we have," Sun Ce said, putting his sword away.

"Luxor, you fool! Why did you not come with me? You let me down over and over. In the former life and in this life. Why is it that you cannot trust me?" Meredox asked, hissing through his clenched jaw.

"I'm so sorry, Meredox. I have failed you. I know I have. I thought I had found love and I didn't think you wanted me in your life anymore," Luxor said, his pleading eyes looking up.

Meredox felt his face twitching with anger. So many emotion welled up inside of him all at once. He felt out of control and it was driving him mad. He had expected defiance and lies from his brother but for once the man was pleading with him.

"Strike me down, brother. I no longer wish to continue this burdensome life," Luxor said, a tear streaming down his face.

"Kill him and the traitor!" Cal said, scrambling to his feet.

Meredox could have avoided the spear, he was quick enough but he let it land for many reasons.

My body is iron.

The spear head drove at Meredox's exposed neck, Cal's man growling as he thrust. The bronze spearhead hit against his flesh and the shaft snapped in two. He stared at the man for a moment relishing the growing fear in his eyes. Then he snatched the man by the throat and squeezed.

Meredox's fingers like metal tongs, crushed the man's windpipe. He felt the life slowly leaving him and it gave him more satisfaction than the applause of all the thousands he entertained over the years.

Scipio and Cal's last man gave a cry and struck out at Meredox. He held the lifeless corpse in front of him blocking their thrusts and then tossed it aside pulling both their spears with it. In another instant his sword flashed cutting down Scipio with ease. Cal's last man managed to back up and draw his blade. Cal too was back on his feet and set in a defensive posture.

With a crazed shout, Meredox burst forward. His sword arced and Cal moved to block the strike. He felt the man's feeble arms give way and metal sliced flesh, cleaving him shoulder to chest. Cal's last man dropped his sword and put his hands in front of him pleading for his life.

Meredox took his head with one stroke.

Ah the control!

Turning around, Meredox saw that Sun Ce was the only one left. He stood over his brother and held a dagger to Luxor's throat.

"Meredox, stop this! I don't want to kill him but if you do not surrender your weapon, I must! I thought we had resolved our differences?" Sun Ce askcd.

Meredox stopped in his tracks. He realized the he was covered in all sorts of blood from the Wyrm and the other soldiers. He had just killed them all. Even his brothers in arms whom he was supposed to trust. A pang of guilt choked him up for a moment and he dropped his sword.

Luxor cringed as the cold edge of the soldier's dagger licked at his throat. He felt the man's shaky hand on his other shoulder, gripping tightly. Ahead of him, he had just witnessed his brother butcher his fellow soldiers.

Why would he do that?

Before he could rationalize an answer, Luxor saw Meredox drop his sword. For a moment he thought his brother was indeed going to surrender but there was a rush of wind and a cry of pain. Suddenly, he was free of the man's grasp and the harm which had been holding the dagger was bent and broken, twisted in the grip of Meredox's hand.

Rolling out of the way, Luxor looked back up at Meredox who plunged his thumbs into the man's eyes and squeezed as he screamed and fell to the floor in a heap.

By the gods.

The cavern fell silent and for the first time. Luxor heard the crashing of the storm outside. It had finally hit and a deluge of wind and rain battered the mouth of the cavern. Fortunately they were well inside out of its reach.

"Meredox what has happened to you?" Luxor asked slowly.

Luxor's brother turned towards him, his face softening into a version of Meredox which he recognized.

"I am weary, brother. Wicked men have pushed me to my limit and I am tired of being ordered and forced to do things that I do not want to do," Meredox said, finding a rock to sit on.

"Your strength and speed. How is it possible?" Luxor asked.

"The bonds of our former world no longer hold us back, Luxor. I can teach you these things and we can become so powerful that no one will ever tell us what to do again."

Luxor sat up and pushed himself to the cavern wall here he finally relaxed letting his arms flop in his lap.

"How will you explain what has happened here to your superiors?" Luxor asked looking around at the bodies mangled on the ground.

Meredox looked at the floor and Luxor could see the thoughts jumbling around in his head. "We can stay here, brother! Forge ourselves a new life."

"We cannot stay here, Meredox. This world is cursed. Everywhere you turn it seeks to take your life," Luxor said, shaking his head furiously.

"You no longer wish to stay? You, who chose to come here willingly?! Meredox said, almost laughing.

"I was following the one that I loved."

"And now she has gone. She betrayed you, didn't she?" Meredox said.

"How...How did you guess?"

"We are connected brother, we always have been. In this world that connection is tangible. How do you think we found you in this vast wasteland?"

Luxor furrowed his brow, processing this information. The logic made sense but the strange abilities of this world still amazed him.

"I will not stay in this world, brother. It truly is the underworld. Will you please end my life? I have nothing left to live for," Luxor asked.

Many moments passed in silence but soon Luxor felt his insides lurch as Meredox rose from his rock and walked over to him.

He is really going to do it.

Even though it was what he wanted the natural fear rose inside of him and shouted for him to move, fight, run. His hands began to shake and he had to squeeze them together as Meredox lifted his sword.

Meredox appraised his poor brother as Luxor sat on the floor shaking. His tattered fur armor was in shambles, covered in soot and filth from his time in this desolate place. Pity enveloped him and all at once he forgave his brother's foolishness. He met his brother's eyes for a moment as he raised his blade and then they squeezed shut expecting the final blow.

What a fool.

"Open your eyes brother. I will not be the one who strikes you down," Meredox said, proffering his sword.

Luxor gasped and looked up at him in surprise.

"You refuse to live here, but something about the solitude of this land calls to me. Besides I can no longer return to Helios. They have discovered ways of finding the truth in men without torture. Take my sword and my name, brother. Go live out the rest of your days in peace.

Meredox offered his brother a smile as Luxor took the sword. His blackened face looked back in wonder.

"Why are you doing this for me after everything?" Luxor asked.

"Call it the last act of Adomos, A man who loved his brother, and promised to always protect him," he said.

"The last act?"

"Adomos, is dead, and now I am leaving behind the name of Meredox. They called me the Basileus in Helios for a time. That title is growing on me."

The Basileus unbuckled his armor and let it crash to the floor carelessly. The new Meredox watched without a word for a few moments then began taking off his own clothing.

CHAPTER FORTY FIVE
A Third Chance at Life

Meredox waded into the luscious grasses of Archonia and fell to his knees, basking in the warmth that spread over him. He didn't care how of why the cold was gone, instead he hugged the ground which smelled sweetly of herbs.

Rolling over, he pulled one of the water-filled roots free and drank his fill. The savory flavor of the root itself exploded in his mouth as his teeth tore into the dirt covered skin.

I think I'll call you Lifegrass.

The Archonian sun which had been shrouded by clouds for as long as he could remember was shining brightly. Blinding him even as he looked at it with joy. He thanked whatever gods he could think of for helping him escape that horrible wasteland they called Dichonia.

There, Meredox rested. On the edge of two worlds reveling in the golden light. He would need a long meditation. His recovery would be the least of his problems however because his brother had apparently made quite a mess of his life before leaving it behind.

Meredox's sibling, the self-proclaimed Basileus, had broken ranks and been imprisoned. Assaulted an officer and been imprisoned a second time. Finally he had been sentenced to be trained in some mysterious art. This combined with the fact that he was returning alone would mean a grand series of fables. Such a web of lies would not be an easy thing to spin especially to these souls who could sense the truth in people.

Meredox thought long on these things. He had also been told to memorize certain facts about certain people maintain his illusion.

Achilles and Zeus command the army. Socrates leads the Synod.

Meredox wondered if he could keep everything straight. It would be his finest deceit yet. Hopefully, after this he would never have to lie again.

Eventually, Meredox continued his journey back to civilization. All the while he wondered how his brother was faring in the bleak underworld. He also felt a surge of guilt and panic as he realized he might never see his brother again.

For now, Meredox had more important things to think about and as he dutifully put on foot in front of the other, his plan began to formulate in his head.

Walking slowly, it took Meredox several more days and many more roots before he saw the outline of Helios in the distance. He was astounded to find that it and Valhalla were visible, their silhouettes rising higher than they had before. Not only that, but they seemed to be growing together. As if eventually they would become one great civilization.

Meredox marveled at the changes that had been made in such a short amount of time. His brother had described many very strange things but it still seemed unbelievable.

Stopping to stare for a moment, Meredox's eye began to see movement ahead. Droves of people were walking out of the city. It took him perhaps another hour before he met them. Hundreds of souls carrying an array of belongings on their back or leading beasts of burden by cart.

"What is going on here?" Meredox asked a passerby.

The man gripped who could only be his wife in a half hug. The woman was weeping. The man didn't respond.

"A great purge is happening," said a man wielding a spear and shield. He wore a long blue cape and his silver armor gleamed brightly. "Who are you? Are you one of the judged?"

"I am Meredox of Helios. I'm returning home from my quest in the underworld. Commander Achilles is expecting me to report in," Meredox lied.

The blue-caped soldier peered at him through narrowed eyes. Meredox worried that this was one of the men who could discern the truth through mere sight. Luckily the man nodded in approval.

"Report to Valhalla, we will ensure these judged do not impede you."

Meredox proceeded without another word. The refugees walking around cursed at him. Some even spat as he walked by. For some reason they were being forced from their homes.

What happened to your promise of peace and equality, brother?

Growing tired of the jeers and scowls, Meredox swung wide giving the exodus plenty of space as he continued on toward Valhalla which now appeared to be a huge fortress made from stone. He could still recognize the initial shape which still bore the craftsmen ship of the north men.

A large wall rose above him as he approached. It surrounded the mighty keep. He was met by more blue-caped soldiers who recognized his brother and led him inside. The tents and yurts which he lived in during his time with Brock and the others was gone, replaced by stone structures which were also growing together to create one enormous building.

As Meredox took in the incredible details his mind strayed away from his plan until it was at the back of his mind. His anxiety got the better of him and he found himself digging in his pocket for the wooden coin. He let the calming motion of his twirling take hold and in moments he was standing before the great Achilles and the legendary Zeus.

Torches blazed on the walls, as Meredox saluted his superiors the way his brother had shown him. Droves of weapons dotted the walls glimmering in their orange glow.

"You have returned...Alone," The large bearded man said.

He must be Zeus. His height gives him away.

"I have indeed. I must report a terrible tragedy has befallen our men," Meredox said.

"Speak," Achilles said.

"Commander, as we waded in the depths of the underworld we encountered monsters of which you could scarcely imagine."

As Meredox said this another figure emerged from around a pillar to their side. A terribly beautiful woman in gilded armor wrapped in a long purple cape which sported fine golden trim. When she met his eye he felt a shiver run through his back.

Who is that?

The woman nodded at Achilles in a peculiar manner and turned away sitting at a long table which lay behind his superiors.

She is one of them. She can tell if I'm lying. Blast it all.

Luckily Meredox's first statement hadn't been a lie. He and his clansmen had run into such atrocities.

"And then? These monsters overcame everyone but you?" Zeus asked, incredulously.

"The creatures stood no chance against the special training from commander Achilles. The others fell to the might of a terrible monster," Meredox said, again circumventing his truth.

Meredox knew that it was Achilles training which had allowed his brother to defeat the Wyrm and even the

Basileus himself admitted that Meredox was destroyed, replaced by some monster. He waited patiently while the strange woman stared at him. After a few moments she nodded again and he let go of his breath. He had gotten lucky twice. He didn't know if he could continue to trick them much longer. The conversation was slipping away from him.

"What of your mission? What of the rogue faction known as Clan Bjorn?" Achilles asked.

"Clan Bjorn is no more. They all fell to the horrors of Dichonia as well," Meredox said, this time with utter confidence.

"He speaks the truth, will you turn him over to me now?" the woman asked?

"Yes, Themis, you may take him. Soldier, as promised you will take the path of the Adjudicator and shed your former life for one of truth and justice," Achilles said.

"Yes, commander, as promised."

But not by me.

Meredox saluted once more and the woman Themis indicated that he should follow her. Without hesitation he hustled over and fell in behind her. They walked for a time in silence until they had passed into a completely new part of the fortress. The dark wood themes gave way to a brighter more open sort of hall. Light poured in through windows set in the ceiling and fresh air moved freely through the chamber.

"What is your name?" Themis asked suddenly.

"Surely you heard it said before by the commander?" Meredox replied.

"I would like to hear you say it," Themis said, stopping and turning. Her eyes were a bright blue color and didn't seem natural with her dark hair.

"I have gone by many names in this life and the previous one," Meredox said.

"You do a splendid job of feigning the truth. I can see that you are a practiced liar. None of your body's natural responses indicate such, and I can sense no falsity in your soul when you speak."

"That is because I am not lying, my lady..."

"However, a report was written by Commander Zeus of his encounter with you and your twin brother in the dungeon at many weeks ago. When you were assigned to me to begin training I was sure to learn everything I could about the man I would be reforming.

"In this report Zeus spoke of how your brother recognized you. He asked that you be searched for a wooden coin, assuring the commander that you would never part with the trinket," Themis said.

Oh Hel.

Meredox took a step back and hid the coin which he still had hidden in his hand.

"You're skilled at hiding it but I saw you playing with it when you walked in. A nervous habit I suppose," she said.

"Please. My brother wished for me to live," Meredox said.

"I have no intention of killing you, Meredox, or whatever name you currently call yourself. What I do intend is to use you as a tool for truth and justice. Your knowledge of lying will be quite beneficial in the third phase of your training. You already know quite well how to spot a lie. We must simply teach you to stop lying yourself," Themis said.

"Very well," Meredox replied.

"There is another problem. This path that I have chosen must be selected by you as well. They were going to force your brother to do it if he returned but it cannot be done. The sacrifices you will make in doing this can only change you if you do not resist."

"What will become of me if I do not choose to undergo this change?" Meredox asked.

"Then unfortunately the others will find out the truth about you. And you would be escorted to the edge of this land and cast out as the impure ones have just been."

"Impure? What trait do they have that made them unworthy to live here?"

"You will come to understand in time. Now. Decide," Themis said, crossing her arms.

The decision was an easy one for Meredox. Even now he didn't have much of a choice. He did however want a change. A new start on life. This would be the second time he would be starting over so the change wouldn't be so terrible. He would give anything to wash away all that happened so after a few moments he made his decision. Themis nodded to him and continued to walk. No words needed to be said. She knew. Somehow, she knew.

CHAPTER FORTY SIX
Blissful Agony

The Basileus walked lightly through the soot and ash. He whistled an old tune from his youth and twirled a barbarian axe in his hand. The cold nipped at his skin but he could hardly feel it. The heat burning within him was profound.

Everything had worked out after all and now he could finally be alone. He could make his own way and not be responsible for anyone but himself.

For no reason at all The Basileus broke into a sort of dance. His exuberance burst forth and his whistle turned into a song and he twirled about. After a minute or so, he realized he was being watched and he stopped spinning and smiled at the newcomers with his hands still awkwardly in the air.

The Basileus quickly lost count of the creatures before him but noted they were being led by a fair-haired woman. The short black creatures looked like tiny men and walked like them too.

Must be some demon or another.

"Hello friends!" The Basileus said, waving obnoxiously at them.

"Luxor!?" The woman cried, screwing up her face.

Running his hands through his hair several times, The Basileus realized that the woman was wearing the garments of a barbarian. She must have been one of them. She also recognized his brother.

This must be his little whore. The one who betrayed him.

"Ah, yes. Uh, you must be Eerika. Am I right?"

You're not Luxor. You're his brother. The one who begged him to stay with you in the land of light!" she exclaimed.

"Quite perceptive of you, wench. You hurt my brother's feelings. I might have to punish you for that," he said stroking the axe in his hand.

"Attack! Kill him!" Eerika shouted motion to her tiny minions.

The Basileus cackled loudly to himself as their little legs moved them closer. When they were close enough that he could smell their putrid stench, he leapt into the air and bearing down with his axe rending one of them in two. Then he flailed his axe about, singing his song loud enough to hear over their dying cries.

Cheerfully cutting them down, The Basileus picked one of them up holding him like a dance partner as he spun. Then, he ripped its arms off and tossed the dying monster out of the circle of death. They couldn't comprehend his speed and strength and soon he was standing face to face with Eerika dripping in fresh, black blood.

"Let's have a chat," The Basileus said, leaning in.

Eerika's wide eyes betrayed her fear and she fell to her knees dropping her weapon. "My Jarl!" she said.

"What? No. I am not your...What do you call it? Jarl? No, my dear, what I am is the Basileus. Say it with me now. Bass. Sill. Eus," he said.

The Basileus waited for Eerika's frightened mind to stop racing. He placed his hands on his hips and wiped the blood from his face upwards running his fingers through his hair. The dark liquid finally kept his tangled hair down.

"Ah finally something that will hold this nest of hair in place," he said aloud to himself.

"Forgive me, Basileus. Please allow me to take you to my master. He would be pleased to have you among his army," Eerika said.

"I thought you barbarians never submitted, never gave up? Whatever, never mind. Look, if anyone asks, my name used to be Luxor, do you understand? From now on I wish to be known only as the Basileus. If anyone utters the name Luxor to me I might very well cut off their head," The Basileus said.

"Yes, Basileus."

"Furthermore, I don't care about you or your master. I have no master and will no longer cower before man or beast!" He spat, his voice rising in a crescendo.

The Basileus watched the woman shuddering under him. He could take her virtue right now if he wished. He could bleed her to death drop by drop and avenge his brother. The prospect made him smile.

"Now run along to your master and spread the good word. I will not be trifled with."

The Basileus watched with a cocked head as Eerika fled the field full of corpses. He took notice of the direction she was headed and decided to go the opposite direction. After an hour the blood had completely dried, mixing with the ash at his feet it formed a second skin of sorts which he enjoyed.

Bursting forth in fits of speed he tested his swiftness. Then with nothing but his fists he crushed stones testing the limits of his strength. As his fist broke apart a large boulder he giggled turning it to gravel.

"You are enjoying the gifts I have given you." a voice said.

The Basileus twirled again, this time his giddiness faded. Nearby, leaning against a rock, stood the scraggly old prisoner he met in the Dungeon. Walking in a curve around him, but keeping his distance, the man began to change. It was the greatest illusion he had ever seen and soon a tall handsome man stood before him in silver garb.

"You are the strange being they called an Archon. Gabriel is it?"

"Adomos, it doesn't matter who I am or what my name is. All that matters is you and your happiness," the Archon said.

Very True.

"I agree with you. I must ask though. Why did you give me this gift?" he asked.

"Because I could."

The Basileus looked around to the open plains scrunching his face in confusion.

"And what do you want with me now?" he asked.

"I just wanted to ask you what you thought about doing now. Your life interests me," The archon said.

"I honestly have no idea. I thought I might just wander around killing things. It feels ever so good. Now that I know I don't need food or water to live I can go anywhere and do anything."

"Not a bad plan. Might I make a suggestion?" The archon asked.

"You may. Though I probably won't take the advice."

"I understand completely. Nor should you unless you want to. But hear me out. To the south there is a vast void in the land. In the center of this void floats a city. I think you might enjoy the things this city has to offer."

The Basileus eyed the Archon and bit his lip. Socrates had told him these beings always had their own agenda. But the idea of there being a city in this wasteland much less a floating city piqued his curiosity.

"A floating city? How is that possible? How would I get there?"

"Why you would fly of course."

"Fly!? Are you mad? Wait can I do that?" The Basileus asked getting more serious.

"Of course you can, I showed you how. You simply have to tap into the knowledge as you did when finding your brother."

"Well I just might do that, Archon. Now if you will excuse me I want to find another of those large snakes to kill. That was a fun thing to kill."

The Basileus blinked his eyes and the Archon was gone. He looked about for a bit but was satisfied that he was alone. Then looking over his shoulder, he headed south. After all, the idea of a crowd was tantalizing to him. Maybe he could do his tricks again. Except for the greatest of them of course. He would just have to find a new trick he thought, skipping away.

CHAPTER FORTY SEVEN
Indoctrination

Meredox lay on his meditation mat covered in sweat. His body was stiff and sore, still healing from the Purge. He thought the horrors he faced in Dichonia would be the worst of his life. Next to the images and feelings that Themis had exposed him to, they were nothing. She had truly broken him.

Craning his neck, Meredox spotted Merideus across the room. He too was leaning against the wall covered in bruises and blood. It wasn't uncommon for the pain to manifest physically on their bodies after so much exposure.

Meredox knew that he smelled. Themis would not let them bath, nor would she allow them new clothing. His filth ridden linens clung to his skin their stench wafting into his mind every few moments.

A loud clank interrupted the solitude of the meditation room and Meredox squinted as light poured in through the doorway. Themis' stood arms on her hips and seeing her made both he and Merideus recoil. Her heavy boots thumped against the floor and he footfall made him shudder.

"Rise, Meredox. It is time for you to be indoctrinated," she said.

Meredox looked up at her trying to keep his head towards the ground at the same time. He turned towards Merideus who had been undergoing the purge far longer than he had and still hadn't begun his indoctrination. His feelings on the subject didn't matter though and he needed to rise before Themis told him again. If he did not obey there would be consequences.

Struggling to flex his limbs, Meredox rose from the ground with great difficulty. First to his hands and knees then to his feet. Finally, he did his best to stand up straight with military posture.

"Come, student. Today you will begin your journey towards truth and justice," Themis said, exiting the chamber.

Meredox followed, his tattered tunic sagging on his thinning frame. He watched with anxiety as Themis headed towards the purge chamber, and he began to shake, his body preparing for the worst. Following her in, where normally there was a blood covered mat for him to kneel on he found a simple wooden chair.

"Sit, student," she said.

Pausing to consider, Meredox knew this was some kind of trick. She had tricked him before. When he sat down the chair would likely torture him in some brutal way. His thoughts caught up with him though and he realized if she asked twice he would receive a far worse punishment.

Swiftly, Meredox scuffled over to the chair, his legs protesting each motion. Then, he sat and awaited the pain. After several moments, nothing happened. Despite this, he remained tense until Themis began to speak.

"Truth is reality. Justice, is balance. Repeat," Themis said.

"T-t-truth is reality. J-justice is balance," Meredox said, meekly.

"Repeat, louder."

T-truth is reality. Justice is balance."

"Louder!"

"Truth is reality! Justice is balance!"

"Continue. Do not stop until I tell you to," Themis said, sitting down on a mat and closing her eyes.

Meredox continued. The first hour passed and Themis made no move. His throat began to pain him around what he thought must be hour two. After an indiscernible amount of time his voice was nearly gone. As his words softened and faded, Themis rose from her seat and a brilliant flash of light burst from her fingertips. The glowing substance, like liquid clung to the wall and formed into a large rectangular slab of smooth black stone.

She walked forward and handed him a long white piece of chalky mineral and pointed to the rectangle. "Write it."

Rising, Meredox stepped to the rectangular surface and with his white stone began to write the words which he had been speaking for hours. He wrote until the stone was filled with these words and then Themis wiped them away with the wave of her hand.

After his white chalk was little more than a stub a new one appeared, suspended in mid-air. This continued for some time until his arms become too heavy for him to lift.

Eventually, Meredox's body could take no more and he fell to his knees, keeling over on his side. He vaguely registered that someone was dragging him along the marble floor and thought he heard the clanking of the lock over the door. The dark meditation room usually gave him some respite between the terrible visions and tortures that he endured but tonight, the words kept running across the darkness. The same words over and over again.

Truth is reality. Justice is balance.

Meditation was rough for Meredox that evening because his mind refused to shut off. The light of morning broke and the door swung open again with a creak. Once again, he rose as he was told and followed Themis to the purge chamber. Sitting down in the stout wooden chair he patiently waited his instructions.

"There are no versions of the truth. The truth is not subject to interpretation. Truth is reality. What happened and how it happened. It is fact, it is certainty," Themis said pausing.

Meredox absorbed this statement, waiting for some sort of strenuous activity to follow. His eyes flickered to the rectangular stone hanging on the wall and prayed that he didn't need to write these words over and over.

"The truth cannot be bent. Anything other than the truth is a lie. If a man is walking along the road and comes upon a bandit who tries to kill and rob him. But the man instead kills the bandit. Then, he says he took the man's life defending himself. Is that the truth?" Themis asked.

Meredox's heart pounded. If he didn't answer he would be punished. If he answered incorrectly he might be punished as well. He thought about her example for many moments and with each passing breathe he could feel her eyes piercing through him.

"This is the truth," he said.

A tremendous crack, issued across the room and Meredox felt pain shoot through his body. Though it was just an illusion the whip crack had sounded and felt real. He fell off the chair onto his belly and his eyes watered.

"The truth is that one man killed another man because of material possessions. The lie is what comes out of the man's mouth. Their reasons and feelings mean nothing. You must learn to differentiate between the two. As a practiced liar, Meredox of Archonia, you should be able to tell the difference with ease," Themis said.

Meredox climbed back up to sit back in the chair not leaning against the backing because of the throbbing pain still scouring his back.

For the next few days, Meredox listened and learned about the intricacies of truth and being objective. Removing both his feelings and other's feelings from the equation. The quizzing was brutal but his body began to grow tougher and more accustomed to the abuse. Each blow made him stronger.

Eventually, Meredox studied the laws of the new Archonian government and practiced finding the tedious balance of Justice in which Themis spoke of. Each day that passed grew easier and less painful. And as they did he become more committed to the ideals being ingrained in his mind.

One morning, Meredox was led By Themis into the Purge chamber but she did not enter with him. Inside steam rose from an ivory bathing vessel. He entered without word and the door clicked shut behind him. He approached with caution. The surface of the water was perfectly still while wisps of steam danced across the air.

Slowly, Meredox dipped his hand in. The water felt warm but not overly hot. His arm sank in and he closed his eyes, enjoying the heat. Moments later he had tossed his raggedy clothing aside and climbed in. bit by bit his body sank into the relaxing liquid until all but his head was fully submerged. Letting out a tremendous sigh of relief he sank deeper into the water almost up to his eyes.

When he needed to draw breath, Meredox came back up and began rubbing down his disgusting skin. The dirt and grime melted away to the scent of lilac and juniper, which wafted from the tub.

After a time, the water cooled and he exited to find a table with several clothing choices laying on it. All the choices had the same color theme of purple just like Themis' many cloaks. He selected a simple yet sleek tunic which he buckled with a dark leather belt across his waist.

"You will follow me," Themis said.

Meredox jumped at the sound of her voice. She must have entered while he was dressing. He obeyed without question and soon found himself standing in a long hall filled with shelves. The sturdy wooden structures were laden with thousands of dusty tomes.

In the center of the room a simple wooden table hefted at least a hundred such books. It was obvious what she wished of him and he took his seat at the table in the same wooden chair he used in the purge chamber.

"You will read these tales, and then judge the characters within. I expect a list of names, crimes, and judgements when you are finished. For every incorrect assessment of each you will receive one lashing. There are a total of four hundred and fifty two characters. Nearly all of these characters have committed a crime and therefore must receive a judgement."

That would be over thirteen hundred lashes. Fifty lashes might kill me.

"How long do I have, Grand Justicar?" Meredox asked.

"You have as much time as is needed. However, you will not know the taste of food until your task is complete," Themis stated exiting the room.

"And if I refuse this task, what will happen?"

"Then we will revisit the Purge. There is no escaping this fate you have chosen. You will be an adjudicator."

Meredox didn't flinch. These things were expected. He and Merideus weren't receiving much sustenance anyway. Dutifully accepting his task, he began immediately. Next to the large stack of tomes lay a newly bound title marked "The Laws of the Archonian Synod."

They have been formally published.

Taking a book off the top of the stack, he set it upon a tilted wooden stand meant to hold the title while he took notes. Then, he found a blank stack of parchment and a quill. Flipping open the book, he began to read until the first character was introduced several lines down. He dipped the end of the feather into an inkwell and quickly scrawled the woman's name.

Samson.

Meredox dove into the story soon realizing that Samson's lover Delilah was guilty of numerous instances of lies and deceit. With each lie he noted, the number of lashes he might feel increased. Within the first chapter he discovered that thirteen hundred lashes was a terribly inaccurate estimate.

Hours passed until Meredox set down the first book. He looked over his notes and re-read them to ensure they were accurate and complete.

Delilah:

- Lied about her true intentions three times – imprisonment three cycles
- Stole a man's hair – Imprisonment one cycle
- Accepted a bribe – Imprisonment two cycles

Total sentence – imprisonment for six Archonian cycles.

Samson:

- Killed numerous men – imprisonment fifty Archonian cycles per soul
- Dis-obeyed a direct order by engaging in lewd behavior with Delilah – imprisonment one cycle
- Destruction of property and murder of numerous men and women in a religious site – imprisonment fifty Archonian cycles per soul plus one.

Total sentence – number of years likely exceeds maximum of four hundred cycles. The criminal is sentenced to death or banishment to Dichonia. Due to the severity of his crimes, recommend execution.

Meredox placed his notes just inside the cover of the storybook, satisfied with his judgements. The tale itself made it seem as though Samson was a victim of a treacherous deceiver but in truth the Israelite killed more people than could be counted in the record.

Days passed and Meredox continued to read and take notes. He took breaks only meditate and let his mind recover. His body grew stronger despite the lack of food because he was no longer being tortured. One by one the stack of books unread grew smaller and his piles of notes grew larger.

One thing stuck out more than anything in Meredox's mind. In every book the storyteller attempted to connect you to the characters but for some reason he could not or would not grow close to them. It was his duty to remain unbiased. Instead he treated each name as a faceless set of facts and offered no empathy to their situations.

Have I become a monster? Or truly objective?

Shoving his conscience to the back of his mind, Meredox read each book one after the other until the stack of tomes was finally depleted. They were now each stacked neatly on the other side of the table from where they had started and they all had pieces of parchment folded within their front covers.

There was no telling how much time had passed but Meredox guessed it had been four or more days. The rumble of his stomach grew ever louder with each passing day but he had been taught that his Archonian body didn't need food stuffs to sustain itself. Perhaps this was part of the training? If he didn't need to depend on such things he could truly become infallible nobody could leverage these things against him forcing him to betray true justice.

It was all training, carefully crafted training. Meredox set the quill down and placed the last piece of parchment with its respective book. Then, placing his hands in his lap, he looked at the completed stack.

Six thousand seven hundred and eighty three potential lashes. I better check them all again.

Without a second thought, Meredox picked up one of the books and began to read once more.

The second pass through the books took half the time. Meredox had found his rhythm and reading became easier for him. His routine helped him monitor the hours and days as well.

Finally when he was satisfied that he had worked through all the books thoroughly he set to checking his judgements against the Laws of the Synod to ensure he hadn't made any errors in sentencing. After nearly a full Archonian week, which he had learned was now ten days. Meredox stood up from the desk, completely satisfied with his work. The rumble from his stomach had ceased, his mind finding nourishment in meditation rather than food.

Meredox moved to the door which he knew to be locked from the outside. He banged his knuckles against the fine wood and waited. Clean crisp footfalls soon thudded outside and Themis unlatched the door.

"You're finished?" she asked.

"I am, Grand Justicar and I await my assessment."

"You will wait in the purge chamber. Strap yourself to the whipping post and await my return," She said.

Meredox lowered his head and moved down the hall to where the purge room sat. His mind flooded with the feeling of Themis' illusionary whip strikes. Perhaps if his mind could overcome the illusion he could handle a higher number of them before his body shut down. He was curious as to why he needed to strap himself into a whipping post.

Perhaps it was a metaphor.

As he turned to enter the purge chamber, Meredox spotted a short stone post with two leather binds on the top.

Not a metaphor. She is really going to whip me.

Resigning to his fate, Meredox slid his wrists into the looped straps and pulled them tight so that he could not escape. Then, he rested his head on the stone post and waited with bated breath.

Somehow, Meredox's teacher had completed her review in a matter of minutes because she entered the room with calm even motions and unfurled a long whip. The tightly wound leather made his mouth go dry.

Meredox watched as Themis swung the whip around her head to loosen her wrist. He flinched as she cracked it two times to warm up her swing. Then without warning he heard a third lash and the leather strap binding his left hand to the post burst open. A fourth snap released his right from its binding.

"Congratulations, Meredox of Archonia. You have completed the indoctrination phase of your training and are one step closer to embodying truth and justice."

Meredox looked back at her and finally released the air from his chest. She exited the room without offering further direction so he assumed that he should retreat to the meditation chamber.

Squeaking open the door to the dark meditation chamber, Meredox spied Merideus heaped against the wall where he usually was. He still wore the horribly defiled garments from when he had started his journey.

"You have not yet begun the indoctrination?" Meredox asked.

Merideus didn't reply.

"You must let go. Submit and things will get better," Meredox finished.

After many moments Meredox still hadn't received a reply and resigned to meditate on what he had learned and accomplished. Crossing his legs he worked to empty his head so that he could focus on the important parts of his brutal training.

CHAPTER FORTY EIGHT

The Order of the Guardian

Socrates adjusted his ridiculous headwear. The tall conical headdress was a strain on his neck as he tried to keep it from tipping off. Therefore, he sat as still as possible on a terribly uncomfortable slab of granite. The stone had been carved into a throne of sorts. Eight identical seats formed a semicircle around him.

In each of these seats were the elected representatives that had been chosen to speak for the people. There were some new faces after the impure had been escorted from the land the people had demanded more representation. The directive to expunge those that were judged wasn't a popular one. It had almost resulted in another civil war.

Socrates hadn't agreed to the motion but the others outvoted him. They all stated that sometimes bad things must happen so that good can flourish. Begrudgingly he held his tongue and in the months that followed things did get better by leaps and bounds.

Across from Socrates, two enormous doors creaked open and a handful soldiers walked in. He recognized Themis who carried herself with such grace. Beside her were her two pupils who had successfully undergone the process of becoming an adjudicator. Finally the two military commanders.

"Good morning. Thank you for coming, soldiers of Archonia," Athena said, standing to greet them.

"What is it that the Synod can do for you?" Isaiah asked leaning forward on his throne.

Achilles stepped forward. The soft clanking of his boots echoed around the high pillars which reached to the ceiling above.

"The army of Archonia is growing each day with new recruits. The laws of your council are being spread and acknowledged throughout all of Archonia. It seems we have found a period of peace. However, as you may know this adjudicator, Meredox, was assigned to go on a mission to the land which some call the underworld. After reading his detailed account of the journey he and I both agree that our armies could not stand against the denizens that dwell there," Achilles said.

"So far these creatures have not passed into our realm. The Archon Gabriel has assured us that there is a barrier which separates the two lands," Anubis said sipping a drink from a silver chalice.

"That does not mean that this barrier won't someday be breached," Themis chimed in.

"What do you propose we do to prepare for such an unlikely scenario?" Socrates asked?

The Adjudicator Meredox strode forth, his billowy purple cape swishing as he did.

"I have your leave, commander?" Meredox asked.

Socrates watched Achilles step back with a curt nod as Meredox took the floor.

"Do we not still bear swords in times of peace? We keep them close in case the atrocities of war ever resurge. Well I say to this council now that we would be wholly unprepared if somehow the evils of Dichonia broke through. I would plea with this great Synod to build a wall, the largest ever seen, along the barrier line. Man it with soldiers who can move and fight like the great Achilles here. The darkness I have seen in the underworld will be with me for the rest of my days. I implore you to prepare for the worst. Perhaps the day will never come and my worry will be for nothing. But if there is even the slimmest of doubts I feel we should be ready," Meredox said.

Socrates appraised the adjudicator. He looked so different, his well-kept hair draped elegantly to his shoulders curling slightly at the end. His uniform was crisp and clean. He was not at all the lost man who stumbled into Helios and launched the movement for equality.

"If this is the recommendation of our military leaders then of course we will authorize the commission of a wall. As for these brave warriors you speak of. Are we not already training men to fight like this?"

"I have one squadron ready to fight at my level. But if what I have read is true then we would need many more to follow. This order of warriors would be far more exclusive. They would have to undergo the most brutal of training and be tested at length. That is why I have prepared a document describing the creation of an order of soldiers called Guardians," Achilles said, stepping back up.

One of the sentinels standing guard took the parchment and handed it to Anubis who flipped through the document. Socrates peered into the man's mind and absorbed the same things he was for a moment.

"These Guardians would have a secondary and more logical purpose," Socrates said.

"Yes. One of your fellow scholars thinks he has discovered how to return to the shadowy world between the mortal plain and Archonia," Achilles replied.

"Right, they dubbed it Valchonia did they not?"

"They did indeed. This purgatory would be an excellent place for these soldiers to see real combat and if possible, save wayward souls who we might deem pure," Achilles finished.

"A fine proposition. Commander. You will have to find willing recruits to do this. We will not force such things on anyone. And what of the sentinels currently trained and ready to help keep the peace?" Anubis asked.

"I will remain commander of this force and select my own captains and generals," Zeus said, stepping up to tower over Achilles.

It sounds like you have everything in hand. Very well. This Synod does authorize the creation of the Guardian order. You will send representatives to report to us weekly. Is there anything else?" Socrates asked.

"There is not. Thank you, great Synod," Achilles said turning on heel and exiting.

Socrates scratched his brow. When Meredox had been up speaking to them he sounded and acted so different. The process that Themis had put him through must have changed him a great deal. He had also felt something off about him. About his soul. It was fleeting and he decided to ignore the feeling. There was still much to attend to, and only so many hours in the day.

The End

Epilogue

Meredox strode briskly down the corridor towards his chambers. His boots clattered noisily in the marble hallway. After a full day of purging recruits his mind had grown weary.

Ahead, Meredox saw Merideus perusing some parchment. It was no doubt the list of recruits that had completed the suffering and were ready for indoctrination. He had sent it over earlier that day.

Not surprisingly, Meredox looked to bid him good evening, but the man ignored him entirely. Things had been like this for hundreds of years since Themis had passed on and chose him to take her place.

Rolling his eyes, Meredox adjusted the sigil of Grand Justicar on his chest and continued on. In moments he was unlocking his chamber door. He closed it softly behind himself with a click and his armor faded away, leaving him standing in his soft white tunic.

Meredox stood there for a moment, admiring his room. The wall to wall bookshelves held all manner of tomes and artifacts which he had collected over the past millennia. His eyes flickered to his prize possession gilded and framed on his desk. His old wooden coin. He had stopped carrying it several hundred years ago, deciding that it wasn't befitting of the Grand Justicar to have such a bad habit. Still, he couldn't part with it.

What in Dichonia? It's moved.

Meredox rushed over to his desk where he found a peculiar piece of parchment. The paper was blackened and the heavy handwriting scrawled over its surface glowed orange like fire.

Reading the letter hastily he recognized the handwriting before he even saw the signature etched at the bottom of the page. His heart throbbed, pumping his body with Adrenaline.

He's still alive. He's coming here.

Trying to keep his emotional response in check he realized that after nearly two thousand years he still had not sorted out the qualms he had with Luxor. After the Purge he had just sort of forgotten. Now suddenly it was being shoved back in his face.

How could he possibly come here though? He is clever that's how. He has found a way.

Meredox calmed himself. Slowly and carefully he sat down in the plush chair set before his desk. Letting the letter drop to the tabletop, he leaned back resting his head in his hand and began to formulate a plan.

Read next

Amelia of Archonia
DAMNATION

Coming Soon.

Locations:

Alexandria:
A Medditerranean port city in Egypt. This renowned settlement boasted one of the Seven Wonders of the ancient World in the form of a magnificent lighthouse.

Archonia:
The immortal world outside of the physical boundaries of the universe. It was created by the Archons as a place for mankind's souls to dwell after their mortal life.

Dichonia:
The immortal world that was created by the Archon's Kronos and Othin on the same plane of existence as Archonia, made as a prison for their brother Lucifer who betrayed them all.

Helios:
One of the largest settlements in the burgeoning world of Archonia. This predominantly Greek and Roman city boasts some of the most decedant living spaces seen for its time.

Jerusalem:
This city in western Asia is one of the oldest in the world and is considered holy to three major Earthly religions. Judism, Christianity and Islam.

Valchonia:
The spirit world between the mortal and immortal worlds. Archonian essences that have not been chosen to live in Archonia linger here until they are either taken to Dichonia by demons known as reapers or are destroyed.

Valhalla:
Comprised of nearly every Scandanavian and Norse culture this mead hall towers above everything for miles. The rowdy inhabitants are known for liking the fermentation of honey and brawling like savages.

Jarod Meyer

www.ingramcontent.com/pod-product-compliance
Lightning Source LLC
Chambersburg PA
CBHW060307100726
47907CB00002B/322